W9-BEK-142

DEATH UNDERTOW

Also by Dennis Casley

Death underfoot (1993)

DEATH UNDERTOW

Dennis Casley

St. Martin's Press
New York

DEATH UNDERTOW.

Printed in the United States of America.

For information, address St. Martin's Press,
175 Fifth Avenue, New York, N.Y. 10010.

Library of Congress Cataloging-in-Publication Data

Casley, D. J.
Death undertow : a Chief Inspector Odhiambo mystery / Dennis Casley.
p. cm.
ISBN 0-312-13643-9
1. Kenyans—England—(Cornwall : County)—Fiction.
2. Police—Kenya—Nairobi—Fiction. I. Title.
PR6053.A8234D43 1995
823'.914—dc20 95-34500 CIP

First published in Great Britain by
Constable & Company, Ltd.

First U.S. Edition: December 1995
10 9 8 7 6 5 4 3 2 1

Prologue

Chief Inspector Odhiambo gazed idly at the greyish-white china clay pits visible in the distance as the train meandered its way through Cornwall. The train had lived up to its former name of the Cornish Riviera Express until it reached Plymouth. Thereafter progress was slow, the train becoming a local, stopping everywhere, including places that, as far as Odhiambo could see, were little more than platforms set in the middle of fields and hedgerows. Odhiambo was reminded of the train from Nairobi westwards, which took such a time to climb the great Rift escarpment that one could leave the train at one station, have a drink, and catch it up at the next, assuming a car was available. This was not quite that slow, but slow enough, and Odhiambo was impatient.

His destination was an old estate, now used as a conference and seminar centre by the British Overseas Development Administration and the Commonwealth Secretariat. He knew he would be one of a dozen or so participants in a seminar on rural development in the Commonwealth but there were no obvious signs amongst his fellow passengers that they included any of his co-participants. This was not surprising: Odhiambo was arriving a day later than scheduled because of a sudden toothache which had required urgent dental attention.

Approaching the end of his six-month senior police officers' course in England, Odhiambo had not felt inclined to accept an invitation to a one-week seminar on rural development. It was suggested to him that it would provide a mind-broadening experience not without relevance to police work, as well as a chance to visit a beautiful part of England and mingle with other Commonwealth visitors. All part of the great Commonwealth scheme of things. Odhiambo was unimpressed – to see more of England, he would have preferred to wander off on his own. Although he was reluctant to admit it, his mind changed when he glanced for the second time at the brochure advertising the Centre where the seminar was to be held. Director, Peter Deane, it read, but it was the next entry that caught Odhiambo's attention: Seminar Administrative Officer, Ms H. Shropshire. It had to be the same, he thought. The haunting and disturbing image of Helen Shropshire as he had last seen her returned to his mind.

It was foolish, Odhiambo knew, to seek out a renewed encounter, but his interest was piqued. He persuaded himself that he should know something about the theory of rural development and accepted his place at the seminar.

DEATH UNDERTOW

1

Peter Deane surveyed the latest batch of 'guests' from his vantage point by the window of what had once served as a reception room but now went under the more prosaic title of Seminar Room 1. This room was used for informal meetings of small groups. Armchairs and Victorian lounge chairs were arranged in an approximate arc with a small table and chair acting as the focal point. It was at this table that Deane, Director of the Polsand Seminar Centre, was presiding over a general discussion on the future of the Commonwealth, designed mainly to serve as an ice-breaking, introductory, participatory session that would enable the individuals in the group to get to know each other. The official opening ceremony with speeches had been held before lunch – the two visiting dignitaries from the Commonwealth Secretariat and the Overseas Development Administration were staying on for the first two days before returning to London and were now intent on half-heartedly demonstrating that they were just part of the crowd.

The participants were the usual varied bunch representing between them seven Commonwealth countries, three African, three Asian and the island of Montserrat, the last being represented by an extremely attractive young woman. As all the other participants were male, including two from Nigeria, Deane hoped there wouldn't be trouble over the woman.

Deane listened to one of the three Indians droning on about the need to make the Commonwealth a force for equality in the world, but that this needed a change of heart in Britain. Oh God, he thought, how many times have I heard this from Indians: they must learn it by rote in school. He was waiting for his chance to interrupt the high-pitched declamation and pull into the discussion those who had remained, as yet, silent, including the lone female from Montserrat, a Tanzanian, and a small but rather sinister-looking Sri Lankan, who seemed the shyest of the bunch. Then it would be tea-time – and none too soon, he thought.

In his audience the Director of International Liaison of the Commonwealth Secretariat, Javi Mahendra, allowed his mind to drift on to thoughts more stimulating than the future of the Commonwealth. No doubt Deane would ask him to round off the discussion, complimenting the speakers on their vision and giving his own thoughts on the subject. But this sort of thing, like his opening remarks that morning, was routine to him, so he allowed the picture of the naked Penny Deane to take precedence in his mind. There had been no opportunity since he and the others had arrived, but he expected a chance for a private session that evening as her fool of a husband would be fully engaged in supervising the opening cocktail party and dinner. He regarded the short, sandy-haired Director as an amiable nonentity. A failed Foreign Office man, a failed academic, he had finally found a niche in this remote corner and, in Mahendra's view, was botching this job too. He wasn't on top of what was happening in his bailiwick and, Mahendra smiled inwardly, he certainly wasn't on top of his wife. Yet, Mahendra thought, Deane could be dangerous. He was the sort of innocent who believed in his fellow man, but if belief was shattered the consequences could be unpredictable.

As Mahendra glanced idly along the arc of chairs his eyes fell on Hugh Gregson, representing HMG in general and his department, the Overseas Development Administration, in particular. Muriel Gregson was accompanying her husband and Mahendra was a little concerned that matters could become complicated if she and Penny Deane shared a tête-à-tête. He didn't rate her husband's perspicacity much higher than that of Peter Deane, but if the two women came to blows their menfolk would be the least of his problems. And, he thought sombrely, he had things to worry about on this visit other than jealous mistresses.

The door from the hall opened and in walked the Administrative Officer, appointed since Mahendra's previous visit. Not bad, he thought. Really there was an embarrassment of riches around. He did not include the girl from Montserrat; his one rule in terms of sexual conquest was not to seek dalliance with those on Commonwealth scholarships who were, in a sense, under his protection. This rule was based not on moral considerations, but on the need to protect his position in the Commonwealth Secretariat – a position which suited him very well. Frustrated females, unwilling to accept a one-night stand for what it was, could be troublesome if they were under the patronage of his institution. The Shropshire woman was attractive, certainly, the pleasantly proportioned face spotted with freckles and framed by a lively reddish mane of hair atop a shapely figure; but there was something about her that gave a man of his experience the warning light. He had a feeling that to her sex would imply more than a transitory physical commitment. Nevertheless, he watched closely as the woman bent over to whisper in the ear of Peter Deane and hand him a slip of paper.

Helen Shropshire was nervous; the tension had been building up within her since she took full notice of the names of the participants. When the list first arrived she scanned it briefly, but without looking closely at the names; it was only last week when she returned to it in order to allocate bedrooms that the name seemed to jump off the page. Disbelief gave way to dismay that the past was thrusting itself back, and dismay was quickly followed by anger. How dare he do this to her! She had made it clear the last time they met that she never wanted to see him again. Eventually, reason prevailed; after all, there was no reason why he should know she was here. Her name appeared in small print on the new brochure advertising the Centre's seminars, but she didn't suppose he would have spotted it. Once she had decided to give him the benefit of the doubt her next thought was to absent herself for the duration of the seminar; plead illness or whatever. But, in the end, she decided to stick it out. It would be a test of how well she had succeeded in starting a new life; and at the very back of her mind a tiny thought insisted on intruding – she wanted to see Odhiambo again.

Deane nodded and initialled the paper. The Centre's minibus was being serviced and the garage needed authority to replace a part. With the minibus out of commission, Deane had sent a Nissan saloon to meet the train from London and pick up the late participant. He hoped the train was on time – he needed the car later to pick up some supplies for the cocktail party, a standard feature on the first evening of a seminar. As he handed the paper back to his Administrative Officer he heard the sound of tyres on the loose gravel of the drive. A glance through the window confirmed it was the Nissan, from which a large African man was now emerging. Deane fancied himself as an amateur psychologist; he looked at the new arrival, tall, strong-looking, but, also, yes, definitely, about him there was a distinct air of unease.

As he turned back to the seminar room he noticed that Helen Shropshire seemed to have suddenly tensed, with added colour in her cheeks.

Gregson's attention was not on the by-play at the front of the gathering; he was covertly watching Mahendra. He knew him from other ODA/Secretariat meetings and now had reason to study him more closely. As Mahendra eyed the Administrative woman Gregson could detect the salaciousness behind the eyes. He was everything that Gregson, a squarely built, bluff, hearty man's man, despised: suave (oily was the word that sprang to Gregson's mind), sleek, slim, he carried himself with the careless arrogance that only the combination of birth into a superior Indian caste and education at Oxbridge could produce. The voice of the seminar participant who had the floor suddenly rose in volume and pitch and Gregson was startled to find that he was the subject of attack. The speaker, he saw, was one of the Tanzanians.

'. . . I say this, Mr Chairman. The policies of the British ODA are not in sympathy with African socialism. The representative of ODA who is with us said to me over lunch it was difficult to increase assistance to my country until we accepted the need for structural adjustment of our economy. Structural adjustment, Mr Chairman, is neo-colonialism pushed by former colonialists using the World Bank as their agent. I find it unacceptable if this gentleman . . .' gesturing towards Gregson, '. . . this representative of ODA, uses a Commonwealth gathering to promote such ideas. We are entitled to support for our development, not the imposition of foreign ideologies . . .'

'Don't forget the IMF,' interjected a Nigerian, who, Gregson remembered, was called Asuna.

'What, what . . . ?'

The Tanzanian found himself put out of his oratorical stride.

'The IMF,' said Asuna. 'They're the main cause of our problems in Nigeria. You mentioned the Bank and ODA, but don't forget the IMF. Sod 'em all, I say.'

Deane hastily intervened from his seat at the front.

'Yes, well, I think perhaps at this stage we're, er, wandering a little away from our topic. These weighty economic matters are perhaps better, er, pursued later in our discussion. They are, of course, er, relevant to rural development, but this afternoon our emphasis is on the cultural relationships and exchanges within the Commonwealth. Perhaps, as it's almost time for tea, I could ask our distinguished guest Dr Mahendra to sum up.'

Gregson coughed gently and half stood.

'Mr Chairman, Peter, perhaps I could just presume on your patience and exercise, very briefly, my right of reply.' He paused for a moment as a gesture of seeking Deane's approval, but pressed on before Deane could respond. 'My friends here are free to air their misgivings regarding any current theories of economic development, but I would regret it very much if my Administration is seen as having any objective other than the rapid development of Tanzania consistent with the Arusha Declaration. The need for serious adjustment of policies is becoming well recognised at the highest level of your governments. Of course, various options are controversial and need debating and, as I will not be present at all your deliberations, I take this opportunity to wish you a fair wind during your sessions.'

'Thank you, Hugh.' Peter Deane was anxious to move on. 'I'm sure your clarification is well taken. And now, perhaps, Javi, your summing up.'

Mahendra was genuinely amused. With an anti-British Tanzanian and at least one abrasive Nigerian, Deane might have his hands full this week. It only needed the girl from Montserrat to turn out to be a Marxist and a jolly time would be had by all. He moved into his smooth, sincere-sounding platitudes regarding the bright future that lay awaiting the people of the Commonwealth if they seized on the opportunities to cultivate the feelings of fellowship and brotherhood that were the bedrock of the Commonwealth ideal.

'Shit,' said Asuna to his fellow Nigerian neighbour. 'If this is how it stays it's going to be a long week.'

2

Odhiambo had given considerable thought to the moment when he would encounter Helen Shropshire once again. As the car entered the narrow road of the estate through a gate flanked by unadorned granite pillars, he wondered if he was doing the right thing. He didn't want to embarrass the woman, or serve to recall bitter memories. Well, it was too late now. He glanced out of the window as the car turned slowly around a right-angled bend. The estate was bigger than he had expected. They were already half a mile into it through a wooded valley, and the old manor house was only now coming into view, set in a sizeable area of lawns and flower beds. Odhiambo was not well up on British architectural periods, but he recognised the solid rectangular shape with uniform distribution of windows on either side of a pillared front entrance as typical of a rich man's house of a couple of hundred years ago.

He could see that the track along which they bumped went on past the house and then turned right, presumably to the sea, which Odhiambo knew was close by. On the left side of the track and about twenty feet below he could see the waters of a lake. If it was open to the sea one would expect some sign of tidal movements but, in fact, it was calm and still. He turned to the driver, a young man dressed casually in jeans and checked shirt.

'Is that a freshwater pool or a creek from the sea?'

The driver smiled.

'Yeah. It's freshwater. Y'see, way back whenever, the sea went and threw up a bar along the beach – sand-bar, I mean. It blocks the water here getting down. So we've got the sea one side of the bar and this pool the other, do y'see? Sort of creepy, some see it as. Specially when it's dark.'

'Is this common? I mean, do you often get lakes like this so close to the sea?'

'No, no, sort of unique this is. Quite famous, actually. All sorts of stories about it.'

Whatever the stories were would have to wait for, as he spoke, the driver braked the car at the front door and Odhiambo alighted. As he waited for the driver to unlock the boot, or trunk as his American-raised wife would call it, in order to retrieve his bag, Odhiambo felt his pulse quicken – the awkward encounter was close at hand.

Odhiambo climbed the few steps and pushed open the heavy door. Stepping through, he found himself in a large hall, bare except for a table on which various papers and documents lay spread and two chairs on each side of it. As he approached the table he saw on it a bell with a notice requesting it be rung. However, his arrival had been noted and a young woman emerged from a door behind the table, smiling at him.

'Mr Odhiambo? Welcome to the Polsand Centre. We'll get you booked in, then you can join the others for tea.'

'Inspector Odhiambo, actually, Jane.'

The voice came from behind him and Odhiambo spun around. Helen Shropshire was emerging from a door marked as a meeting room. She looked at Odhiambo and a nervous smile came and went like a light bulb that blows as soon as it is switched on. The red hair still glowed, he thought, even here away from the Equatorial sun. She was as he remembered her, attractive, with a face that he had not been able to slip into the recesses of his memory. Odhiambo bowed slightly and lied.

'Mrs Shropshire. I only noticed your name when I read the brochure on the train. I'm sorry if my presence here is a source of upset to you.'

The smile returned, stayed just a little longer, but the voice was strained.

'No, no. There's no need to apologise. The past is over. Nairobi seems a long way away and a long time ago.'

Odhiambo advanced towards her and held out his hand.

'Well, I'm pleased to see you. You're right, this is a different time and place and I'm just an African wanting to learn about rural development.'

'Was I right about the Inspector bit or did I hear you were promoted?'

'Yes, well, it's Chief Inspector now, the prize for being a good boy – and a course in England thrown in as well. But here it's plain Odhiambo, or James if first names are the form.'

'Yes, we are informal and try to cultivate a friendly atmosphere. My name is – well, that's silly, isn't it, you probably remember, it's Helen. And this . . .' the voice recovered stability and poise, ' . . . this is Jane who will settle you in and direct you to your room.'

Once more the smile came and went uncertainly, and then she was gone through the door from which the other girl had emerged earlier. Odhiambo turned his attention back to the girl at the table, who was waiting with a scarcely concealed curiosity.

'Yes, well, if you would just sign here, Mr . . . er . . . Inspector . . . then I'll show you to your room.'

Odhiambo bent over the table and completed the formalities. The girl, pleasant-looking, but overweight, came around from behind the table and gestured for him to follow. As they mounted the stairs she could restrain her curiosity no longer.

'So you know Mrs Shropshire, then?'

The glance over the shoulder was almost conspiratorial.

'Yes. Slightly. We both live or lived in Nairobi.'

'Oh, yes, I know she used to be there. Sad about the accident to her husband. Did you know him too?'

They had arrived at a door which opened to Jane's push. Odhiambo took the proffered key, smiled his thanks and went into the room, shutting the door as the girl turned away, without a response to her last question. He sighed. It was a mistake, he shouldn't have come. Not only because of the past; it was the future he must guard against.

The room was large, well appointed with furniture that pretended unsuccessfully to be of an age with the room. There was a door on the right that Odhiambo assumed to be the bathroom, but the main feature was the big double sash window. Crossing to it, Odhiambo took in the striking view of the woods, glimpses of dark water at places through the trees and just a glimmer in the distance of the sea. I wonder if everyone's got a room like this, he thought, or have I received a favour from the Administrative Officer?

Half an hour later, Odhiambo found himself clutching a cup of tea and chatting to the two Nigerians, who were doing their best to make it clear that they regarded Kenya as a backward East Coast country and policemen as belonging to a lower form of human life. He had met his fellow participants, although he had not grasped all their names, as well as the visiting officials and staff of the Polsand Centre – the Administrative Officer, however, was absent and the Director of the Centre, having made his apologies about 'things to see to', had slipped away, leaving his wife to act as hostess. Odhiambo's inner sense, which he attributed to his Luo ancestors, together with his policeman's eye, combined to tell him that there was something other than an official connection between the Indian from the Commonwealth Secretariat and the attractive wife of the Centre's Director.

'Of course, you've no oil, have you?' one of the Nigerians was saying. 'Only pandering to tourists and coffee. And selling your rhino horns. Can't expect rapid development in those conditions.'

'We do as well as we can,' Odhiambo gently riposted. 'And better than most, including some countries blessed with greater resources.'

The Nigerians seemed unimpressed. The second Nigerian – Asuna, Odhiambo recalled, was his name – turned the topic to soccer, or football as the game was known in most English-speaking countries.

'Our national team are through to the finals of the Africa Cup. Will Kenya be there? In Morocco, isn't it?'

Odhiambo had no idea of the fate of the Kenya team, but was spared an answer because they were joined at this point by the British official.

'Hello, Inspector, Gregson is the name – don't suppose you caught it when the introductions were made. So you made it, albeit a little late. Had trouble getting down from London?'

Odhiambo explained about his toothache.

'Sorted it out for you, did they, all right? Good man. You're from Kenya, are you not? Policeman, too. Were you there when there was that nasty business some months ago? Made a lot of splash in our papers – there's a lot of fascination here with the doings of tourists in Kenya. Goes back to the old settler days, the wild ones.'

Odhiambo avoided the question.

'Are you helping to run the course?'

'No, no, helping to pay for it together with Javi Mahendra over there. Joint ODA, Commonwealth effort. We're only staying a couple of days. Brought the wife with me. It's a lovely spot, this, and she has connections in these parts.'

Asuna took his cue.

'Too remote for me. Stuck here with no transport. Isn't there somewhere to go in the evenings?'

Gregson considered for a moment.

'There's a village just a thirty-minute walk away. Penleith. Through the woods and along the cliff. Perhaps an excursion after dinner, eh? Visit a village pub.'

'You say your wife is with you,' Odhiambo asked. 'Is that the lady over there?' He gestured towards a tall woman with a definite air of wife of diplomat talking graciously to the natives.

'Yes, that's Muriel,' said Gregson. 'With the Montserrat girl.'

Asuna started a lewd remark about the younger woman, but stopped as if realising that the audience was an inappropriate one. She was pretty, thought Odhiambo, but Muriel Gregson seemed to him to be the more interesting study. She was well built without being matronly, dark hair framing a narrow face with a full mouth. Overall, she gave an impression of sensuality.

As the Nigerians resumed their enquiries of Gregson regarding the prospects offered by the village of Penleith, Odhiambo slipped away to deposit his teacup on the nearby table. He was intercepted by his hostess, Penny Deane.

'Another cup, Mr er . . . Odambo, is it? And a slice of cake?'

'Odhiambo, but call me James – it's easier to remember. No, no more, thank you.'

'Oh, I'm sorry, er . . . James – it's difficult remembering names the first day or so. I'm Penny, by the way. I expect you're trained to memorise things quickly. I mean, Javi said you're a policeman. Is that right?'

'Yes, yes it is. But no, I find it difficult too – names, I mean. And particularly when I'm in a strange place. It's odd that. But although the place is new to me, I could see enough on the drive in to know you have a beautiful location here.'

'Yes, it is, isn't it? It was a manor once, of course. A family that owned lots of land around here and in Dorset. The latest generation decided to focus on Dorset and dispensed with this.'

Odhiambo watched the woman closely as they chatted. She was very different to Mrs Gregson. Small, petite, blonde, pert face with an upturned nose and a small mouth. But there was a hidden tension there, he thought, and instinctively, his eyes moved to find the Commonwealth Secretariat representative now talking animatedly to the ODA man's wife. Penny Deane followed his gaze and Odhiambo sensed rather than saw the stiffening of the mouth. She turned back to Odhiambo, excused herself on the grounds of seeing to another of her guests, and headed resolutely towards another small group of participants.

An introductory cough heralded a new companion for Odhiambo. He turned to find the Indian with the Oxford accent and the affectations of the upper class – what was his name? Yes, Mahendra, that was it, Javi Mahendra.

'Attractive lady, do you not think, Inspector? I expect she finds life in this rural outpost somewhat quiet.'

'Yes, I suppose she might. You, yourself, a moment ago were with another lady. That's why you took me unawares.'

'Ah, yes. Mrs Gregson. Also interesting. Different type altogether, of course. Actually, I wanted a word, if you have a minute?'

'Of course. What about?'

'We have a mutual friend in Nairobi, Inspector, who speaks highly of your powers of observation.' A smile flashed briefly. 'Your reputation precedes you, you see. No, no, let me finish.' Mahendra raised a hand as Odhiambo was about to interrupt to claim that he was but a participant in a development seminar. 'I am leaving here tomorrow evening, but you will be here for the rest of the week. I merely ask you to keep your eyes open. That's all.'

'What do you mean? Keep my eyes open for what? The scenery?'

Odhiambo's irritation showed clearly on his face, but Mahendra again raised a placatory hand.

'We, that is the CS, provide a substantial contribution to the funding of this place. We wouldn't want to be embarrassed in any way. One has heard this and that. A trained pair of eyes might be helpful. Then, perhaps, we can get together when you're back in London.'

'Mr Mahendra, your request is preposterous. If you have any problems concerning this Centre you must surely take it up with the Director.'

'No, no, nothing like that. Mr Deane is, I'm sure, a pillar of rectitude. I mean exogenous happenings. Wouldn't want to prejudice you by saying more. Wander about – make yourself known to others on the estate. Pay a courtesy visit to the local constabulary. Chat to the local fishermen, that sort of thing.'

'You've either said too much or too little.' Odhiambo's voice had risen with exasperation. 'I'm supposed to be attending a seminar not prowling around the district. What are you getting at?'

If a reply was intended it was destined to be postponed, for now at the door Peter Deane was clapping his hands for attention.

'Time to resume. Case studies in rural development with a very experienced speaker, Dr Hargreaves, formerly of Cambridge University.'

'Ah,' said Mahendra in Odhiambo's ear. 'Deane must be grateful that old Hargreaves retired to these parts. Always ready to pontificate on the developing world and how he advised all and sundry. One country that listened to him more carefully than most was Tanzania and look what happened there. You'd think that would have chastened him a little, but not a bit of it. Nobody more confident in his faith than a socialist economist, Inspector. You've done well to avoid them in Kenya.'

3

After dinner, Odhiambo reluctantly allowed himself to be persuaded to join the foot-party to the village pub. He didn't wish to be unsociable, he did need a walk and he did want a chance to see the locality, although he would have preferred to accomplish these latter objectives alone.

Odhiambo was not in the best of moods. He felt gloomy and irritable. It was probably a mistake to have come. Helen Shropshire had seemed to avoid him during the drinks and dinner. And Mahendra was missing at dinner, sending his apologies via the Administrative Officer, so Odhiambo had not been able to pursue his strange request. Penny Deane was also missing; Odhiambo supposed there was no necessity for the Director's wife to join in all the communal activities, but he speculated to himself on the nature of Mahendra's other engagements. Yet another absentee was Muriel Gregson, so the group contained only two females, Helen Shropshire and the girl from Montserrat. Odhiambo found himself next to the latter at dinner, but at the other end of the table from the former. The conversation was depressing: a lot of hot air about development and the sins of the richer countries combined with the cynical derision of all things local by the Nigerians.

Despite himself, Odhiambo found the walk to the village impressive. It was a clear evening and still daylight. They walked along a track, wooded on the right with the lake on the left. The noise of the sea hitting the sand-bar could be heard before the coast came in view and contrasted with the eerie stillness of the dark water of the lake. Odhiambo had been raised near a lake, Lake Victoria, but that was the size of a small sea and it had waves and movement. This lake seemed as if it was made of dark glass, and Odhiambo's sharply tuned ancestral instincts told him it was evil.

After a ten-minute walk, the group turned a corner and reached the boundary of the estate marked by a lodge guarding a gate. At this point the scenery dramatically changed. Below them lay the huge sand-bar with waves continuously dissipating their energies climbing part-way up the sloping ridge of pebbles and sand. Beyond the gate the track turned right and headed along the cliff edge and down to the village, still visible in the twilight, but with lights coming on as they approached. 'The Crab's Claw' was gained via a narrow cobbled road that ran alongside the small harbour towards the heart of the village. From there the houses rose up a hillside, straddling the road that connected Penleith with the main trans-Cornish highway a mile or so inland. The pub itself was old, with a thatched roof, low beams and dark wood, and gave out a masculine smell of beer, tobacco and mustiness that seemed genuinely to have built up over many a year. The party from the Centre, consisting of Gregson, a staff member named Brown, the evening's lecturer Hargreaves, the two Nigerians, a Tanzanian and Odhiambo, elicited no significant response from the locals. Although, as Odhiambo knew, there were very few non-white people on this far western coast, the locals of Penleith were used to exotic visitors from the Centre.

Odhiambo settled himself into a corner of the bar with a lager – he had not been able to acquire a taste for English bitter – as the group gradually merged with the local customers. The Nigerians were the most forward in opening conversations. Hargreaves seemed to be known – as also, Odhiambo observed, was Gregson, at least to the publican and his wife.

'So, you're from Kenya,' said Trengrouse, the publican, Gregson having made the introductions. 'Odhiambo. What line of business are you in, Mr Odhiambo?'

Odhiambo evaded the question by answering a different one and then posing one of his own.

'We're here for a week on a course in rural development,' he said. 'Everyone keeps telling me about the mystery of the lake around the Centre. Is there a long-standing local legend?'

Trengrouse laughed. 'It's pretty creepy there when it's dark and the wind is blowing through the trees. Us believe in ghosties down this way.' The last was said with a broadening of the local accent as if Trengrouse was poking fun at local superstition that he did not share. 'It's also supposed to claim a victim every five years.'

'It looks calm enough today,' said Odhiambo. 'I'd have thought it was OK for swimming.'

'Ah, that's where danger comes. 'Tis a strange pool, that one. Calm on top, but a terrible pull underneath. Undertow, 'tis called. No one thinks of swimming in 'un, until word gets round that five years is nearly up, then some great fool thinks he'll challenge the legend. Usually after a few pints, mind. Goes in and the undertow gets him. Y'see, the pool drains somewhere under the bar, so stands to reason there's an undertow down there someplace.'

'And when was the last victim claimed?'

The publican considered a moment.

'It was a visitor. Been drinking – not here, mind. Went up with his girl. She watched while he went in and disappeared. Was in, let me see now . . . Well, I'll be darned, I think we're about at the five-year mark again.'

Gregson said with a laugh, 'So we'd better ensure that none of us goes for a dip this week. I understand Mahendra enjoys a skinny dip, preferably with company.'

Odhiambo saw a reaction from a burly local who was talking to the Nigerians. Turning away from the Nigerians he addressed himself to Gregson.

'You telling me that gentleman from the East is here this week?' Sarcasm was loaded on to each syllable and Odhiambo felt the radiation of real animosity.

Gregson asked, 'You know him, then? Mr Mahendra, I mean.'

'There's a few of us here do know 'e. Took him out on me boat once when he showed interest. But like a few of you people from out along he needs to mind his business and let us mind our'n.'

'Don't say he caught you breaking EC fishing regulations.' Gregson laughed, but his curiosity was piqued by the local man's obvious animosity. 'Or smuggling, perhaps?'

The burly man got up off his stool and moved closer to Gregson and Odhiambo.

'You're another quizzy bugger, are ye? I'll tell ye sump'n, mister . . . ' A large gnarled and wind-browned finger thrust towards Gregson's face. 'I'll tell ye . . .'

Trengrouse, from behind the bar, quickly intervened. 'Now, now, Daniel Menherian, you've had a pint too many. Mind your tongue, man. Now, sir . . . ' to Gregson, 'how long you staying for this time?'

The fisherman, if such he was, looked truculently at the publican for a long moment then suddenly turned and moved away.

Trengrouse turned back to Odhiambo.

'Don't mind Menherian, sir. Bit of a loudmouth, specially when the beer's in 'im. Good fisherman. Best boatman hereabouts.'

Odhiambo smiled and nodded. He was intrigued by the fisherman's reaction to the mention of Mahendra.

'No problem. He seemed a mite touchy about our Indian friend.'

'Yes, Mr Mahendra's been down a few times. He and Menherian didn't hit it off for some reason. What about you, Mr Odhiambo? Your first visit to these parts?'

'Yes, yes it is. 'Fraid I don't know much about Cornwall, except stories. I remember reading *Jamaica Inn* at school. Smugglers and worse. What was the name?'

Trengrouse laughed.

'Wreckers, you mean. Luring ships on to the cliffs and killing the crew before taking the cargo. Long time ago, that were. Mind you,' Trengrouse leaned conspiratorially across the bar, 'there's things that go on today nearly as bad in my book. Drugs, I mean.'

Odhiambo looked at the publican quizzically.

'Come on. Don't tell me there's drug smuggling down here. Around London, yes, but this doesn't look like a drug gang area to me.'

'It's gotta come in somewhere and where better than parts of the coast? Little coves all over and no one to see. You mark my . . .'

Trengrouse's wife interrupted, indicating that it was time he assisted with the pulling of pints, and with a friendly nod the publican turned away.

Odhiambo watched a little longer as Gregson circulated around the party. He was a large-framed man of above average height, but light on his feet. Probably played a lot of cricket and tennis in the exotic places he'd been stationed in when younger, thought Odhiambo. Now greying, but muscular-looking rather than flabby, he was still a handsome man.

He saw the truculent local gesturing to the Nigerians and then the three of them disappeared through a side door. After finishing his lager Odhiambo, too, left the same way. The door led to the toilets and to a rear exit. A visit to the men's toilet revealed no other user, so the trio must have left together. He returned to the bar, but tired now of company he muttered his excuses to Gregson and left the pub, emerging on to the lane that led to the cliff. It was dark now, but a near-full moon promised some light on the return walk. Odhiambo enjoyed the solitude as he retraced his way towards the Centre. From the cliff top the sea was lit by the moon, giving it a shimmering effect that suddenly reminded Odhiambo of his home lake in Western Kenya. What was a Luo boy doing here on the tip of England? What would his father have thought? And then as his memory switched to the last time he was on that lake, his mind was invaded by the figure of Helen Shropshire. So sudden and vivid was the image that Odhiambo thought for a moment that she was there on the cliff path ahead of him. Oh, come on. What's the matter with you? he muttered to himself, and then consciously conjured up a picture of his wife, Cari, currently staying with her parents near Washington whilst working at the Washington office of her employers. I ought to write her a letter tonight, it must be a week since the last.

These musings brought him to the lodge at the entrance to the estate. Light shone from two windows. Odhiambo had noticed signs of habitation when they passed it on their way to the village. He passed through the estate boundary gate and started past the lodge towards the corner that would bring him back to the lake and the path to the Centre. Odhiambo had his share of Luo superstitions, but he was confident that Cornish ghosts could be relied on to be invisible to men from another continent. It was certainly not a ghost whose raised voice now impinged on his solitude.

'No. No. Can you understand that, you slimy bastard? No more. You hear me? No more. Now, get the hell out.'

As Odhiambo turned towards the lodge he traced the source to a window open to the balmy evening. A different voice was speaking now but, without the volume caused by anger, it was merely a faint susurration of sound waves. The original voice returned, however, still operating at full volume.

'I don't believe you. You're bluffing and I'm calling your bluff. Are you going to go or do I have to throw you out . . .?'

Odhiambo hurried on. He had no wish to be awaiting the exit of the lodge owner's unwelcome guest. As he walked he found himself startled more than once by the trees, which, exposed to the strong westerly winds from the Atlantic, had grown slanted and twisted. Now that it was dark with the moon picking out branches at random, individual shapes took on strange anthropomorphic forms. This was coupled with the occasional sound of water disturbed by a fish or nocturnal animal. Odhiambo had a vague memory of an old rhyme he had once come across – something about looking over your shoulder with dread because you didn't know what behind might tread. Well, he had made his guess about who was likely behind him to tread, so he increased his pace, not from fear but from reluctance to become involved.

The manor house came in view as he turned another corner and the trees suddenly gave way to the open meadow that led from the edge of the lake up towards the house. He could see little of the intervening land but the house shone brightly enough to outbid the moon in terms of illuminating the lawn.

Odhiambo followed the path, which changed from an uneven fixed stony surface to gravel as it threaded its way towards the house. As he climbed the steps to the entrance he looked back. It was an instinctive act, but no one was to be seen in the darkness under the trees. As he turned back to the door, however, he gave a start: there was a figure seated on the stone balustrade leaning against the pillar that supported the stone canopy. Although whoever it was must have heard his footsteps on the gravel, the figure did not turn towards him. Diverting his steps he approached the silent watcher – somehow it came as no surprise to recognise Helen Shropshire.

'Good evening, er, Helen. Enjoying the Cornish night air?'

Now, at last, the figure turned, the light from the window catching her face.

'Oh, Inspector – I mean, James.' The voice was cool and composed. 'You're back ahead of the rest; the pub not to your liking?'

'It was OK as long as you avoid the flat English draught beer. I wanted a solitary walk back. It's a lovely evening.'

'Yes, it is. There's usually more wind than this.' Her voice became more animated. 'Although we're sheltered here in a sort of bowl surrounded by trees. But on the cliff sometimes it's unbelievable.'

Odhiambo stood over the woman who, as if uncomfortable at his looming presence, rose to her feet, her head failing to reach the level of his shoulder.

'I passed a lodge at the sea end of the estate. Do you know who lives there?' Odhiambo was careful to make his question sound casual.

'Yes. There's two lodges, as a matter of fact. One at the end of the other path, going the other way. But that one is empty. The one you passed is lived in by a man called Bastian. Lives there with his son. Well, he says he's his son. Village gossip has other views.'

Odhiambo remembered this trait in Helen's conversation. The tendency to blurt out a little more than she seemed to intend when she started to speak.

'Bastian, eh? Does he have any connection with the Centre here?'

'No, none. The lodge was sold off years ago. Why do you ask? Did you meet him? He runs a seafood restaurant in Penleith. We don't see him about the estate.'

'How do you like it here? It's a bit isolated, but I suppose there's plenty of folk about – staff of the Centre, I mean. Including Mrs Deane.'

'Yes, there's no need to be lonely. They're all very kind. But it's also possible to be alone. Walk into the woods and it's as if you're the only person on earth.'

Her voice trembled on the word 'alone'. Odhiambo cursed himself and changed the conversation back to the previous topic.

The woman started to walk towards the door with Odhiambo following.

'No, I didn't meet the man in the lodge. I heard him, though, as I passed the lodge just now. Eavesdropping in a way, although I couldn't help it.'

For the first time, Helen Shropshire seemed to relax and a genuine smile of amusement gave her face the cheeky gamin look that he also remembered.

'My dear Ins . . . James. Once a policeman always a policeman, eh? Oh dear, it wouldn't do if your fellow participants thought you were listening at the keyhole.' She chuckled and then checked her demeanour to a more neutral stance as Odhiambo opened the door for her to enter. 'I'm sorry, I didn't mean to be rude. I must be off. One or two things to finish off in the office. Good-night.'

Back in his room, Odhiambo gazed from his window towards the trees, but there was no sign of a returning figure. He sat down at a chair near the window and turned his attention to one of the papers to be discussed tomorrow. It failed to engage him and with a sigh he put it down and stood up once more. This time he could see movement between the house and the trees. He leaned over and switched off his table lamp. The figure came into the light from the lounge window – it was Penny Deane, wearing jeans and pullover and carrying something under her arm. She was hurrying but, as she neared the door, Odhiambo momentarily saw her face illuminated by the light. It was the face of a disturbed woman. Whether she was frightened or worried Odhiambo could not be sure. Perhaps it was both, he thought. He debated with himself as to whether to return downstairs. But to what purpose? He opened the door and listened. All was quiet in the hall. Presumably Mrs Deane had gone straight to her private accommodation. In any case, she wasn't raising an alarm.

Odhiambo prepared himself for bed by the light afforded by the moon. He found himself looking repeatedly through the window. He saw some more of the Crab's Claw party arrive – the two locals and the Tanzanian. The Nigerians were missing, which didn't surprise Odhiambo; the local fisherman had presumably guided them to some local night-life more stimulating than the company at the Crab's Claw. What did surprise him was that Gregson was also missing.

Well, he thought, he's old enough to look after himself so there's nothing to be done. But he felt uneasy. Something was amiss – but what, he didn't know. Oh hell, he muttered, what's the matter with me? I'm letting this place with its legends get to me already. Better get to bed.

4

Gregson had wondered whether he should have offered to accompany Odhiambo on his walk back to the Centre. Probably not, he decided. Odhiambo seemed to be something of a loner, not a club or pub man. Gregson himself was both; he genuinely enjoyed a boozy evening with his friends where the conversation was aimless and gossipy. It didn't matter to him whether it was the somewhat more genteel atmosphere of his London club, or a gathering such as this in the public bar of a pub. Both reminded him in their separate ways of the colonial clubs he was old enough to have experienced just before they faded as the Empire disappeared. But now it was time for him to go.

With Odhiambo and the Nigerians already gone, the walking party was now down to four. Gregson made his excuses to the other three, who seemed to be enjoying themselves as Hargreaves droned on about the evils of the colonial regime in Tanganyika, and started his own trek back towards the Centre. He had put off thinking about the situation that was worrying him. His suspicions had been aroused over some time that Muriel was playing fast and loose again, but it was only when he arrived at Polsand and observed the two of them that the possibility that Mahendra was her amour came into his mind. My God, he thought, what was she thinking of? Yes, these were not colonial days, but still, he could surely expect that she would avoid a scandal involving an Indian. And Mahendra at that: a womanising, supercilious Indian who sneered at him with all the contempt of an Oxford classics man for one with a poor history degree from a provincial university. What was he to do about it, that was the question. Yes, he could talk to Muriel, but it was Mahendra he would like to see taken to task. Smooth-talking bastards like him should be castrated.

As he passed the lodge at the entrance to the estate and entered the wooded path, Gregson saw in the moonlight a figure ahead of him and recognised it as the man he was thinking of. He followed discreetly at a distance; he certainly didn't want to catch the fellow up or for him to know he was being followed. As he turned a corner he could see Mahendra nearing the next curve in the path. Gregson paused to allow him to extend his lead, but suddenly he disappeared – not, it seemed, around the corner but off the path itself. Gregson walked on and discovered a track leading off the main path which headed down towards the lake. He remembered his remarks at the pub; was Mahendra about to enjoy a nude frolic with his wife? Muriel was a strong and avid swimmer too. He hesitated for a moment only, then turned on to the track and made his way slowly along it.

Penny Deane normally enjoyed the solitude of the lake at night. She was not sensitive to any feelings of isolation in a supposedly haunted or bewitched place. On the contrary, the fact that the locals were not prone to wander in these woods at night meant that she was more sure of her privacy and could strip for a swim, when she wished, without fear of being seen. Tonight, however, her thoughts were not conducive to enjoying the peace. Indeed, her very purpose tonight was to confirm the intrusion of others into her private domain. She had introduced Javi to her secret beach as befitted the trust to be given to a lover, but now she was sure that her trust was to be betrayed. And betrayed within hours of her leaving his bed! He didn't know she had caught sight as she dressed of a few words on the crumpled piece of paper he had carelessly left on the bedside table. She had managed to conceal her surprise and anger then, but the anger had been growing steadily since.

She took a track that brought her to the lake nearer to the house than the small sandy area she called her beach and made her way cautiously through the trees to a point closer to it. She sat down, her back to a tree. There was no sound of human intrusion into the normal night sounds of the lake and trees. The slap of the water on the lake's edge was soft, for there was no real movement in the lake. Only the leaves of the trees trembled with a soft rustling; there was insufficient breeze to make the old bent tree creak above the water. Penny was wearing a swimsuit under her jersey and jeans and was carrying a towel, although she wasn't sure why: she had no clear plan, only a jumbled mind and a pain like a stab wound in her heart.

Daniel Menherian fingered the note in his pocket and smiled to himself as he walked along the cliff. He had extracted a price for directing those two blacks to Joe's place. Wanting a little more excitement indeed – he knew what the buggers were after as soon as they approached him at the bar. A couple of pints and a few quid better off, he was now on his way to pay a late evening visit. The mention of that Indian being back worried him. Last time he was here he'd been sniffing about and Menherian felt himself partly responsible for putting him on the scent. He wondered if they knew he was back. Indian or not, he probably had fancy connections in London. Could be a lot of trouble. So, better call in and give a warning.

Once down from the path on to the sand, he had a change of mind precipitated by a stumble caused by unsteady legs. He had drunk a few pints and he knew what sort of reception he'd get if it was thought he was drunk. Tomorrow would do as well. He moved over to the lee side of the sand-bar and settled himself into a declivity in the undulating sand and pebble surface. It was a nice night, just right for a quiet pipe and time to think matters through. His thinking made little progress for the beer took its toll and he dozed off, the pipe dangling loosely in his fingers. It was a movement nearby that jerked him awake.

As he made his way along the narrow footway that led from the main path down to the lake, Javi Mahendra was hard put to focus on the delights to come rather than on his other preoccupations. He was not pleased with the events of the evening and was in some doubt as to his next step. There was that policeman fellow from Kenya; Mahendra had made an overture thinking that his fortuitous presence might come in useful, and with the forcefulness of the resistance he was facing the Kenyan was probably the next card to play. He could, of course, play the honest citizen, forgoing any personal advantage, and if it came to that he would, rather than let them get away with it.

But now it was time for pleasure. He had been delighted to get the note suggesting a nocturnal swim. He should have had more confidence that her desires would overcome restraints. He had assumed she would find the present circumstances too restricting for he had a feeling that her husband was suspicious. Then of course there was the fact of having two mistresses in the same house. It was clear to him that both were exhibiting signs of jealousy. Penny had put the question directly to him in his bed that very evening, but he was used to coping with jealous women. What intrigued him was the invitation naming the time and location. He had swum there before, but not with tonight's date – it was as if she knew of his previous indulgence.

The moon was temporarily obscured as Mahendra arrived at the minute sandy beach, but in any case a huge overhanging tree rendered the area pitch black. A splashing sound told him that he had been beaten to it. At least she wasn't late like most women.

'I'm here,' he called softly. 'Be with you in a moment.'

Another splash of a swimmer's arm and what sounded like a muted giggle spurred him on. He had left watch, wallet and other incidentals behind at the house, so it took but a few seconds to strip off his plimsolls, trousers, pants, shirt and pullover and dive into the water.

As he surfaced his first thought, oddly enough, was that he hoped she had brought the towels. He hadn't noticed them or her clothes on the sand. He turned on his back, looked and listened in order to locate his fellow swimmer. He felt without concern a disturbance in the water beneath him: he had swum in this part of the lake several times – any dangerous currents would be closer to the main sand-bar marking the barrier to the sea. Suddenly he felt the pressure on his ankle – strong, irresistible and calculating. His head went below the surface, but briefly he forced it up again only to succumb once more to the unrelenting pressure which cut off a half-emitted cry. As the water entered his lungs and he sank lower, the thought that killed his mind before his bursting lungs stopped his heart was that the hidden dangers of the lake were not to blame – what held him under were fingers locked like talons around his ankles.

5

Odhiambo had barely gained his bed when the sound of voices coming through the partly open window reached him. He got out of bed and crossed to the window. Gregson was on the steps leading to the front door talking to someone Odhiambo did not know. Gregson was agitated, and very wet.

Odhiambo hastily pulled on his trousers, a pullover and shoes and hurried down the stairs to the hall. Gregson was there, having entered with the other man.

'I think I'd better wake the Admin lady,' the man strange to Odhiambo was saying. 'I don't think Mr Deane is in. Leastways I haven't seen him come back.'

Odhiambo addressed Gregson.

'What's going on, Hugh? Have you had an accident?'

Gregson stared at Odhiambo for a moment as if he didn't recognise him. His hair was stuck wetly around his face and his clothes hung heavy with moisture. He squelched as he took a step towards Odhiambo.

'Ah, Odhiambo. No, not me. Well, me as well, I suppose. But I think there's been a serious incident. In that damned lake. Mahendra – I think he may have drowned.'

Odhiambo had a sense that had come to him once or twice before; the feeling that somehow his fate was preordained, that he was about to be thrust into a situation that he had not sought, but could not avoid.

'OK. We'll have to organise a search. Did you see him? In the lake, I mean. You know where it happened?'

Gregson waved an impatient arm which sent droplets on to Odhiambo's face.

'Of course I know where. I've just come from there. Bit confusing actually, but yes, I know. We need the police, man! We need to phone the police. You're as bad as that night-watchman or whatever he is. You think I'm joking.'

Gregson looked down at himself as if realising for the first time how wet he was. There was a note of hysteria in his voice and Odhiambo spoke to calm him.

'Yep. We'll get on to that while you get into some dry clothes. Just tell me where it happened.'

Behind him a door opened, heralding the return of the night officer accompanied by a slightly dishevelled-looking Helen Shropshire clad in a white dressing-gown. Odhiambo admired the way she took charge, addressing Gregson quietly but firmly, laying her hand in a comforting manner on his arm.

'Mr Gregson, I will call the police and the Air-Sea Rescue if you think Mr Mahendra is missing in the lake. Can you just give me the basic facts so that I can relay them?'

Her manner did the trick. When he spoke, Gregson sounded calmer.

'Yes, yes, Miss er . . . Helen, isn't it? I was walking home when

I heard a sort of shout . . . cut short it was . . . from the direction of the water. It was a few hundred yards this side of the lodge. I made my way down to the lake edge. There were clothes piled up – Mahendra's clothes – but after what seemed like further splashes some way off, nothing! I called but no reply. Then I thought I saw something caught in the branches in the water's edge. I tried to determine what it was . . . I thought it might be his arm . . . but I slipped in. Anyway, it wasn't . . . his arm, I mean. It was another partly submerged branch.'

'Are you sure he didn't come out somewhere else after finishing his swim?'

This was the other male again, still sounding dubious, and ruining Gregson's equilibrium once more.

'Don't be ridiculous, man. You don't suppose he's wandering around the woods with nothing on, do you? His clothes are still there.'

Helen muttered an acknowledgement and disappeared. Odhiambo stepped into the awkward silence that ensued.

'Did you see anyone else in the vicinity? Either before or after you investigated the shout?'

'No. No one else. This is a bad business, Odhiambo. I tell you, I think he's bought it. That damned lake. Trengrouse was saying the five years was up; time for another victim.'

'You were coming home alone? The rest of the party still at the pub?'

'Some had left ahead of me. You, of course. And the two Nigerians, Asuna and Adimojo. The others were still there when I left, listening to old Hargreaves. Why do you ask?'

'No reason. Right, I think you'd better change your clothes. We're obviously going to have to return to the spot where you think he went in.'

Just then Helen reappeared, clutching a large blanket which she gave to the now shivering Gregson.

'I've phoned the police, they're sending a car. I said we'd meet them at the lodge. They'll be coming from that direction. I'll go and see if Peter, Mr Deane that is, is in his flat and tell him there's been an accident. Jimmy, if you could get the jeep out.' She looked at Odhiambo. 'Will you be coming with us, Insp . . . Mr Odhiambo?'

Her last question was put in a neutral tone, but Odhiambo believed there was a plea hidden underneath. He nodded.

'Of course. I think we'd all better go and get ourselves ready. Reassemble in a few minutes?'

They went their separate ways, Gregson and Odhiambo making their way up the stairs. No one else seemed to have heard or seen Gregson return. The bedraggled ODA man laid a hand on Odhiambo's arm.

'Muriel, my wife, she was going to see an old friend the other side of the lake. Staying the night.'

Odhiambo noted the urgency with which Gregson imparted this news, although why he should think it relevant was not clear. Odhiambo was thinking about the movements of another Centre resident, namely Penny Deane. If Mahendra had decided on a moonlit dip, it seemed unlikely he would have gone alone.

Odhiambo returned to the hall, hearing as he arrived the crunch of tyres on gravel as the jeep pulled up at the door. He was not the first at the assembly point. Peter Deane was pacing up and down, his natural woebegone expression accentuated now into one of real concern. Odhiambo noticed that Deane was fully dressed, including a jacket and tie. Obviously he had not been in bed when Helen contacted him. Deane turned and watched Odhiambo approach.

'Hello. Mr Odhiambo, isn't it? Are you involved in this incident I've been informed about? Were you with Hugh? Gregson, I mean.'

'Not involved exactly. I saw Gregson return, wet and agitated. I agreed to join the search party.'

'Oh, I see. Yes, I suppose that's all right. Helen will be here in a minute. She's putting some clothes on. But I'll ask her to stay here and keep an eye on things. We'll go and have a look. We need Hugh, of course. Where is he?'

'Changing into dry clothes. He fell in the lake.'

'Oh yes, of course. You say you saw him returning. You were watching? From your room?'

Odhiambo looked at his companion more closely. Was there more to this question than idle curiosity? Was he wondering if Odhiambo had seen his wife?

'No. I'd gone to bed, but I heard voices. Hugh and the night officer. I had been looking out earlier. Saw some others returning from their walks.'

Deane opened his mouth and then shut it again. He looked a if he was struggling to formulate his next question, but hi attempt was interrupted by the virtually simultaneous arriv

from separate directions of Helen Shropshire and the originator of the current alarm. Helen did not seem too pleased to be assigned the role of looking after the base camp while the expedition set forth, but accepted with as much grace as she could muster what was virtually an order from the Director. The three men moved to join the driver of the jeep, who was hovering at the door.

As he passed Helen, Odhiambo pressed her arm lightly and whispered, 'I'll keep you posted. Will you be OK?'

She managed a slight smile.

'Go on, join your other male chauvinists. I'll put some coffee on. A traditional woman's role.'

During the rattling, bumpy ride to the lodge, Odhiambo, clutching the rear seat to avoid being jarred out of the open vehicle, pondered on the likely movements of the missing Indian. If, as he suspected, Mahendra and Penny Deane were engaged in a liaison, they could have gone for a swim together. Why would Penny not raise the alarm if something had happened to him? Fear of her relationship with Mahendra becoming known to her husband? And where had Peter Deane been? Dress at the Centre seemed to be informal; Deane was still formally dressed at midnight – had he been away from the Centre? Did he know of his wife's solitary return from the direction of the lake? And if Mahendra was with Penny Deane, then Odhiambo's guess that he was the unwelcome guest at the lodge when Odhiambo passed was wrong.

Arriving at the lodge they dismounted, Gregson feeling his lower back as if checking that his vertebrae were still in place. There were no lights now emanating from the lodge; the residents presumably had retired and the arrival of the jeep did not arouse them. Conversation had been impossible in the jeep but now, as they waited for the police car, Deane, the worry creases across his brow showing deeper in the headlights, cross-examined Gregson on his story. Gregson took a proffered cigarette from their driver, Jimmy the night officer, and drew on it deeply, showing agitation at Deane's persistence. Odhiambo watched them. There was more than the tension of a possible accidental death about these men; Odhiambo detected on the sea breeze the smell of fear.

He succeeded in intervening by asking the question that was puzzling him.

'Why is it taking the police so long to get here? Where are they coming from?'

Deane answered as if his mind was on other things.

'Redbourne. That's the nearest station. At night, at any rate.'

The driver added the extra relevant information.

'It's about a thirty-minute drive. They should be here by now, even assuming there wasn't a car nearby.'

His words were prescient. As he spoke, Odhiambo could see behind him lights approaching up the cliff road. The four men left the estate through the gate and awaited the police sergeant who emerged from beneath the flashing blue light, torch in hand – something which the party from the Centre had omitted to bring along. Introductions were criss-crossed through the night; the sergeant, Odhiambo learned, was called Trewin. He and Deane knew each other and, as the torch passed across the group, the sergeant showed no surprise at seeing an African who was taller and broader than himself. Gregson, regaining something of his professional poise, gave a succinct version of his story.

'Right,' said Sergeant Trewin, almost cheerfully, 'let's go and see if we can find the spot.'

This proved to be less than easy. As the jeep and police car made their way slowly back towards the Centre, Gregson seemed confused. Eventually they found what Gregson believed to be the track down to the water, and, when they reached the lake, his belief was justified – there in the torch's beam on a tiny area of sandy soil was a pile of clothes, haphazardly flung down as if the wearer had been in a hurry.

Sergeant Trewin shone his torch first on each garment in turn and then around the perimeter of the tiny sand area, as if he expected Mahendra to be lurking in the undergrowth. Then he aimed the light on to the water but with the air of a man going through the motions. The moon was still high in the sky and the lake was visible for some distance as a reflector for the already reflected light, but no detail could be seen and the prospect was far from inviting.

The policeman took Gregson through his story again and got him to show where he had seen, or believed he had seen, something that led to his own immersion in the lake. Odhiambo had the tangible sense that the policeman and everyone else assembled were on the verge of shouting something like 'Hello. Anyone there?' But nobody did, for nobody wanted to look ridiculous.

Finally, Sergeant Trewin turned his torch and attention on to the Director of the Centre, who was, in a sense, squire of the estate where they stood.

'Now, Mr Deane, can you confirm that a gentleman from the house is missing? And who that gentleman might be?'

Deane drew himself to attention, but still gave the impression of a worried rabbit transfixed by the torch's beam. He answered in a tone that scarcely concealed his mild irritation.

'No. No, of course I can't. I didn't wait to wake everyone up to take a roll-call. But Mr Gregson says it was a Mr Mahendra, so I have no reason to doubt it.'

'Ah, but Mr Gregson didn't see anybody, according to his statement. He's identifying the clothes.' The sergeant turned back to Gregson. 'Did you have a torch when you were here earlier, sir? And how certain were you these belonged to your Mr Mahendra?'

Gregson kicked at the sand, petulantly.

'No, I didn't. Have a torch. But the moon was bright and I've seen Mahendra wearing this shirt. So either it's Mahendra in there or someone who was wearing his shirt.'

The sergeant was unruffled.

'And this Mr Mahendra. A visitor to the Centre, I assume. And a foreign gentleman, I take it. Like this gentleman here.' The torch moved and shone its beam on to Odhiambo. Deane tried to preserve Commonwealth distinctions.

'Well, yes, foreign – that is, he's from India, not like Mr Odhiambo. But he's based in London at the Commonwealth Secretariat. He's here to open one of our courses. Well, he has opened it, as a matter of fact.'

Odhiambo decided it was time to intervene.

'Ah, Sergeant. If, as seems unfortunately to be likely, there has been a fatal accident here, I'm sure we will all be happy to give statements. But, perhaps, we should first decide what to do to organise a search of this lake.'

'Yes, you can leave that to us, sir. We'll organise the necessary, but there's not much to do until we get some light. And you, sir, would you be the police officer from Africa or some such?'

The question was put almost as an accusation. Odhiambo cursed to himself. He had hoped to keep this knowledge away from the local police; it could only serve to complicate matters. How the hell did this sergeant know?

'Odhiambo is my name and I'm from Kenya, yes.'

Trewin smiled.

'And a police officer. And you're wondering how I come to know that. Well, sir, the lady that phoned said something like

"We've got a senior police officer here but he's from Africa so that's no good is it?" She was right, of course.'

'Of course.' Damn Helen. She was always likely to say too much. 'I'm here as a student, so what I am back home is irrelevant.'

Trewin was about to concur with this when he and all present were startled by a loud splash. Everyone jumped, turned and scanned the dark lake as if expecting to see Mahendra rise from the water. But, of course, no Mahendra appeared and the large fish that had broken the surface now returned to his hunting depth. When they had all blundered around some more, Sergeant Trewin decided to move operations to the manor house and they all shuffled off up the track.

Back at the Centre Helen Shropshire greeted them at the door, together with another member of the staff unknown to Odhiambo and one of the seminar participants, who had been awoken by the comings and goings. Helen guided them through to the room that had been in use when Odhiambo arrived, so that Trewin and his constable driver could start to take notes. She claimed to have been as good as her word and to have coffee and biscuits ready. Odhiambo followed her as she made her way across the hall to the kitchen to fetch the tray. She turned to Odhiambo as the kitchen door shut behind them.

'I realised after you left. I told the police who you were. You might not have wanted me to do that.'

She looked at him, hoping to be exonerated. Odhiambo smiled.

'Yes, our friend the sergeant has referred to it already. It doesn't matter. They'd have found out sooner or later if this business turns out to be serious.'

Helen interrupted.

'I've knocked on Mahendra's door. There's no reply. You didn't find him?'

She realised the futility of her question and looked down. The likelihood of a fatality seemed to suddenly sink in on her and as she placed the coffee jug on the tray her face crumpled.

'Oh, my God, James. The poor man. He must have been pulled under. They talk of the undertow. What made him do it?'

'It's no good worrying until we know more about it. But from talk in the pub this evening, or rather . . ." with a glance at his watch, " . . . last evening, I gather he was in the habit of moonlight swims.'

Helen turned her head away. Odhiambo was sure she had been about to say that she too had heard the gossip. But acknowledging the gossip, as she was sharp enough to realise, would lead inevitably to the question of who had accompanied him on any earlier occasions. He changed the subject.

'When you went to call Deane he was still up, was he? Fully dressed, I mean.'

Helen looked at him, puzzled.

'Yes, yes, I think he had just returned. From some meeting or other.'

'What about Mrs Deane? Did you see her?'

'No. He came to the door and he came straight away. Come to think of it, he didn't call out to say he was going or anything. Perhaps she was sleeping. Why do you ask?'

'No reason, really.' Odhiambo picked up the loaded tray. He hesitated, but then went on. 'It's just that I saw her – Mrs Deane, I mean – returning from a walk. Before Gregson came back. I just assumed she would be in her apartment when you knocked.'

Helen looked at him appraisingly and then blurted out, 'Did she look as if she'd been swimming?' She looked down, embarrassed. 'Oh dear, what am I saying? Forget it, please. Let's take the coffee through.'

Odhiambo managed three hours of sleep, but woke and rose at dawn. It was a bright, clear morning, with a stiff breeze from the sea. He went into his bathroom, returned shaven and showered, pulled on slacks and pullover and walked quietly down the stairs and out of the door. No one was about, although he heard noises from the direction of the kitchen. Only as he walked down the drive did his conscious mind accept that this was no casual early morning stroll, but a desire to return to the scene of the drowning. As he walked along the main path he came to a track that led towards the lake some distance before the track down which Gregson had led them the previous night. On impulse he turned down it and soon found himself at the water's edge. The sun had not yet cleared the wooded hill on the far side so the lake still retained the darkness of the night now gone. He had reached a point in the lake where it curved towards the manor house, consequently he could see neither its major portion nor the sand bank dividing it from the sea. After some moments' casual observation, he noticed that a few yards to his right was a heron, standing motionless, eyes focused intently into the water as the bird sought an early breakfast. It was nature's *trompe-l'oeil* – the peaceful, graceful scene that contained the everyday life and death struggle of predator and victim – and into Odhiambo's mind came an image of Mahendra gasping for air as the water closed over him.

There seemed to be a way through the trees in the direction of the sea and Odhiambo picked his way along it, avoiding the nettles and brambles that occasionally traversed the faint signs of an infrequently used path. It was necessary to watch where one put one's feet and it was because he was looking down that Odhiambo saw a wisp of cloth under a creeper. He retrieved it and saw it to be a woman's handkerchief. It was not soiled or damp and retained its folded crease. It had been dropped, and recently. He looked around and noticed a small cushion of grass at the foot of a tree – it too showed signs of a recent visitor. The grass was crushed; Odhiambo guessed that someone had sat with their back against the tree. He thought of his Scottish game warden friend in Kenya. With his old game-tracker's background he could probably have read a lot more into these signs, but Odhiambo could tell no more than the obvious. He thought he was probably close now to the sandy strip where Mahendra had chosen to take his fatal swim. As he moved on he heard the sound of a helicopter approaching over his head and as he watched it came into sight, hovering low over the water and then slowly traversing the width of the lake. Odhiambo had seen helicopters in the distance as he was driven to the Centre the previous day: presumably there was an air base nearby, the services of which had now been solicited by the police. Confirmation came as into Odhiambo's sight nosed a small motor boat containing two men in wetsuits and a third man at the rudder. The police were at work early. Somehow Odhiambo had expected a less energetic approach to the matter. Perhaps the fact that the missing person was something to do with a big organisation in London had led Sergeant Trewin or his superiors to demonstrate their efficiency.

They soon gained their reward. Odhiambo was about to retrace his steps, for he had no wish to insert himself into the investigation, when a member of the helicopter crew appeared in the open doorway and signalled to the boat. The helicopter remained stationary as the boat approached and the two divers entered the water. The activity that then ensued, involving the divers and a winch lowered from the hovering craft, was sufficient for Odhiambo to be convinced that the search was over. Despite his better judgement he found himself making his way through the trees to the little beach. There, as he expected, he found Sergeant Trewin, who turned in some surprise as he heard Odhiambo's approach.

'I'm afraid I must ask you to . . .' The policeman started to warn off the visitor, but then he recognised the large black man coming towards him. 'Ah, it's you, sir. Up and about early, you be. And what brings you back here, if I may be so bold? Just curiosity, as they say?'

Odhiambo was nonplussed. To say he was on a casual stroll would stretch credulity, but he was loath to admit any other concern.

'Good morning, Sergeant. It would appear you've struck paydirt early. They seem to have found what you're looking for.'

Trewin considered. He was about to say that he would prefer no onlookers as the boat brought its grisly burden to land. But there was the fact that, even if African, this fellow was a police officer. Probably didn't mean much from what he knew of the goings on in Africa but there it was. Then it occurred to him that Odhiambo might have his uses.

'Yes, well, now you're here, tell me – you knew this chappie we're looking for, did you not?'

'Yes. I only arrived yesterday, but I met Mr Mahendra – certainly I can identify him if that would be of help.'

'Well, for the record, you know. Hardly likely to be anyone else, of course. Be a bit much if we had two bodies in here, wouldn't it now? Only supposed to claim one victim every so often, not two in the same night.'

The boat nudged its nose on to the sand and the two wetsuited men raised with some care a bundle wrapped in shiny plastic. With some manoeuvring the bundle was laid on the sand and gingerly unwrapped, revealing Mahendra's naked body. The effect of immersion was already evident and there were some signs of damage inflicted after death by denizens of the lake, but there was no doubt of the identity.

'Yes, that's Mr Mahendra, temporarily staying at the Polsand Centre, but normally resident, I understand, in London where he is employed by the Commonwealth Secretariat.'

As he spoke, Odhiambo was surveying the body more carefully. His instincts told him that something other than a bewitched lake with a curse on it was responsible for this pathetic shape in front of him. And that's all it was, a shape. Not only had life been extinguished; it was difficult to envisage that this sodden, soiled and already swollen lump had ever had life in it. His eyes ran down the body in a practised assessment. He noticed the contusion and bruising around one ankle and bending closer he could see a series of what seemed like little cuts or gouges in the skin.

Trewin completed his formal note of Odhiambo's identification.

'Thank you, sir. Now, how do you spell your name? And you're an inspector, I believe. In the African police, is that right?'

'Kenya Police and Chief Inspector, but for your requirements a student at the Centre here.' Odhiambo was determined to maintain his masquerade of being just another seminar participant, even though his eyes and intuition had aroused his professional interest. He raised a hand as the body was about to be re-covered by its attendants. 'But have a look at that ankle, Sergeant.' He paused as the other men shifted their attention to where his finger pointed. 'What d'you think? See the bruising and the skin damage?'

The sergeant looked closer and then turned to Odhiambo with a peevish expression.

'Superficial damage, sir. To be expected, I've no doubt. No need to worry yourself about that now.'

'I'm no pathologist, Sergeant, but I recommend you ask yours for an opinion. That looks a lot to me like it was done before death. And I don't wish to think where that might lead you.'

Trewin adopted his most supercilious manner.

'You leave the body to us, if you please. Now you've identified it. Very helpful, that was. No need to get into any speculation. Has to be a post-mortem given the nature of death. That's the law in this country, sir. As I expect they'll be explaining to you while you're on your course.'

'As it is in mine, Sergeant. You're quite right. But you might make a note of my comment. I think it may be a material fact. And now I'll leave you to your labours. No doubt we'll be seeing you at the Centre.'

Trewin watched him go – this time up the track to regain the main route to the manor. Don't need these sort of people to come and tell me my job, he thought. He knew what the chap was driving at. Well, perhaps it would all turn out all right. Here's another foreigner doesn't know what he's about. No one local would swim in there. Not without drink to dull their common sense.

But Odhiambo, as he strode along, was in no doubt. He didn't need further confirmation. What he had seen provided proof of what his instincts had already told him: Mahendra had been murdered. What irritated him was his own reaction. It was not his *shauri*, as he would put it in Swahili. Not his business. But somehow the Mahendra affair seemed more inviting than lectures on rural development.

6

Back at the Centre, life was stirring and the kitchens were alive with the sounds and smells of an English breakfast in the making. The women of Penleith who were making these preparations had heard the helicopter, seen the police car and heard the rumours; they spoke in grave voices of 'another victim for the lake,' 'funny how some folk'll never learn,' 'mind you, if it were that Indian, he weren't to know, how could he,' 'educated man, too, always very polite he were, been down here several times.'

Peter Deane looked at his wife as she sat on the bed, half dressed and staring vacantly at the floor.

'I must get to my office. There'll be a lot to do. London to call. And the police will be back soon.' He sounded defensive, even to his own ears. The face that had looked back at him from the bathroom mirror seemed to have aged overnight. 'Are you all right? Can I leave you?'

Response was slow in coming, but, at last, Penny Deane looked up and towards him. Neither of them had slept, but both had pretended, for the alternative was conversation that neither desired.

'Of course you can leave me. What are you talking about?'

Her expression was blank. Deliberately so, Deane believed. She was trying very hard to keep her feelings to herself. Is this what it has come to, he thought, and he felt an inner despair threatening to overwhelm him.

'It's just . . . well, it's all upsetting. I mean, it's not just someone missing who you . . . we . . . hardly know.'

Her eyes had focused now and the look she gave him frightened him. She couldn't hate him, could she? She was the one to blame. Whatever he'd done was a consequence of her behaviour. And she didn't know, did she?

Another silence descended on them. Eventually he shrugged,

reached for his tweed jacket from the chair-back and left the room. Penny heard the door of their flat close behind him. Slowly she allowed her emotions to take over. As the tears welled up and started down her cheeks she hammered her fists against the mattress and cried aloud.

'No. No. It can't be. It didn't happen, please, it didn't happen . . . Oh God, what am I going to do?'

Hugh Gregson was another of the Centre's early risers that morning. He arrived at the secretarial area outside the offices of the Director and the Administrative Office to find it deserted. He knocked at the two office doors, opened them on receiving no reply and satisfied himself that he was alone before returning to the secretarial desk to make use of the telephone. The call was unanswered for what seemed to Gregson an eternity; finally a voice responded.

'Hello, this is Hugh Gregson . . . Yes, hello, how are you? I apologise for this early call, but do you suppose I could speak with Muriel?'

He waited for another protracted period, before he heard his wife's voice. He interposed quickly.

'Listen, Muriel. It's important you get back here and we have a talk. Have you heard anything yet? . . . No. Right. Well, I can't go into details over the phone, but we must talk. Mahendra has gone missing – drowned in that bloody lake . . .' He heard the gasp and then a wordless cry. 'Muriel – are you there? Listen. I was there when it happened or just after . . . Are you there?'

There was a pause then the original voice returned.

'I'm sorry, er, Hugh. I think Muriel is upset. Your news is bad, I assume.'

'Yes. I think one of the people here was drowned last night. She knew him. I mean, we both did. The police are involved. I think she should get back here.'

He saw the door open and Deane walk in.

'Don't worry. I'll get her back as soon as she's collected herself and had a coffee. Oh, she wants a word with you . . .' Gregson looked at Deane, rolling his eyes. Deane smiled and moved towards his own office door. 'Hugh. This is awful, awful. Oh my God. I must think. This is . . .'

'I'm sorry, Muriel – this is not the time to talk. I'll see you as soon as you get back. You understand. I'm sorry, I've got to go.'

He replaced the receiver. Awful was an understatement. Whatever had she thought she was doing? He hoped she would pull herself together. Wearily he went to explain to Deane the use of his facilities.

Deane managed to ease Gregson out of his office and get down to more pressing matters. Gregson had seemed to want to talk without quite being able to bring himself to say what he intended. He seemed more upset than Deane expected. It had not seemed as if he and Mahendra were close friends. Anyway, now he was alone. He made one call to Penzance and passed his message briefly and, he hoped, with clarity. He emphasised that the need for a statement was unlikely, but there was just a chance, in which case embarrassment was better avoided. The reaction was, he supposed, to be expected – surprise, assurance and then evidence of some uncertainty. Oh, well, he would need to shore up the commitment.

Next, after checking his address book, he called one of the only senior Commonwealth Secretariat officials he happened to know well enough to have his personal number. He told him what little he knew and was assuring him that he would provide regular updates when a knock at his door heralded the arrival of the large Kenyan, what was his name? James Od . . . Odhiambo, that was it.

'Good morning, James. You're up and about early. Have you been out?'

Odhiambo looked at the Director with interest. The strain was showing; the haggard look revealed more than a shortage of sleep. Odhiambo's impression on meeting him the previous day was of a face of blandness portraying faithfully a personality lacking any aura; now looking at the eyes that shifted nervously under his gaze he was reminded of a Luo proverb – 'Beware the one who casts no shadow.'

'Yes, I've been back to the lake. The police have found Mahendra's body. I was there when they fished it out. They'll be coming here soon, obviously.'

'Poor Javi. Poor, poor man.' The words were appropriate but lacked any emotion. 'He liked to swim, although I warned him more than once of the undertow. That was a CS man in London I was talking to. I must call back with the news. He can inform Mahendra's office.'

Odhiambo hesitated for a moment, but could see no reason

why he should not warn Deane, in his formal capacity, of the complications ahead.

'I've got to tell you, Peter. It's just possible it wasn't an accident. We have to wait for the post-mortem, but there are signs on the body that he may have been pulled underwater. Not by the current, but by a hand.'

'Good God, man, what are you saying?' But it was clear that Deane knew exactly what was being told him. His face paled further and there was a distinct tremble in the hand that rose and clutched his thinning hair. 'It can't be. You mean, someone meant him to drown?'

'I'm just saying we could be dealing with something other than an accident. In which case there will be a full enquiry into everyone's movements, as someone must have been with him. Or at least following him.'

The mouth opened, but no words came. Odhiambo stared into the face of a very frightened man.

A tap on the door heralded the entrance of Helen Shropshire bearing a cup.

'I thought you would like . . . oh, hello, James, I didn't know you were here. Can I get you a coffee, too? Oh dear, you must think I spend all my time making coffee.'

She put the cup on Deane's desk and looked from one serious face to the other.

'You've got some news. Have they found him?'

Odhiambo nodded and her clenched hand went to her mouth. She looked vulnerable, as Odhiambo remembered her looking when events had brought them together in Nairobi. Vulnerable but appealing. He turned back to the man at the desk who was stirring his coffee aimlessly.

'You'll have to decide what to do about the course. If things are as I suppose, the police will want everyone to stay for a while, so you may as well keep them occupied by keeping things going. To the extent possible, anyway.'

The reply was vague. Deane was not focusing on rural development. Odhiambo took Helen's arm and shepherded her towards the door.

'Yes, I could do with that coffee.'

Once inside her office she wordlessly went over to the coffee percolator, poured a cup and handed it to him, gesturing to the milk and sugar. Odhiambo helped himself and looked around. Her office was smaller than Deane's but pleasantly arranged and with a more personal touch, including flowers on the corner of the desk. Helen had her back to the room and was gazing out of her small window, which looked out on to a walled garden. She spoke without turning.

'It's bad, isn't it? You don't think he simply drowned. Someone was with him.'

'I don't know. It could be. But what makes you jump to that conclusion? Why do you think he was not alone?'

'Because of the way you looked when I came in. I know you, you know. And Peter – he looked shell-shocked. Oh, I might have known you would be the catalyst for trouble. It's all starting again, isn't it?'

The shoulders dipped, and Odhiambo, to his embarrassment, heard the muffled sobs. He crossed over and gingerly took the woman's shoulders in his hands.

'Don't upset yourself. I'm sorry I'm causing you these memories. I shouldn't have come.'

Helen turned and for just a moment he felt the touch of her breasts upon his chest, before she pulled away, wiping her eyes with a finger.

'No, no, it's me that's sorry. It's not your fault; how could it be? And you want to know what I know. I can read you like a book, James Odhiambo.' The laugh was brittle, but at least it was a laugh. 'Mahendra has a reputation, you know. A ladies' man. He's attractive. I mean, he was attractive.' Again, the voice nearly broke but control was reasserted. 'Jane, the girl who met you when you arrived, told me he'd been seen in the lake with a woman. And one of the participants once told Peter he couldn't keep his hands off women in London.'

There was a pause. Helen looked as if she was about to resume, but her mouth then clamped shut. Odhiambo prompted.

'And I told you I'd seen Penny Deane walking back from that direction and you wondered if she'd been swimming.'

'Oh, I shouldn't have said that. It was bitchy. You mustn't repeat it.'

'Does Peter Deane have any suspicions?'

'I don't know. Honestly. I didn't think so, but yesterday he seemed to withdraw a bit. In the evening. Then he went out.'

Odhiambo remembered that both Penny and Mahendra were missing at dinner. If this had happened before during Mahendra's visits, Deane would have to be particularly obtuse not to get wind of something.

'What about Mrs Gregson? Is this her first visit? Of course, you haven't been here long yourself.'

'No, only two months. I don't think she's been to the Centre before, but I think she knows the area. I heard her telling one of the participants about the range of wild plants on the cliffs around here. I think she said something about having relatives or friends or something in this area. But I can't stay here chatting to you. I must go. Your point about keeping the course going. I'd better see Peter about it, now he's had a chance to gather his wits.'

'Just one more thing. What about the people in the lodge – Bastian and another man? You said something about them last night. Before the fuss started.'

'Oh, God, I talk too much, don't I? I should have learnt my lesson with you. Well, it's only that the willowy youth who passes as his son is thought by some to have a different relationship with Bastian. You know – gossip is, Bastian's gay and the boy is his companion, shall we say. Why do you ask? What's Bastian got to do with it?'

'Nothing, that I know of. Just trying to familiarise myself with the cast of characters darting about the fringe of this business. Anyway, I've kept you from your duties. I'm off.' Odhiambo turned and went to the door, then he looked back, 'And I am sorry. Really sorry. I don't bring you much luck.'

'Well, you're no lucky black cat, that's for sure. Oh, go on with you. I'm sorry to be such a ninny.'

Well, at least, Odhiambo thought as he closed the door, her voice was back to normal and her naturally ebullient spirit was returning. It was fortunate for his peace of mind that he didn't see her face as she gazed at the closed door.

Back in the hall, feeling himself ready for breakfast, Odhiambo glanced through the front doors, now open to the morning sun. Up the drive appeared two cars, one with a light attached to the roof, the other a plain dark saloon. The police were arriving and Odhiambo thought that rural development was about to take a back seat. Well, it was Deane's responsibility to handle the initial contact; Odhiambo considered himself well advised to partake of a good English breakfast while the opportunity was available.

There were only a few people in the refectory, most unknown to Odhiambo; from their dress he presumed them to be various outside workers on the estate. One member of the lecturing staff he recognised by sight and the female participant on the course, the attractive girl from Montserrat, was also there. Odhiambo passed down the service line, helping himself to a large portion of fried eggs, baked beans, sausages and various trimmings plus coffee and toast. His wife, Cari, would look askance, he thought, at the fried food. It was true that he had put on a few pounds since he arrived in England, but, like all men, and with better cause than most, he believed his frame could absorb some extra flesh without detriment to his appearance.

The Montserrat girl and the lecturer seemed to be in a deep private conversation so he crossed with his tray to a vacant table. The girl looked worried – Odhiambo wondered to what extent news of Mahendra's disappearance was already in wide circulation. His solitude did not last. A cough behind him and a perfunctory 'May I?' heralded the arrival of Gregson. Plumping himself down with a tray that added to Odhiambo's guilt, for it contained only a bran-type cereal, toast and coffee, Gregson wasted no time in bringing Odhiambo back to the main business in hand.

'So what's happened? I saw you coming back when I was dressing. You've been to the lake? And I see the police are here.'

'They've found Mahendra's body. They had a helicopter and boat out early.'

'So, he's gone then.' There was no sign of regret in the voice. As if to correct this impression, Gregson went down one octave and spoke in a sombre tone. 'Poor man. Not a nice way to go. Tragic.'

Odhiambo swallowed the last piece of sausage, considering how best to approach his questions.

'Tell me – you said you heard a shout last night when you were on your way back here. Did you recognise the voice?'

Gregson looked up from his cereal and seemed about to question Odhiambo's curiosity. But when he answered, it was in an even tone, almost, Odhiambo thought, as if it was a rehearsed reply.

'No, not really. It wasn't words, if you know what I mean. More a kind of strangled cry.'

'It must have been loud. It's quite a way from the lake to the road at that point. And dense trees in between.'

'Well, it was damned faint to my ear, but it certainly seemed to be someone in trouble.'

'How did you find that path down to the water in the dark? Or did you know it was there?'

Just for a moment Gregson seemed taken aback. He took his time spooning up cereal and chewing it.

'I think I'd noticed it before. Why are you asking me all this? I've given all the details to our friend the sergeant. And no doubt will have to do so again.'

'Yeah, I'm sorry. Just my old habits, I guess. How are you, anyway? It must have been a nasty moment when you fell in. Good job you can swim. I'd have been a goner.'

'Yes, yes. Hardly necessary, actually, right by the shore and so on. But I swim a bit.'

Odhiambo hesitated only a moment. What the hell, he might as well go for it.

'Not as well as Mrs Gregson, perhaps?'

The reaction was sharp, puzzlement giving way quickly to anger.

'What are you implying, Odhiambo? What are you suggesting?'

'Nothing. I'm sorry, I didn't mean to pry. I seem to remember hearing someone say she was a good swimmer, that's all.'

The lie was smooth and Gregson made a visible effort to appear official.

'I'd better go and talk to Deane to see how he wants to play it. Whether to go on with the seminar, I mean. What to do with the body. Lot to decide.'

Odhiambo watched him go. There was an air about the way he walked that probably reflected a normally confident, even arrogant, man. But since he had arrived back last night he had been defensive in conversation. Odhiambo was sure his account of how he came to be at the lakeside was not correct. But why should he blur the truth? He couldn't have been planning to meet Mahendra. Nothing in his demeanour in the pub supported such a hypothesis.

He finished his coffee, handed in his tray and made his way out to the front lawn. The police cars were there: the dark saloon with driver in attendance indicated that someone senior to Sergeant Trewin was now in charge. Odhiambo wandered around the side of the building. Looked at from the front, the main house was flanked on the left by a high wall and then a complex of buildings, once the stables and lofts for the handlers, now converted to cottages and flats for the staff of the Centre, including the estate manager. Odhiambo found a gate in the wall; yielding to his push, this revealed the walled garden he had glimpsed from Helen's office. The back of the garden as he looked at it was not a plain wall but the front of what appeared to be an apartment – clearly of more recent construction than the rest of the complex. Odhiambo guessed correctly that this was the Director's accommodation. Confirmation came quickly as out from the door came Penny Deane. Her attire suited the peaceful rural scene, a pretty blue dress, a pale cardigan and sensible shoes. Odhiambo approached along the path that circled the well-kept lawn.

'Good morning. I'm sorry, I'm intruding on your private domain. I was exploring. You know – getting a feel for the geography of the place.'

The practised official hostess smile came and went without illuminating the face, which looked far from welcoming.

'Oh. It's, it's Mr Odhiambo, isn't it? James, that's it. No, it's quite all right. This is not my private garden. It's part of the Centre. Like everything here.'

The note of bitterness was not, perhaps, intended, but audible nevertheless.

'I expect you've heard. Mr Mahendra's body has been recovered. Very sad. Your husband will have told you about the accident last night.'

The pretty face stayed composed. Cosmetics had been carefully applied, but seemed to create a mask. It was as if she was on a stage, made up and dressed for the 'anyone for tennis' scene in a country house light romance. The voice was equally under control and equally false.

'Yes, it's a terrible tragedy. I hadn't heard that the body had been found. Thank you.'

Odhiambo felt an urge to shake this slim little thing; to get her to say what she had seen and done the previous night.

'He had been here before, I believe? A regular visitor to the Centre.'

'Not regular, but certainly this was not his first visit. He was Peter's liaison point in London.'

'Did he swim in the lake often? When he was here, I mean?'

But the official hostess deemed that diplomacy had been served. A brief smile came and went and she turned to leave him.

'I really couldn't say. It's Liberty Hall here, Mr Odhiambo. Not a school. Now I must see if Peter needs anything.'

Odhiambo nodded as she passed him and entered a door on the side of the manor leading to the administrative offices. Behind the mascara the eyes seemed to see something other than Odhiambo's face – haunted, Odhiambo thought, by the vision of a drowning man.

7

Detective Chief Inspector Bill Pendham was cross and was not attempting to disguise the fact. A drowning was not usually a matter for his attention. On the Cornish coast such deaths unfortunately were not uncommon. However, the complication of foreigners being involved made it a sensitive matter, complicated further by the fact that one of them was, apparently, a Chief Inspector in his own right. The report of a missing Indian diplomat had reached his superior's ears in the early hours of the morning and that alone was sufficient for him to wake Pendham and put him in charge of the investigation. At first Pendham's disgruntlement had been due to his assumption that he was wasting his time, but the first report he got at the scene was that this foreign policeman was claiming suspicious circumstances. Pendham's boiling point was easily reached, although the police doctor, worried by his blood pressure, wished it were higher. His recommendation that Pendham see an anti-stress therapist and a dietitian had merely achieved one of Pendham's famed outbursts, involving, on this occasion, colourful remarks about doctors from fancy medical schools who tried to send honest men to quacks. Suspicious circumstances were all very well, but Pendham preferred to detect them for himself.

'So where's the body?' he had asked the sergeant as they stood beside the lake. 'Gone? What do you mean, gone? Thrown the bugger back in, have you?' He went on at some length to make it clear that if a body had suspicious marks it should stay where it was until somebody with intelligence could have a look. He did not count the local pathologist amongst that number: in his view he was likely to add more suspicious marks.

Now he and Trewin were in Deane's office. He had interviewed Deane and had not been impressed. A ditherer, was his summary. He had seized on a half-hearted offer and taken over Deane's office for other interviews. Gregson was the next to encounter Pendham's irritability. His story seemed plausible enough, but to Pendham it did not ring true. Shifty character, like all these civil servants from Whitehall. He checked his notes. Overseas Development Administration – just the sort of poncy organisation he would belong to.

'So what you're telling me, Mr Gregson, is that on the basis of some sort of faint noise you find your way down an unknown track in the dark to where you thought the noise came from. Is that right?'

Gregson adopted his most officious manner.

'Quite. You have correctly summarised the facts, Chief Inspector, omitting only the light from the moon, which was considerable.'

'Never mind what I've omitted. I'm interested in your omissions. Omissions such as that you went down there together for some reason.'

'Are you contesting my statement, Chief Inspector? I have witnesses who were with me in Penleith, and Mahendra was not with us. Why on earth would I want to go swimming with Mr Mahendra?'

After dismissing Gregson, Pendham sat for a while drumming his thick fingers on Deane's polished desk-top. His inclination was to allow the African policeman to stew in his own juice for a while. He had asked Deane to tell him to stand by. But apart from Deane and Gregson there were no other obvious candidates. And until he saw the body for himself there was only the one witness who was raising this case from an unfortunate accident to that of a potential murder. He dispatched Trewin to fetch Odhiambo. There was the Admin woman of course, but all she had done was call the police on Gregson's say-so. But if there were suspicious circumstances involving a naked male, Pendham assumed it would be a matter of finding his female companion. Unless he was a queer. Odhiambo's arrival interrupted his reverie. A big laddie, he thought as he waved him to the chair opposite, and no doubt about his place of origin. After the minimum of introductions he settled back and viewed Odhiambo with a jaundiced eye.

'So, you're from the Kenya CID, Mr Odombo, is that right?'

Like his sergeant the previous night, Pendham made it sound like an accusation, but Odhiambo was placatory.

'Yes, that's right. But I want to stress, Chief Inspector, that, as you know, my being a policeman is a coincidence and an irrelevance; I have no standing, obviously, and seek no involvement.'

'But you were present when the body was landed and made certain observations.'

'I noticed the markings around the deceased's ankle, yes. I guess this raises questions, but the autopsy will, no doubt, give you the answers. I merely thought it helpful to draw Sergeant Trewin's attention to the ankle.'

'Did you have any reason for suspicions? I'm told that lake is dangerous to swim in. Why wouldn't an unfortunate accident be the most likely?'

Odhiambo shrugged. The exchange of words was reasonable, on the face of it. But there was a tension between them that was palpable. It was the old story, as Odhiambo expected: one lion did not appreciate the presence of another on his territory even if it had crossed into it by accident. But there was more to it than that and Odhiambo thought he could recognise it well enough. Resentment was becoming mutual as the two men faced each other, with Sergeant Trewin taking notes at the side of the desk.

'Sure. Probably that's the way it was. Let's wait and see.'

Pendham pressed on.

'Mr what's his name, Mahendra – the Director of this place tells me he has swum there before, on previous visits.'

Odhiambo shrugged again.

'This is my first visit and I only met him yesterday. But so I understand.'

'Now, Inspector Odombo. The sergeant here tells me you were quickly on the scene last night, and again this morning. Can you give me an account of your movements?'

Odhiambo gave a short but detailed summary of events following the return of Gregson. Pendham was quick, however, to pull him back a step in time.

'You saw Gregson arrive at the house?'

'No. I had just gone to bed. I heard his voice, through the open window. My bedroom is more or less above the front door.' Odhiambo hesitated, but there was no real doubt what he was duty bound to say. 'I did see one person returning. Just before I went to bed. It was Mrs Deane, the wife of the Director here.'

Pendham sat up. Now this was more like it.

'Coming from what direction?'

'By the time I saw her she was close to the house. But coming from the direction of the lake road, yes.'

'And how did she look? Dress and manner? Running or strolling?'

Odhiambo described Penny Deane's appearance and demeanour as he had viewed them. He paused again, but this time more for theatrical reasons than through doubt as to how to proceed.

'And this morning, while walking near where the incident

occurred, I found this.' He produced from his pocket the small handkerchief he had retrieved.

Pendham viewed Odhiambo's offering suspiciously before picking it off the desk. Odhiambo had not yet seen him standing, but guessed that Pendham was only of medium height, but bulky, with the beefy shoulders that caused the back of his jacket to rise and curve forward, giving him a hunched look. Fifty, Odhiambo judged, with a full head of brown hair, greying only at the temples.

Pendham had finished his examination of the cloth.

'You're quite the Sherlock Holmes, aren't you? One step ahead of the clod-hopping police. You'll be producing some cigar ash next.'

Odhiambo struggled to maintain his dispassionate status of willing witness.

'You don't need to be Sherlock Holmes to deduce whose this is. The coin embroidered in the corner. I bet it's Penny Deane's little affectation. A penny as her logo. Where I found it, it looked as if someone had been sitting. From there in the moonlight she could see the water where Mahendra drowned.'

'Why didn't you tell all this to Sergeant Trewin earlier? You're a policeman. You know better than to hold back evidence.'

Odhiambo had had enough. He leaned forward and pointed his forefinger at the man opposite him.

'Look, Pendham. You can have whatever views you want about me. I'm telling you all I know, whether you appreciate it or not. If there was foul play last night then Penny Deane may have seen something. That's what I'm trying to get across to you.'

Pendham smiled. At last he had pierced the chap's defences.

'Would you mind answering my question?'

'I hadn't seen the body then. When I found the hanky. Then when I saw Mahendra I forgot about it.' He didn't want to admit that Trewin's attitude had annoyed him. Actually, give me Trewin any day now I've met you, he thought. 'But so what, you've got it now.'

'OK. We'll let your little memory lapse pass. So what you're telling me, Mr Odombo, is that you think Mahendra was murdered by a person unknown who held him under the water and then swam off before Gregson arrived. Not knowing, however, that Mrs Deane was also present, leaving all sorts of things behind. Mrs Deane, despite having been present, arrives back, possibly overwrought, but does not see fit to raise the alarm and hasn't exactly been beating at my door since I got here. You get that sort of thing in Kenya, do you?'

It was Odhiambo's turn to smile.

'You're beginning to get the picture. Yes, if I'm right about Mahendra, those are the facts you have to chew on. From what people tell me about Mahendra it seems unlikely he would go for a swim alone.'

You're right there, matey, Pendham thought. Maybe you're not so daft. He took Odhiambo through the previous night's events once more, got him to specify more precisely the spot where he had found the handkerchief and then terminated the interview.

'Right, Inspector Odombo. Thank you. That's all for now. I'm sure I don't need to give you the usual rigmarole; may need you again and all that.'

Odhiambo nodded, got to his feet. No handshake was proffered so he tendered none. He went to the door and turned back.

'Od-i-am-bo, not Odombo. I think your sergeant has it correctly in his notebook.'

When the door closed, Pendham sighed and, while still looking at the door, said, 'There's a deep one there, Trewin. As dark and deep as the bloody lake. We need to watch our step, mister. Can't have a wog policeman doing our job for us, can we?'

Helen Shropshire had given up her office to her boss as he had relinquished his to the police. She was operating now in the outer area used by Jane and a part-time typist. The decision had been made to carry on with the course regardless. Deane, when all were assembled, intended to acquaint everyone of the basic facts and say a few words as a eulogy for Mahendra. Everyone was now up and about and news of Mahendra's death, often embellished by exaggerated tales of the legend of the lake, was spreading. When Odhiambo emerged from Deane's office she left Jane to explain arrangements to the Tanzanian, who seemed to expect a period of tribal mourning, and walked with Odhiambo into the main hall.

'Good morning, again. You know we're carrying on? With the seminar, I mean.'

Odhiambo turned towards her. He's looking very serious, she thought, serious and angry.

'Yes, I suppose that's sensible. But . . . but I'm not sure I can attend this morning. I want to go and see someone.'

'You don't have to tell me. I didn't think you would be able to concentrate on rural development when there's a mystery to solve.'

'It's none of my business, of course. But there are one or two things I need to clear up to my own satisfaction so I can complete my evidence to Pendham.'

They wandered together on to the verandah. The sun was now up above the trees, the sky was clear and a fine day was obviously in prospect. Helen looked around but there was nobody about.

'The police wanted to see Mahendra's room. The master keys are in my office. The one I needed was not where I left it, but on a different hook. I went to the room with them. It looked OK at first sight, but then I saw something that wasn't quite right.'

She now had Odhiambo's complete attention. He drew her further away from the door to the steps down to the sunlit drive.

'What? You mean someone had been going through his things?'

'No, not that. Our ladies, they make the beds in the morning in a certain way. You know – fully tucked in with the eiderdown fully covering the bed including the pillows. Mahendra's bed was unslept in, obviously, but it had been made differently, eiderdown folded back and one corner turned up.'

Odhiambo looked at his companion. She blushed slightly. He knew what they were both thinking. Mahendra and Penny Deane had missed dinner last evening. If there had been a dalliance in Mahendra's bed, Penny Deane would not have wanted it to be seen to have been used. She might have gone to Mahendra's room when she returned last night. But that then presupposed she already knew Mahendra was not returning.

'Did you tell Pendham?'

'No. It seemed sort of silly and tale-telling. And I need to check with the room maids before being sure.'

Odhiambo sighed, hesitated, and then made a decision to bring Helen into his confidence.

'Look, we need to be sure before proceeding much further. But it looks as if Mrs Deane was somewhere in the vicinity when Mahendra drowned. If it was an accident, OK. But if it was something else she's got a lot of explaining to do. That's Pendham's job. But if she was involved with Mahendra and is too embarrassed to say so, she could get herself in deep. How is it best to proceed? Should I have a word or would it be better coming from you?'

As he hoped, Helen took the bait.

'Oh, I'm sure it would be better coming from me. What with you being a virtual stranger, and . . . er . . . and a policeman.'

'OK. But be careful how you go about it. A friendly shoulder to cry on, that sort of thing. Not impugning her actions, I mean. May not do any good, but we can but try.'

'I understand. I'll be discreet. Or as discreet as I can.' A genuine smile lit up Helen's face. She placed a hand on her companion's arm. 'I'll be a good Dr Watson, honest.'

Odhiambo took her hand and lowered his head to establish direct eye contact.

'This is not a game, Helen. And we're not going into the private detective business. We just need to be sure Mrs Deane doesn't have another explanation before we fill Pendham in, that's all.'

'Oh, go on with you. I understand.'

And with that Helen detached her hand, turned and re-entered the house. Odhiambo watched her go. He hoped he was doing the right thing.

Another pair of eyes also watched Helen's departure. Gregson was in his room, looking down from his window. He didn't like the look of the close conversation he had just seen. He had a nasty feeling Odhiambo's interest in the Mahendra drowning was more than that of a passive spectator. He could do without Odhiambo getting involved as well as the local police. Someone in the ODA had told him that Odhiambo was reckoned to be pretty smart and determined once he'd got the scent. Gregson turned away from the window. Where the hell was Muriel? Perhaps he should ring again.

Pendham had decided to interview Penny Deane in her own living-room rather than her husband's office. He knew what local gossip could do. She received them politely, offered them coffee, sat demurely in her armchair, but revealed little.

'Yes, I did take a walk last night. I often do. Peter was at a meeting in Penzance, it was a nice night and there was no more official socialising to do. I enjoy a walk.'

'And where exactly did you walk.'

'Oh, I don't know. In the woods.'

'Were you at any time near the lake close to the area where Mr Mahendra went missing? You've heard Mr Gregson's account?'

'From Peter, yes. No, I was never by the lake. I was in the woods the other side of the road to the lodge.'

The face was that of an innocent teenager, but Pendham was sure he was looking at an experienced liar. He pressed her on her memory, suggesting she might have been mistaken, but a shake of the head was his only response.

'How well did you know Mr Mahendra?'

'He was a colleague of my husband's. As he lives in London we only saw him occasionally.'

'Did he often swim in the lake?'

'I've no idea. I was not responsible for his movements.'

'But you must have heard rumours if he did. People talk hereabouts.'

She looked at him gravely. Her hands were clasped together tightly.

'I find as the Director's wife it's better not to encourage rumours. Some of our guests see their stay here as part holiday. If they relax and socialise in the evenings that's their business.'

'Mrs Deane, this is not a formal interview, but I'm asking for your co-operation. We're investigating Mr Mahendra's accident. Are you sure you cannot help us?'

Another shake of the head and the hands tightened further. Pendham rose, produced the handkerchief and dropped it in her lap.

'I believe this is yours.'

She looked at it suspiciously, then looked up at the figure looming over her. She closed her eyes momentarily as if to blot him out of her mind.

'Yes, this is one of mine.'

'It was found by the lake near the spot where Mr Mahendra went for his last swim.'

'I don't know how it got there. It may have been there some time.'

Pendham allowed the silence to convey his disbelief. Suddenly she burst out.

'Why are you questioning me? I've told you. I was not with him and I don't know who was.'

Pendham heard the door open behind him. He cursed to himself. Peter Deane's voice was sharp.

'Are you all right, dear? There's no need to upset yourself. Is there, Inspector?'

8

Odhiambo walked briskly along the path, familiar to him now from the previous evening's excursion. In the full light of a crisp sunny day the estate was beautiful. It was difficult not to have one's spirits raised, but Odhiambo's mind was too preoccupied to be affected. If his assumptions were correct, Mahendra had an assignation in the lake last night and whoever was in the water with him pulled him under and drowned him. He was sure that Penny Deane knew something about it; it was likely she was Mahendra's swimming partner. But had she been in the water with him? If so, she was almost certainly the killer. Gregson had been in the water, albeit with his clothes on; Odhiambo did not believe he was telling the truth, but it could scarcely be that Gregson had a date with Mahendra, and certainly not for a swim fully clothed. Then there were the missing characters – the spouses of Penny Deane and Hugh Gregson. Fair enough so far, he thought, a reasonable array of suspects. But his mind kept coming back to Mahendra's request for him to keep his eyes open. That could scarcely be in connection with Mahendra's own affairs. His irritation at the time was intensified now. Mahendra had intended to use Odhiambo's presence for some devious reason of his own, of that Odhiambo was instinctively certain. But what reason? And did it have any connection with Mahendra's death?

Odhiambo rounded the corner and there was the sea rolling in, but with a gentler motion than the previous evening. There also was the lodge, marking the end of the estate. Odhiambo approached the lodge and, when level with it, hesitated. Then, as he was about to open the little gate leading to the lodge's small garden and front door, he saw a slim figure carrying a shopping basket come through the main gate from the cliff road into the estate. He waited and the figure approached; it was a young man dressed in trainers, bright yellow slacks and a V-necked cricket-type sweater with a brightly coloured cravat. He looked as if he'd stepped off the stage of a Noël Coward 1930s comedy.

'Hello. Can I help you? Or are you resting on the gate?'

The voice was friendly enough. Odhiambo stood aside to allow the young man to open the gate.

'Good morning. I'm staying at the Centre, as you can probably guess. I was hoping to have a word with Mr Bastian.'

'Ah. Bastian senior that would be. Come with me, my dear cousin. I take it you're from some distant part of the Commonwealth if you're at the Centre, so we're all meant to be part of the Queen's family. Or are you from one of those awful republics? No, no offence, you must excuse my little eccentricities.'

Odhiambo accompanied the youth to the door of the lodge and followed him in. They stood in a mini-hall, wood-panelled, slate-floored and gloomy – this last alleviated to some extent by two large, bright, polished brass Indian vessels which framed the door and served as umbrella, walking-stick and fishing-rod receptacles.

Down the stairs came a short, thickset, middle-aged man dressed in slacks and a fisherman's rollneck pullover. Although the body gave the impression of muscle turning with age to fat, the face was incongruous, being lean, lined and sunken-eyed. It was as if it was a face peering through a hole with a corpulent body painted underneath, as found on seaside piers in earlier years. To say the face looked lived in would be an understatement; it was raddled, dissipated. Odhiambo's judgement was that he was looking at a heavy drinker. As the man reached the bottom of the stairs Odhiambo became aware of another feature of the face now close to his: beneath the heavy brow and protruding eyebrows the small but bright eyes radiated intensity, the focused stare of a genius or a madman.

'You have a visitor, Alex,' the youth's voice remained light, bright and affected, 'from the Centre. Or do you know each other from the far-flung reaches of the old Empire?'

'I'm sorry to disturb you.' Odhiambo held out his hand, but received only a slight nod in response. 'Odhiambo. Yes, I'm at the Centre, but I was hoping for a word with you about the unfortunate accident last night. I suppose you've heard?'

Again, a slight nod was the only acknowledgement. The man moved past Odhiambo to a door level with the foot of the stairs, opened it and gestured for Odhiambo to enter. The youth looked as if he might follow, but Alex Bastian had other ideas.

'Thank you, Nigel. I'll see Mr Odhiambo.' He closed the door behind him. 'Now, sir, what can I do for you and what is your interest?'

They were in a small study. Books on the shelves, an ornately carved desk and a swivel chair with curved arms, two leather armchairs flanking a small two-tiered brass table. Desk and table also Indian, Odhiambo guessed. A window gave a view of the woods behind the lodge.

'I have no legitimate official interest. Only I knew the dead man, Mahendra. The police found the body earlier this morning. I was just interested in his movements last evening.'

'And why should you come here?' They remained standing and Odhiambo's host made no gesture towards the chairs. The eyes glittered with animosity, as if he identified Odhiambo as an enemy. 'I knew him slightly, but I certainly don't accompany him on midnight swims.' The lips widened, but there was no humour in the mouth.

'I guess I wondered if you'd seen him. He was not seen at the Centre from the afternoon onwards. As I said, I'm interested in his movements prior to the accident.'

'Idle curiosity, Mr Odhiambo? You say you have nothing to do with the police?' Suddenly, the man stiffened, as if a memory was triggered. 'Perhaps you are a policeman?'

'I am, yes. But not in this country. So it's not relevant here. I told you I knew Mr Mahendra and he's dead. Naturally I'd like to know what happened.'

For several seconds Bastian seemed to be considering what line to take.

'You're sticking your nose into other people's affairs, mister – that's what I think. But I'll tell you this. That Indian man was here briefly yesterday. There's no mystery about that. A social visit.'

Bastian turned and opened the door and awaited Odhiambo's departure. Odhiambo, however, held his ground.

'No altercation? I understand that passers-by heard raised voices.'

'Get out. You have exceeded my hospitality. Go.'

Odhiambo shrugged and moved to leave. As he passed Bastian he could almost feel the heat of the man's pent-up anger. At the front door Odhiambo turned. Bastian still stood at the study door. At the door to the right of the stairs Odhiambo caught sight of movement. Nigel was taking a close interest. Odhiambo delivered his parting shot.

'Mr Mahendra had something on his mind; he had told me as much. I think it might have been connected with you. When you see the police you might remember the law about concealing evidence.'

Bastian's expression did not change. Stony-faced would about sum it up, Odhiambo thought as he closed the door behind him.

As he reached the gate, he was surprised to see Nigel emerge from the side of the house, having presumably come out of a back entrance. The youth was smiling as he approached Odhiambo, laying a hand familiarly on Odhiambo's arm.

'I don't know how long you knew our Asian cousin, my Kenyan friend. But there was usually only one thing on his mind.' Nigel made a vulgar gesture. 'Ask Mrs Deane.'

'How do you know where I'm from? Did somebody tell you? It wasn't me.'

The youth laughed.

'Your fame goes before you, Inspector. You mustn't mind Alex. He gets easily upset. To tell you the truth, neither of us was very fond of Mr Mahendra. Alex owns this property, it has nothing to do with the Centre and so nothing to do with Mahendra.'

'What time did he leave here last night?'

'Oh, didn't Alex tell you? I'm sorry, I can't help – I was in Penleith until late.'

'What was the cause of friction between Mahendra and Mr Bastian?'

'Promise you won't tell? You see, Alex is a bit of a prude. He complained to the Centre's Director about goings-on just below us here one evening. Our Indian friend demonstrating his knowledge of the Kama Sutra. I think he took it amiss.'

Odhiambo was sceptical. The story might be true as far as it went, but he was sure there was more to the Bastian-Mahendra relationship than that.

'Who was the lady involved?'

But any reply was pre-empted by a shout from the lodge doorway. Alex Bastian was gesticulating angrily.

'Send him packing, Nigel. We want no truck with him.'

Nigel's light coquettish manner changed, his face darkening. He turned away, but his spirits seemed to return as he looked back over his shoulder with a feminine archness.

'Goodbye, Inspector. Perhaps we shall meet again. I'm always happy to entertain a celebrity.'

Odhiambo left the lodge but, rather than turning back to the Centre, turned right, went through the main gate of the estate and moved to the edge of the cliff, looking down on the great bank of sand that stretched for half a mile or more before giving way to gently sloping green fields, that replaced the woods as one neared the cliff top. The bright morning had flattered to deceive. As Odhiambo watched, a bank of sea mist rolled in, temporarily obscuring the sand. It eddied across the water of the lake, thinned and dispersed. Out to sea there was a great bank of mist, hugging the water surface and for the moment leaving visible the blue sky above it. It seemed to approach and then retreat but gradually all the time drew closer. Odhiambo shivered.

Now that the sand bank was visible again, Odhiambo saw that he was not the only watcher on the shore. Below him on the sand stood a woman, hands thrust into the pockets of her trousers, who also seemed rapt at the sight of the approaching mist. Knowing not why, but following instinct, Odhiambo picked his way down the cliff path to the sand. By the time he gained it the mist had arrived, approaching in the end at a surprising speed. Visibility fell in the space of seconds to a few yards, so rendering the woman invisible. Odhiambo cursed to himself and was about to retrace his steps before he lost sight of the path, when a voice behind him made him jump. My God, he thought, the atmosphere of the place is getting even to me.

'Hello. It's dangerous to be walking in the mist, you know, if you're a stranger here. It's easy to get lost, believe it or not.'

Odhiambo turned. The woman was there, late thirties was his guess; even with a bulky sweater disguising her figure it was clear she was slim, pleasant-faced, with short curly hair. She continued.

'I'm sorry, I startled you. It's this mist.'

'You're right. I'm sorry, I didn't see you. I could see you clearly enough when I was at the top. Does it usually come in as quickly as this?'

'It happens. When the land and sea temperatures differ you get these very local sea mists. It's a feature of this piece of coast. Sometimes they linger but on a day like this it will disappear as fast as it formed.'

'My name is Odhiambo. I'm staying at the Centre, if I can find my way back to it.'

'Ah. The gentleman from Kenya. A policeman, am I right?'

Odhiambo had a strange sense of unreality. How come he was suddenly known to everyone?

'That puzzles you, right? Actually, it's simple. Muriel Gregson is a friend of mine. She told me about you.'

'Oh, I see. Mrs Gregson. Yes, her husband told me she had gone to see a friend. She was with you yesterday evening?'

'Yes. I live the other side of the lake from the Centre. Over there.' She waved in the direction of the fields. 'Yes, we spent the evening together and she stayed the night. I strolled over with her this morning from the other direction and decided to keep going and complete the circular route.'

Well, there was Mrs Gregson's alibi neatly placed into evidence, thought Odhiambo. He moved to the matter of the day.

'I suppose you've heard there was an unfortunate drowning here last night?'

'Yes, indeed. Poor Mr Mahendra. He liked his moonlight bathes. Foolish, of course. It's not safe.'

'You knew him then? Mahendra.'

'Yes. I had him and the Deanes to dinner once. A friend of mine was staying with me who is also in the diplomatic game. She found him quite attractive. A bit of a ladies' man, wouldn't you say?'

'So people tell me. I only met him yesterday. You don't swim in the lake yourself?'

'Not at this end. No. At the far end of the lake – inland, I mean. It's safe there.'

'So why would Mahendra choose this end? He must have known that.'

'I think it appealed to the romantic in him, Mr Odhiambo. The other end lacks, what shall we say, lacks the glamour of legends.'

'And, perhaps, the other end lacks the privacy of the spot he preferred.'

The woman laughed and as if by cause and effect the mist suddenly eddied and cleared. The sun shone on her face, the glowing healthy skin seemingly unadorned by make-up.

'Perhaps so, Mr Odhiambo. Perhaps so. But there was no one with him to save him last night, it seems. Now, we'd better go our separate ways while we can see.'

'I've enjoyed meeting you. Do you live here all the time?'

'Oh yes. I'm widowed, you see. But one can enjoy solitude here. And I've enjoyed meeting you.'

'Goodbye then.'

Odhiambo turned towards the path. Another bank of mist seemed to be almost on them. The woman's voice addressed his back.

'I didn't introduce myself. That was rude of me. Angela Tamlyn. Better late than never.'

Odhiambo turned back.

'To me you'll always be the Lady in the Mist. You see, I'm a romantic too.'

But he was addressing a swirling wall: Angela Tamlyn was no more.

Back on the path to the manor, Odhiambo trudged through the mist, his thoughts on the Mahendra murder, for as such he regarded it, and the set of characters that had now made their entrances. It seemed very plausible that Mahendra had been threatening Bastian, but what the Indian had on him was unclear. Exposing a homosexual relationship with the precious Nigel was a possibility, but from what Helen had said most people were not deceived by the claimed family relationship anyway. Then there was his latest acquaintance, the Lady in the Mist. The volunteered alibi for Muriel Gregson had been neatly but quickly inserted. Mrs Tamlyn was surprisingly forthcoming, considering they had just met. Of course, she knew who he was, apparently. There seemed little doubt that if and when Mahendra's drowning was confirmed to be murder, Penny Deane would be the people's favourite for the person most likely to have had the opportunity. But where was the motive?

Occasionally the mist almost dispersed and the sun's light would suddenly penetrate, reflecting off the remaining mist clouds, giving the onlooker the impression of being in some fantasy world, a scene conjured up by Tolkien. Suddenly Odhiambo was overtaken by a sense of loneliness – not just the isolation of a lone traveller in the mist, but a loneliness of the soul. He was in an alien world and he needed to be amongst his own people in his own land. Or at least to be with Cari; he remembered with guilt that the events of last night had overtaken his good intentions to write to her.

Around a corner and suddenly Odhiambo left one world and entered another. The sun shone down on the manor house, the lawn and the part of the lake below it. Of mist there was no sign; Odhiambo nearly turned around to assure himself that he hadn't imagined it. He glanced at his watch, it was now approaching eleven o'clock. He wondered how large an audience the morning session on rural development had attracted. His stride increased, his body leaning characteristically forward, and soon he was on the gravel path leading to the house. The door to the walled garden was open and as he passed he caught sight of another truant from the course; Gregson was seated with his wife on a rustic bench deep in conversation.

The police cars were no longer in evidence at the front. No doubt Pendham and Trewin would be back, but it gave Odhiambo a little more time to think his way through the problem.

Inside the house he found Helen Shropshire at her temporary desk. She was talking on the telephone but gestured to him to wait. There was a radio on at low volume on a filing cabinet. The voice was giving the local news headlines 'on the hour'.

'Following the raid on the night-club in Exeter, during which substantial amounts of drugs were found, police warned this morning of increased volumes of drugs reaching the market despite the recent interdiction of a supply line following the successful police swoop on a yacht in Falmouth. "We are having substantial successes but the war is still to be won," said a police spokesman.

'The lake at Polsand on the coast of West Cornwall, which, according to local superstition, periodically claims a victim, maintained its reputation last night. A body of a man was retrieved from the lake this morning. It is understood the victim was staying . . .'

Helen had finished her call, so Odhiambo turned the radio off.

'How's it going? I see you've got rid of the police – for the moment, anyway.'

Helen Shropshire did not respond in similarly cheery fashion. Her freckled face was designed for laughter, but now it was sombre, appearing to dull even her flaming red hair.

'Oh, James, everything's awful.' Helen stopped as the door opened and the plump figure of Jane appeared, giving Odhiambo a shy smile. The two women engaged in dealing with some administrative chore while Odhiambo waited again.

'Right, Jane. I'll leave you to it a minute. I just want a word with James, here.'

Helen gestured towards Deane's office and moved towards it.

'It's free at the moment. The police have gone and Peter hasn't moved back in. I don't even know where he is.'

The voice trembled. Odhiambo closed the door behind them. He kept his voice neutral, almost stern. Showing sympathy was likely to bring on the tears that were obviously close.

'So what's happened? Did you see Penny Deane?'

'Yes, yes, I did. I saw her come out from her door and made an excuse to intercept her. I got around to her movements last night, but she more or less told me to mind my own business. But it's obvious she's worried. Badly worried and frightened, I think.

She knows something, I'm sure, but she can't bring herself to say anything. Well, not to me, anyway. Then Peter came to see me to say he was going out. He seemed like a zombie, looking straight through me. I asked him if anything had happened and he muttered about the police interviewing Penny. He added, "Little fool, why did she have to do it?" and then he went off too. After her, perhaps. She had headed for the woods. I dunno how I'm supposed to cope. He's certainly not helping.'

Odhiambo felt the first stirrings of concern.

'And they're not back? Either of them?'

Helen looked at him closely, seeing the agitation behind the eyes.

'Well, I haven't seen them since. What's the matter, James? What do you think happened last night?'

Odhiambo returned her look. Well, why not – he wasn't acting in any official capacity.

'I think Penny Deane had a date with Mahendra for a moonlight swim. For some reason she was waiting a short distance from the bit of sand where Mahendra undressed. It's possible she saw Mahendra drown and may have seen someone in the water with him. In which case she's wandering about in the same woods as a murderer, so to speak. The only other alternative is that she was the one in the water with him.'

'Oh, God. I don't believe what's happening. I feel as if I've had a curse put on me.'

Odhiambo tried a smile, intended to be reassuring, although he himself felt increasingly nervous in this woman's presence due to his own turbulent, confused feelings.

'It's not you. It's me. Trouble follows me about. Anyway, if you see Mrs Deane let me know. I think I should have a word with her. I didn't before because of treading on the toes of the police. Perhaps she's told them everything she knows, in which case there's nothing to worry about. But I'd like to be sure.'

Helen's self-pity was, once again, short-lived. She returned his smile, although the nervousness in his mind was mirrored in her eyes.

'Right. Well, I must get on. There are things to do.' She moved to the door, but as she passed Odhiambo she paused and looked up into his face. She went as if to touch him, but withdrew the hand that had started towards him.

'And I don't blame you. Honest.'

Odhiambo followed her out and then traced his way to the main seminar room. He eased the door open and sidled into a chair against the wall but, nevertheless, several pairs of eyes swivelled towards him.

The gathering seemed to be engaged in a question and answer session, presumably following a lecture given by a middle-aged woman who was a stranger to Odhiambo. The co-ordinator seemed to be the staff member who had been with them in the pub the previous evening. He gestured for Odhiambo to take a spare chair at the table. As he did so, Odhiambo felt as if a lot had happened since he last sat in this room the previous afternoon.

As far as Odhiambo could tell, all the course participants were present except the Nigerian, Asuna. The girl from Montserrat was commenting shyly on the subordinate role of women in rural society. Her concern was evidently shared by the guest speaker, but Odhiambo did not detect any overt sympathy emanating from the miscellany of Commonwealth men.

When eventually they broke for lunch, Odhiambo found himself next to the one Nigerian present as they made their way to the stairs.

'Where's your colleague? Away without leave, like me, this morning?'

The Nigerian glanced at him as if Odhiambo had cast a slur on his countrymen.

'He wasn't well. He's gone to see a doctor. In the village where we were last night. Why do you ask?'

The last sentence carried the clear intended meaning, What's it to you?, but Odhiambo ignored the truculence.

'No reason. Just noticed I wasn't the only truant, that's all. Given the unfortunate drowning of Mr Mahendra, I'm surprised most people were diligent enough to attend lectures instead of staring morbidly at the lake as people are inclined to do.'

'Staring at it won't bring the Indian back, will it? Stupid guy, anyway. All I've heard about since I got here is how dangerous the water is.'

'What time did you walk home last night? I left early.'

'Yeah. We left that pub you were in. Stopped at another. Bit more relaxed in atmosphere. Know what I mean?'

'I wondered if you saw or heard anything on your way home?'

'No, nothing. We weren't by the water, man.'

'It's just that we were out there with the police for some time and then back here talking. I didn't see you either.'

They had paused at the top of the stairs, but now the Nigerian abruptly turned away and made off towards his room. Odhiambo followed more slowly. He wondered where the Nigerians had spent the night – had they managed to find a couple of girls? One might think that would be difficult in a sleepy village like Penleith, but then this pair of Nigerians were probably expert in flushing out accommodating ladies wherever they were, and they had left the pub with a local who could have guided them to what they were seeking.

9

Odhiambo partook of a light lunch – a sandwich rather than the roast that was available – and went in search of the Deanes. The more he thought about it, the more urgent it seemed to put some pressure on Penny Deane. He was thwarted in his ambition by the lack of response to his knock at the door of their private quarters and confirmation from a chance encounter with Jane that neither Deane had been seen since they left after their meetings with the police. Frustrated, Odhiambo decided to go to his room and write the overdue letter to his wife. As he emerged from the walled garden on to the drive he saw the fleshy figure of Asuna coming towards him. He was dishevelled and bore himself with the air of a man with a sore head. Odhiambo lingered to allow the Nigerian to reach him.

'Hello. You're back. I was asking after you earlier.'

Asuna looked at him suspiciously.

'Why? What's it to you, man?'

'Nothing, really. I was interested whether you found some real life in that village last night, that's all. Seemed dead to me. But your friend said you were sick.'

Asuna grinned.

'He's not wrong there. Someone is beating a big drum inside my head, man. I just got a lift back as far as the entrance off the road back there.' He waved vaguely behind the Centre in the direction of the road from Penleith to Helston. 'Yeah, we found ourselves a little entertainment. Bit of a rave-up in a club the other side of the village. Surprising what was available there, including the local talent.'

A salacious smile widened the heavy mouth set in a broad and chubby face.

'Is that right? That local in the pub plugged you into the local scene, did he?'

'That's it. He seemed to know what was what. If you want a night out, then let me know.'

'Have you heard that Mahendra was drowned last night?'

Asuna's jaw tightened and his eyes focused more carefully on Odhiambo.

'No. You mean the guy from the CS? Shit. You mean he went swimming in the lake? Silly bastard.'

'Yes. He did. Did anyone mention him last night? Your fisherman friend seemed to know him.'

'Yeah, he did, didn't he? He wanted to be sure Adimojo and me weren't friends of his before he'd show us where Joe's place was. "Nosy Indian bugger", he called him.'

'I thought that odd in the pub. Why do you suppose Mahendra would bother with him?'

Asuna's face grew warier.

'Don't ask me, man. Not my affair. Now, I must go and have a shower.'

He moved purposefully past Odhiambo who watched him disappear through the doorway. Mahendra had got wind of something and had upset the locals, at least Bastian and the fisherman, Menherian. Had he been a threat to them? And if so, in what way? Odhiambo sighed and followed Asuna indoors, determined to write his letter.

Feeling satisfied that at least one goal had been accomplished, Odhiambo left his letter in the box placed to receive mail for posting and joined the other participants for the afternoon session on 'Rural Community Structures and their Role in Combating Crime'. He felt duty bound to attend this, in addition to collaborating in the effort being made by the Centre's staff to restore a feeling of normality. The Tanzanian was vocal once more, taking the view that police forces tended to be agents of neo-colonialists impeding the efforts of the people's representatives to achieve true socialism. An Indian put up a spirited defence of law and order and received some backing from the others. Odhiambo quite enjoyed the debate and for an hour or so managed to rest his mind from the matter of Mahendra's death. When they broke for tea, however, his preoccupation with this matter reasserted itself.

As he made his way into the tea room a familiar figure intercepted him.

'Ah, there you are,' said Sergeant Trewin. 'Mr Pendham wants to see you . . . sir,' the last added as a distinct afterthought.

Odhiambo followed the policeman across the hall and into the Director's office, which was rapidly becoming familiar to him. The Chief Inspector was seated once more at Deane's desk, looking aggressive and disgruntled.

'Ah, the great African detective. Sit yourself down, Inspector.' Pendham gestured to a chair at the desk. 'That's it. And now you can tell me why you think it's your business to go nosing about into Mahendra's death?'

Odhiambo looked at the man opposite. Why did he go out of his way to reduce Odhiambo's good intentions to confide all he knew?

'What are you referring to, Inspector?'

'You know bloody well what I'm talking about. After you left here this morning you went straight to the . . .' a quick glance down at his notes, ' . . . the Bastian household. Making a nuisance of yourself, Mr Bastian senior told me. Although the younger one seemed to have a more favourable impression.' A sardonic smile came and went. 'Now, mister, you told me this morning you had no involvement, then you go straight out interrogating witnesses. What are you up to?'

Odhiambo told himself that he should sympathise with Pendham's irritation. He would feel the same if the roles were reversed. But what made sympathy impossible was that Pendham's antipathy was at least partly determined by the fact that Odhiambo had a black skin. He strove to keep his voice neutral.

'This morning there was no clear evidence that Mahendra's death was anything other than an accident. I don't know if you know more now. So I didn't want to spread a lot of irrelevant ideas about before checking. Now I can fill you in on all I know.'

'Not before bloody time. What do you know?'

'First, Bastian. Several of us went to the pub in the village last night. I was walking home alone, several of them stayed on. Gregson, who raised the alarm, was probably half an hour behind me. As I passed the lodge I heard raised voices. Or rather one raised voice; that of the older Bastian, shouting, angry. The other voice was low so I couldn't identify it. This morning I went to verify that it was Mahendra. So if Mahendra's death was not an accident it might be relevant that the last person he called on was Bastian.'

Pendham pondered, gazing at Odhiambo, looking for how Odhiambo might be putting one over on him.

'If you didn't recognise the second voice, why did you think it was Mahendra?'

'I don't quite know. Partly something Mahendra said to me earlier, while we were having tea; somehow, I thought it might link up with Bastian's words.'

Odhiambo went on to recount Mahendra's request to him and Bastian's shouted allegation of being bluffed. Pendham seemed unconvinced.

'Seems a strange connection to me. Don't see why you thought there was one. You're asking me to believe that Mahendra wanted you to keep an eye on someone without telling you who or why. That's ridiculous. You're holding something back again, mister, and I'm warning you, I'm getting tired of it.'

'I'm not holding anything back, but if you don't believe there's any connection, you're probably right. We probably won't ever know what Mahendra meant. But he was there, as you've probably discovered.'

Pendham leaned back in his chair.

'Oh yes, he was there. And now you've admitted you were there too. Or just outside. So you waited for Mr Mahendra to come out, did you? That's natural enough. Ask him what was up. Explain himself. Then what did you do?'

Odhiambo laughed.

'You're something else, Pendham. You can't be serious. While you sit here enjoying slanging me, you are in effect procrastinating. Have you got anything out of Penny Deane? And do you know where she is? These are the important questions.'

Pendham leaned forward again so that his face was close to Odhiambo's. 'Now, you listen to me. You're the one stirring up all the shit in this affair. You know what I think? I think you think you're smarter than us rural coppers. You with your London courses. I'll tell you one thing, Mr Smartass, the preliminary investigation by the doctor says you may be right. Something seemed to have been clamped around his ankle. OK, so you're a smart African detective. Thanks for the intuition. Otherwise us country yokels might have missed it. From now on you leave the investigation to us. I don't want the next person I talk to to start by saying,' the voice rose to a falsetto, ' "Oh, I've already told this to the nice African policeman." '

Odhiambo considered. So he was right. For the moment his antipathy to Pendham faded into the background.

'So, Mahendra was murdered and Penny Deane was nearby at some point around the right time. You didn't answer me. What are you doing about her?'

'For your information, we have interviewed Mrs Deane who denies having seen the incident. I don't know what you're accustomed to, but in this country she's free to come and go as she pleases. Within this vicinity, at least. Have you any other evidence that Mrs Deane and the dead man were more than official acquaintances?'

Odhiambo hesitated and then recounted Helen's account of Mahendra's bed having been made. Pendham looked at him.

'And what do you infer from that?'

'I'm afraid I think Penny Deane went there knowing he was not returning.'

'So you think she drowned him?'

'Not necessarily. It's obvious Mahendra must have had a date at that pool. He had the reputation for being a ladies' man. It's no good thinking he went there on a whim. Someone was waiting for him, and that someone killed him.'

Silence reigned for some moments as if the three men were picturing the scene. The sergeant cleared his throat.

'We're not certain of that yet. It's a possibility, that's all.'

Odhiambo refused to be side-tracked.

'He's a strange guy, this Mahendra. I get the feeling he enjoys, or enjoyed, tension, danger, whatever. Affairs with women, possibly under the noses of their husbands. And Bastian plus others in the village seem to have regarded him as a menace.'

Pendham was quick to intervene.

'What do you mean, "others in the village"? What else are you holding back on us?'

Odhiambo grimaced.

'Oh, nothing. What's the matter with you? Everything I say you jump on. It's just when his name came up in conversation in the pub, some of the locals knew him and didn't speak highly of him. That's all I know.'

Pendham took Odhiambo through an account of his conversations in the pub. Finally, he told him he could go.

' . . . and keep out of my way. Just go to your lectures like a good boy.'

Odhiambo rose and gave his parting shot as he turned to go.

'OK, Pendham. But get on with it rather than sitting here with an inferiority complex.'

Odhiambo felt rather than heard a stifled sound from the sergeant, who had been silently taking notes. Could Trewin have been about to laugh? Pendham, however, achieved the last word to Odhiambo's retreating back.

'And I don't want to find you close to any more bodies. You hear me?'

But Odhiambo was gone.

Pendham turned irritably to the sergeant.

'I told you we'd have trouble with this bastard. I need him out of my hair. Now, what do you suppose this Indian had on that lodge chap, what's-his-name?'

Trewin thought for a moment, but only as to his choice of words. He didn't want to divert Pendham's wrath on to himself.

'There's been rumours that Bastian may be involved in some way in smuggling. I think the drug boys may have looked at him not so long ago. But if they did, they presumably didn't get anywhere. Could be gossip, sir. You know how it is down here. Bastian and that supposed son of his. Tongues wag. And one bit of gossip leads to another.'

Pendham stared at the sergeant as if faced with another African policeman.

'And you didn't think to tell me that when we called in there earlier? Like that black bugger, you like to keep things to yourself.'

'Didn't come to mind then, sir. And there's really nothing I know. It was just a spur of the moment call you made.'

A derisive snort kept Trewin twinned with Odhiambo as part of the travails of Pendham.

'Right. Well, do something useful now. Better find out what's happened to this Mrs Deane. If she is out somewhere, let's find out where. Discreetly, mind. If that isn't asking too much. No. On second thoughts you stay here and get the routine statements off the rest of this assorted menagerie. And that woman we haven't seen yet; the wife of the fellow who reported it. I'll go and see about tracing Mrs Deane and arrange for some more men here. Actually, I'd like to know where both the Deanes are.'

At the time that Pendham was posing the question, the Deanes were in the same place – in a clearing in the woods between the Centre and the Bastian lodge. Peter Deane knew reasonably well the few circular trails favoured by his wife and by luck he had chosen correctly. Penny Deane was sitting on a log with her hands hugging her shoulders as if she was cold. If she heard her husband approaching through the early leaves of autumn she made no sign.

Peter Deane looked at his wife; she looked forlorn, lost and desperately in need of help, but he could not bring himself to comfort her. At last he spoke.

'It's no good, you know. It's all going to come out one way or another.'

Penny looked around. She eyed her husband as if he was a stranger, but offered no response. Deane moved closer.

'You were there. You saw something, didn't you? You were meeting your lover, damn you. Why don't you admit it? You think nobody knows?' Still no reply came from the seated woman. Only her eyes spoke of contempt. 'I can't let you do this, you know. It's too late.' Suddenly the passivity and silence of his wife became too much. He reached forward, almost pulling her to her feet and shaking her by the shoulders. 'Speak, damn you. Who do you think you are? I'll tell you if you don't know.'

Penny Deane pulled herself away and turned to leave her violated sanctuary. As she reached the shelter of the trees she turned back. Her husband was still standing there, irresolute.

'You make me sick. Don't preach honesty and faithfulness to me. You don't expect me to believe you were in Penzance last night, do you? What did you tell the police? That you were attending your precious arty group talking about Newlyn paintings? Don't make me laugh.'

Peter Deane watched her retreat into the trees. Oh, my God, he thought, she's going to blame me now. How did she find out? It seemed she knew far more than was good for her in more ways than one. He would have to do something, however reluctantly.

Odhiambo made his way back towards the meeting room, but then changed direction and opened the door to the room where tea had now been completed. There were two women clearing away the debris and one was Helen Shropshire. Odhiambo moved towards her, as the other woman moved towards the door pushing the trolley containing the urns and used crockery.

'Hi. Sorry to keep interrupting you; after each encounter with Pendham I seem to need a shoulder to cry on.'

Helen looked up and gave a little shake of her head.

'You could of course attend the seminar on "Credit Schemes for Rural Areas", which is why you are actually here.'

Odhiambo returned the woman's grin, and then blurted out, 'Do you swim?'

Helen looked startled at the apparent switch of conversation.

'What do you mean? In this lake, do you mean? Certainly not. It's too cold for a start. Apart from the superstitions.'

'No, I mean, can you swim? And well – underwater and so on?'

'You're not implying that I held Mahendra down, I hope. Yes, I swim pretty well. Looking at the coral off Mombasa and so forth.'

'You see, I can't. Us Luos didn't swim much in Lake Victoria. My mother was afraid of me getting bilharzia. And I avoided it at boarding school. I preferred rugby, even cricket.'

'OK, so you can't swim. You looking for someone to teach you? You'd better find a heated pool or your poor Equatorial blood will freeze.'

'The point is, I don't know much about it. How easy is it to pull someone underwater and hold him there until he drowns? I'd have thought buoyancy would make it difficult.'

Helen's face lost the sunny look; gravity returned.

'Well, it depends, I suppose. If you grabbed a leg and pulled upwards the swimmer's head would tip under and he'd lose buoyancy. And if it was a surprise and he swallowed water as his head went under, he wouldn't be able to struggle long.'

'So it's not a matter of sheer strength; a good swimmer could do it as long as they can stay underwater a while.'

'I would think so. What are you getting at?'

'Just educating myself.'

With a reminder of the spectre hanging over Polsand, Helen's disposition had now swung back to gloom.

'Oh dear. Do you know, I was beginning to fall in love with this place. Now I'm beginning to hate it.'

She shivered slightly. Odhiambo considered a moment and then took the plunge.

'I tell you what. How about getting away for an hour or two? Come with me to the village tonight, we'll have a drink and a meal. We could try that fellow Bastian's restaurant. He should have some good fish there – even if there's no tilapia from Lake Victoria.'

Helen looked at the large figure looming over her. He seemed suddenly almost boyishly shy. She hesitated, but what harm was there in a meal? She could do with getting away from the fraught Peter Deane and the rest of the crowd here. She nodded.

'Thank you, James. I'd love to. Now I'd better get on with my work.'

Odhiambo left, feeling strangely elated, but also guilty. Don't be daft, he said to himself, there's nothing wrong in having dinner with someone. Cari would be having dinners with male business colleagues. But he failed to reassure himself.

10

Odhiambo was enjoying his evening: having resolutely banished feelings of guilt about absent wives and thickening waistlines, he enjoyed the company of a beautiful woman and a generous portion of chips with an expertly cooked sea bass. The only damper on his enjoyment was the knowledge that up to the time Helen and he had left the Centre Penny Deane had not returned. However, the police presence had increased and there were signs that Pendham was taking her continued absence seriously. There didn't seem anything more he could do, so Odhiambo resolutely put thoughts of the Mahendra affair out of his mind and basked in the warmth of female company.

The restaurant overlooked the village harbour. The evening was clear with the sun beginning to set over Land's End. The panorama across Mount's Bay, with the cliffs dark in the evening shadows but the sun still lighting the fields in their various shades of green, was magnificent. The sky beyond the sea was beginning to take on extra colours, pink, yellow and slowly but surely a dominating red. But it was a softer sky than Odhiambo was used to seeing when the sun set across Lake Victoria on the Equator. The comparison in his mind did not this time bring with it the twinge of homesickness; Helen had the power, at least, to dispel that.

Helen, too, was enjoying herself, despite earlier misgivings. She had not dined with a man since . . . well, since. And she had never dined out *à deux* with a black man. She had not been able to avoid wondering whether they would be the object of stares or surreptitious glances, but as far as she could tell this wasn't happening. She supposed Penleith was used to a *mélange* of foreigners, given the proximity of the Centre. Plus tourists, of course, of whom there was still evidence in this tail-end of summer.

She knew Odhiambo as a policeman. Intense, driven, stubborn and something of a loner. She also knew that he had his human side; he seemed to care about people. And, of course, she was aware of the quiet magnetism of his personality. But in the last twenty-four hours and particularly this evening she was becoming aware that he was a humorous man with a sense of insecurity that bordered on inferiority. She also knew deep in the recesses of her mind that she felt a powerful sexual attraction to him, an attraction that would, must, not be fulfilled.

It was as they were drinking their coffee that two men entered the room and sat at a table near the door. They did not appear to be focused on selecting a meal from the menu in front of them. Rather, as soon as they were seated, their heads bent forward and an intense conversation seemed to be resumed. Nor did it give the appearance of being an entirely amiable one. Odhiambo watched with interest. Alex Bastian and Nigel were having an argument and the older man's body language, in particular, was indicative of irritability.

Helen Shropshire watched her companion with amusement. She could tell that his mind had switched from their conversation to another matter.

'Penny for your thoughts, James.'

Odhiambo turned his eyes back to the woman opposite him.

'I'm sorry. I guess I was startled by the two who just came in. It's the men from the lodge – the Bastians. We were talking about them earlier. They are, indeed, a strange couple.'

'Why should that startle you? This may be a small place, but the same range of human eccentricities are found here as in Nairobi.'

'It was just that I was enjoying your company and had forgotten about Mahendra when they came in and jolted my mind back to it.'

'You think Bastian has something to do with it? Or shouldn't I ask? But you're not an official bobby here so I can, can't I?' There was a gentle mocking undertone to the voice and the freckled face looked genuinely happy for almost the first time that Odhiambo could remember. She's getting to me, he thought. This evening could be a mistake.

'Come on,' he said, almost roughly, 'time I was walking you

home.' He placed notes on the bill that was already to hand and emphatically forestalled Helen's movement towards her purse. 'No. This is my treat. We're not used to women paying. Us Luos, I mean. Men give the orders and men spend the money.'

They rose and moved towards the door. The younger man, Nigel, saw them approaching, looked from one to the other. There was a certain air of abandon about him as if he didn't care what he said or whom he offended.

'Ah. The Commonwealth cousin and friend. Sampling the local village scene. You have to seek your pleasures where you can here. Make your own excitement. I hope you've discovered how.'

A grin that was close to a leer and a sneer in the voice made Helen bristle. Odhiambo was anxious not to have her embarrassed so contented himself with a nodded acknowledgement of Nigel's presence. He turned to the older man.

'Good evening to you, Mr Bastian. I can recommend the bass.'

Alex Bastian looked around and up; his face did not reveal any pleasure in his renewed acquaintance with the African.

'Ah. The foreign policeman.' He saw Helen Shropshire and rose to his feet. 'Good evening. You're from the manor house, are you not? Showing the visitors Penleith, eh?' He turned his gaze on Odhiambo. 'I should hope the bass is good, and the rest. It was caught by a local fisherman and I serve it. This is my place.'

Odhiambo smiled.

'I know and I congratulate you. I enjoyed it.'

The scowl remained in place.

'Better you're eating fish than poking your nose in where it's not wanted. I had a visit from the proper police. They didn't seem too enthused that you had been queering their pitch.'

Odhiambo bit back an answer in kind; he didn't want to embarrass Helen. He gave a short nod and guided Helen through the door. Behind him he could feel Bastian's eyes watching him, but he would have liked to hear the exchange between the two diners.

Bastian resumed his seat and switched his gaze back on to his companion.

'I regard that man as an omen of trouble. It's what I was trying to get across to you – this is the time to get away from trouble, not dig ourselves deeper into it.'

The younger man laughed mockingly and watched the indignation on the face of his companion become mixed with hurt and pain.

'Oh, Alex, you are a silly. You're not becoming superstitious in your old age, surely? Just because our visitor this morning is black doesn't mean he's bringing us bad luck. We're not in the Middle Ages. More's the pity. Perhaps we could have some fun burning him as a witch, or the male equivalent – what is it? A warlock.'

'Never mind him. That's just an extra irritant. With that Indian dead the police are all over the place. It's time to get out, Nigel. I don't like the way things are going. What happens if they talk to Menherian? I don't trust him to keep quiet.'

'Ah, now, there you have a point, dear Alex. Menherian is a bit of a menace, specially with the beer in him. But I'm enjoying myself. It's all becoming exciting. Makes a change in this hole of a place.'

The older man looked more closely at his companion. He didn't like the way Nigel was behaving. There was a wildness about him that was getting more noticeable. He sighed.

'I'm telling you, Nigel, not asking. I've got my plans and it's time we acted on them. You've got to choose.'

If he had hoped to see a softening of attitude he was disappointed. Bastian wasn't sure whether the look he received was one of sympathy or contempt, but either was unacceptable.

Hugh Gregson looked irritably at his wife. They were in their room at the Centre.

'For God's sake, Muriel. It's no good moping about. The man's dead. If he was murdered, well, that's terrible, but it doesn't affect us.'

The look he received was withering.

'Oh, you are a fool, Hugh. And a self-centred fool. We knew the man. If he was murdered we're likely to be trapped down here for ages.'

Hugh's reticence could stand no more. He had beat around the bush when he talked to his wife that morning, verifying that she had been with the Tamlyn woman and telling her to avoid giving the police the impression that they knew Mahendra well. But ever since, she had loped around the place looking like the knell of doom. He had been glad when she went off in the afternoon for a shopping trip. But back again at supper she had acted most peculiarly.

'That's not what's worrying you – is it, Muriel, my dear? You're worried that the police will discover you've been sleeping with him. You and half the women in London. You can't bear the thought of being exposed as the tramp you are.'

Muriel leaped to her feet from the bed on which she had been sitting.

'How dare you? How dare you? What an outrageous thing to say.'

'Oh come off it, Muriel.' He sighed, wearily. 'You can't think I'm blind and dim. That's hardly being fair to me. Of course I know what's been going on. Despite my warnings and your promises. You're a tart, my dear, whatever fancy ideas you have about yourself. The trouble is, you used to be able to disguise it, but now you can't even act your part.'

For once, the woman facing him fell silent as if she realised that with these words they had crossed some personal Rubicon. Hugh sighed again and turned away. Then he turned back and his voice took on a hard and brittle tone.

'Thank God you've got a bloody alibi. The last thing you can do for me is look the part of my wife for the remaining hours we're here. Is that too much to ask?'

Muriel found her voice once more.

'You're a very common man, Hugh, do you know that? Javi had more class in his little finger than you have in your whole body. You're common and spiteful. But yes, I will do my duty – as always.'

Hugh Gregson laughed loudly and when he spoke it was close to a shout.

'Class! What do you know about class? He was a wog, my dear. Had you forgotten? Or have you sunk so low you didn't even notice?'

'That's what sticks in your gullet, isn't it? You wouldn't mind if he'd been white. Is that why you killed him?'

The blow knocked her backwards on to the bed. Suddenly Muriel felt very frightened.

Odhiambo and his companion made their way along the cliff-top road in a silence that had lasted for a few minutes. Helen didn't mind the silence, it was companionable enough and it was a lovely evening, but still it was time James was jolted back to his social duties, she thought. They reached a point where a narrow track veered away from the cliff path and up a steep slope. Helen put a restraining hand on her companion's arm.

'If you've got time, we ought to go up there. It's the highest point on this cliff; we'll get a marvellous view of the sunset over the bay. There's a big wheel at the top – a ship's steering wheel. It commemorates the crew of one of the ships wrecked hereabouts.'

Odhiambo looked up the path and looked at the woman at his side.

'Why not? More exercise after the meal won't do us any harm. And the night is young.'

They scrambled up the path with Odhiambo leading. It was steep with occasional large steps in the rock. Once or twice he reached back and took Helen's hand to help her up. Nearing the top, Helen was panting for breath and Odhiambo, himself, was feeling somewhat breathless. He paused where the path widened and as Helen joined him she stumbled slightly. He reached out and steadied her with his hands on her waist. She straightened and Odhiambo felt her hair in his face. As she turned her head towards him Odhiambo gave way to the impulse of the moment and, bending his head, kissed her. For a moment the response was overpowering as her lips parted and her body moved into his. But then Helen pulled away. The words were trite but the voice cracked with tension.

'I'm too out of breath to kiss. And anyway, we mustn't. You're bad.'

Odhiambo felt more embarrassed than guilty.

'I'm sorry. I shouldn't be on the Cornish cliffs with a red-headed beauty. It's too much.'

'Come on. Let's see the old wheel.'

With that, Helen, breathless or not, scampered the last few feet to the crest of the slope. Odhiambo, following, attained the flatter top and could just see in the advanced twilight the shape of a large ship's wheel set on some sort of stone plinth. To his surprise there was a dummy figure at the wheel, presumably the helmsman still steering although the boat had hit the rocks a century or more ago. Helen had stopped to regain her breath, but Odhiambo continued towards the wheel. As he neared it, he broke into a run until his eyes confirmed the awful truth his senses had detected: the figure was no dummy but the stiffened body of Penny Deane.

Odhiambo sat on a rock at the edge of the slope which he had ascended some half-hour ago and which Helen Shropshire had descended again more recently. He had managed to stop her getting close to the wheel and the dreadful helmsman, but she had seen enough to become hysterical and it had taken him some minutes to calm her down sufficiently to listen to his instructions. He had debated which option was the best. Clearly, one of them had to stay, in case some other evening walkers decided to visit the wheel, while the other notified the police. He decided that Helen would be better with something specific to do rather than guarding a dead body, so it was Helen who departed. He was right; once she had assimilated the instructions she became calmer and her mind moved to the task in hand. Following her departure, Odhiambo had surveyed his eyrie. The only easy access was by the path they had used. Behind the wheel the cliff reached its climax in a rocky outcrop; on the Penleith side the slope down was steep and lacking in footpaths; the Polsand Centre direction was guarded by thick undergrowth leading to the estate woods. Odhiambo wondered why the wheel was in such an invisible spot; the only explanation that occurred to him was that it was visible from the sea by the fishing boats going about their business in the hostile waters that had claimed the ship to which the wheel once belonged.

There was an inscription carved into the granite base of the memorial which read:

In Memory of the Crew of the S.S. Agiline
who Perished on the Rocks below
September 12, 1862.
This Wheel was almost the only Artifact
to survive the Storm.

Whatever the horror of their end it was no worse than that suffered on almost the same day of the year by Penny Deane. Her throat had been cut and there was little doubt it had happened on this spot. There was a great deal of blood a short distance from the wheel and evidence of the body being dragged to the wheel and draped obscenely against it. Her arms between the spokes provided the support that prevented the body sliding down to the granite base. Her clothes, though blood-soaked, were undisturbed. There was no sign of a sexual assault.

The body was cold so it had been here for a few hours, Odhiambo assumed. Strange that no one had discovered it earlier. Presumably there were few tourists about and none of those who were had happened to visit the site this evening. The privacy in terms of access combined with the view probably made it a trysting spot for local couples, but none disturbed Odhiambo in his vigil. The view was certainly worth the climb, as Helen had promised. It was almost dark now and the lights of towns and villages shone across the several miles of the great bay. And beyond the last darker shadow of the land sticking out into the sea there came the regular flashing light of a lighthouse. Out on the horizon there were lights from what must be a large ship making its way around Land's End and into the heart of the Atlantic. Closer were two or three smaller clusters of lights marking the passage of local fishing boats. It was a beautiful and tranquil scene, although the memorial behind him was evidence that it was not always so. It was what had occurred at that memorial, rather than the cold of approaching night, that suddenly caused him to tremble violently until he had to clutch himself to control the shaking.

Odhiambo felt angry and guilty. From the time Penny went missing he had had a presentiment of disaster. She had seen something the previous night; Mahendra's murderer discovered this fact with the bloody result now revealed. Had she met the murderer here in order to reveal what she knew? And if so, why would she be so foolish?

His thoughts moved on to the anonymous murderer. This was a sick mind. Mahendra's death was bizarre enough. Swimming up to a man about to enjoy a moonlight assignation and pulling him underwater was hardly a common method of murder. Was it the woman he was meeting at the lake who had done it? Jealousy, revenge or whatever? Now Penny Deane, her throat cut – the murderer, far from hastening from the scene, stages this grotesque flaunting of the crime. The first thing was to establish with whom Mahendra had a date for a swim in the nude. More and more he was inclining to the view that Penny was a bystander, an onlooker, and Mahendra was due to meet someone else. He was not sure why he was coming to this view, other than from the evidence that she had sat under a tree as if eavesdropping, but his instincts told him he was right and he had learned to trust his instincts.

Flashing lights below heralded the arrival of the police and Odhiambo turned his mind to how he was to deal with Pendham, who would hardly be delighted to find Odhiambo in the presence of another body.

He didn't have long to wait for it was Pendham himself who shortly crested the slope accompanied by a uniformed constable with a powerful torch which he directed on to Odhiambo's face.

'So, what mess have you got yourself into now? Where's the body?'

There was no panting for air; despite his bulk and his hurried ascent, Pendham's lungs seemed untroubled. He followed Odhiambo towards the wheel until the torch wavered as it lit up the body, which looked even more macabre in the darkness. Pendham snarled at his companion.

'Here, give me that thing if you can't hold it steady.'

Odhiambo waited as Pendham inspected the body and the obvious evidence of the cause of death. As Pendham returned he jumped in quickly with a brief account of the circumstances of the discovery. Pendham heard him out, restraining any impulse to intervene. As he finished, another policeman arrived and was dispatched back to arrange for lighting and to check that a doctor and ambulance were on their way. Pendham then returned his attention to Odhiambo.

'Yes. Mrs what's her name called from the village. I was at the Centre. We were still looking for her. It seems we didn't have your advantage of knowing where to look. Are you telling me you came up here by coincidence?'

Odhiambo sighed.

'Of course I am. If I'd known she was up here with her throat cut, do you think I'd have taken my time having dinner in the village?'

'Hm. Yeah, we'll check that out, of course. So you take a lady to supper then you bring her up here.' Odhiambo could sense rather than see the smirk. 'I won't ask what you intended to do next if you hadn't stumbled over another body. You don't waste any time do you, you boys from Africa.'

'Pendham, you've been frigging around all day trying to score off me instead of concentrating on what you should be doing. I told you to find this woman and what happens – she stands at that bloody wheel for hours until I decided to admire your Cornish views.'

'How do you know she's been here for hours, mister, tell me that?'

'Oh, grow up, for Christ's sake. I'm a policeman too. I can tell a body that's affected by rigor mortis.'

The police constable shifted uncomfortably from one foot to the other. This was something outside his experience: dead bodies and the Chief having a face-to-face with this black fellow. Fortunately for his peace of mind scrambling noises and muttered curses heralded the arrival of reinforcements.

Odhiambo arrived back at the Centre to find the house a blaze of light and abuzz with its inhabitants, who were eddying around in an atmosphere that mixed curiosity, gloom and incipient panic. Helen Shropshire, as Odhiambo knew from Pendham, had arrived home in a police car accompanied by Sergeant Trewin; he was now organising a new round of interviews whilst his boss continued to supervise the activity at the cliff-top memorial. The car had been dispatched back to the cliffs, taking Peter Deane to his wife's body. Trewin had intercepted Deane on the path leading to the Centre as the car arrived with Helen Shropshire. Odhiambo had been allowed to depart before Deane's arrival. Encouraged to go, in fact, but with no offer of a lift back to the Centre. As he entered the hallway he was accosted by an agitated Gregson.

'Odhiambo, what the devil's going on? I hear you discovered another body: Mrs Deane. It's terrible. This place is becoming a madhouse. And Deane is missing. The wretched fellow never seems to be around. Oh dear, shouldn't say that . . . I mean, his wife and so forth.'

Beside Gregson was Asuna, one of the Nigerians. He accosted the unfortunate Gregson.

'This guy is one of the students. It's your organisation, ODA, that's supposed to be running this place. We didn't come from Lagos to stand around being interviewed every few hours by your policemen.'

Odhiambo looked at the two men. Both in their different ways seemed personally anxious.

'Yes, Mrs Deane is dead. There's nothing we can do at the moment. The police aren't likely to let anyone leave for the time being.'

Gregson was not placated.

'Where's that Chief Inspector fellow? Is he out there? I need to see him to get things sorted out. We can't go on like this, it's chaotic.'

'I dare say he'll be here soon. No good expecting me to be a mouthpiece – Chief Inspector Pendham is not very pleased with me.'

Asuna grinned.

'Don't say he thinks you did it. There's racial prejudice for you. Go for the first black guy you can find.'

He laughed and Odhiambo had to restrain himself from hitting the round fleshy face. He turned back to Gregson.

'I think you'd better get the staff here organised and try to restore some calm to this place.'

He moved away before either man could detain him further. It didn't take him long to track down Trewin, ensconced in Deane's office once more. He waited until he had finished one interview and then slipped in and brought Trewin up to date.

Trewin seemed a bit out of his depth, but also somewhat friendlier than at their previous meetings. He thanked Odhiambo and let him go. Odhiambo went in search of Helen Shropshire. She was not in the administrative offices, but a member of the Centre's staff who was preparing a large tray of coffee and biscuits in the kitchen told him that she had gone to her flat at the back of the house. Odhiambo found his way down the passage and mounted the stairs. There were three doors but name tags were lit by little night-lights. He pressed the bell and as if she had been waiting for the summons the door opened almost immediately. Her hair was dishevelled, he could detect dirt on her cheek from her evening scrambles, and she looked frightened. They looked at each other for several seconds. Odhiambo tried to keep his voice light.

'I thought I'd better check to see if you were OK. You did well out there. I'm proud of you.'

There was a pause as Helen tried to collect herself. But then she broke.

'Oh, James, it's too much. I can't take all this. And I'm scared.'

She came into his arms as if walking through water, slowly, reluctantly, but inevitably.

11

It had been a long night for Bill Pendham. The bizarre nature of Penny Deane's murder together with its circumstantial linkage to the drowning of Mahendra, linkage in terms of time, space and acquaintanceship, would inevitably lead to high media exposure, which, in turn, would lead to pressure on the investigating police for a quick solution. The worst possibility of all was that Pendham would find himself supplanted in his responsibility for the investigation by a more specialised murder enquiry team. Consequently, when he finally left the ghastly wheel on the cliff top, he commandeered space at the small police station in Helston and set about commissioning a fully manned operation. He woke his superior without a qualm and placed his order, including as a high priority someone to handle the press.

'This has got everything, Super, that will bring them here in droves. Local superstition, links with ancient shipwrecks, mad killer wandering on cliff top like something out of *Jamaica Inn*, and a place in the middle of nowhere full of multicoloured ex-colonials. It's going to be a circus, I tell you.'

Despite a grumbling and less than sympathetic initial response, Pendham was confident that support was on the way. Meanwhile, he was going through the results of the night's interviews with the local sergeant. Mugs of coffee were at hand and the local constable had promised his wife's contribution of eggs and bacon.

'Let's get one thing established, Trewin. We're dealing with linked cases. Mrs Deane was at or near the scene of the drowning and then gets butchered the next day. Second, these are not random killings. There's something going on that's causing them and it's linked to that Centre. So start with Mahendra. What do we know about him?'

Trewin coughed and started a résumé of Mahendra's particulars, but was quickly interrupted.

'No, never mind all the crap. I can read that when it's typed up. Why was he killed, if he was killed which now seems more than likely? There's three things account for murders like this, Trewin, sex, drugs or blackmail. So which is it?'

Trewin coughed once more and tried again.

'It looks as if he was a ladies' man, sir. Mrs Deane may have been one of his conquests, as it were. There's the other women on the staff, of course.' He consulted his notes. 'Mrs Shropshire is the only other one who might have mixed with him socially and she's only been there a while. Mahendra himself, of course, was only a visitor.'

'Exactly. And in London he knew the Gregson woman, from what you told me. OK. So he's fooling around with one or both of them and the husband finds out.'

'Or the other lady, if he was involved with both. Jealousy, sir, the old green-eyed monster.'

'Well, that means the diplomat woman. So she kills her lover and her rival. Trouble is, Trewin, she's alibied for the first at any rate. No, stick with the husbands. Gregson was on the spot for Mahendra, and was not in the classroom yesterday afternoon. Deane told us he was at a meeting in Penzance, but that could be a cock-and-bull story. Check it out, by the way. Was he with his wife in the woods yesterday afternoon? I like Deane, if we can break his Penzance alibi.'

Trewin allowed himself a small self-congratulatory smile.

'I did get the Penzance lads to check. Mr Deane was supposed to be at a meeting in the museum. Some committee or other. The meeting is next week.'

Pendham sat up sharply, pounding his fist on the desk, causing coffee to slop from his mug. He ignored it.

'Well done. So why would he lie? I'll tell you why, 'cos he was spying on his wife. Found her frolicking with that Indian, jumped in and drowned the bugger. Wife frightened, won't speak to us, but Deane knows she'll crack, so she has to go too.'

'Not exactly a husband-type killing though, is it? Bit bizarre, I mean. Hit her on the head and bury her somewhere in the woods would be more like it.'

Pendham nodded, thought for a moment and entered the case for the prosecution.

'He's a clever bugger. Dress the murder up to look like some madman is on the loose. Divert suspicion.'

Trewin contemplated the theory.

'He'd have to be a heartless bastard.'

Pendham grimaced.

'You're right there. God, what a scene that was. Turned my stomach. OK, so we pull Deane in for further questioning. What about the other motives? Somebody supplying drugs in that Centre. Mahendra and Mrs Deane suspect someone so they get eliminated. The way the killings were, could be someone high on drugs.'

'We know there's drugs coming in along this coast, Chief. Drug boys caught one smuggler at Falmouth the other day, but with all the coves and caves along here they're pretty sure a lot is still coming in. I told you they had a good look at the guy in the lodge, but nothing doing. Mahendra was with him that evening.'

'Yeah, which brings us to our African police friend. He's always on the spot.' Trewin looked sceptical. 'Yeah, I know. It's not him, but there's other foreigners in that place. Can't eliminate blackmail at this stage. I don't like the look of those other black fellows there. Then there's the fellows from India. They might have known Mahendra.'

Their scan of suspects was interrupted by the constable bearing breakfast. Before turning to his eggs, Pendham came back to his chosen candidate.

'Get a car back to the Centre and bring in Deane.'

Although he had waited until daylight was established, it was still dark under the trees as Odhiambo picked his way along a footpath he could but barely see. He had noticed a track into the trees when he was in Bastian's study yesterday and now, having found his way around the back of the lodge, he was heading towards a destination he could anticipate. He had left Helen's bed in the middle of the night, leaving her asleep, racked with his guilt of marital betrayal. He had gone to his room to shower then had spent the rest of the night sitting in his chair trying to come to terms with himself and his situation. Having condemned himself repeatedly and with the jury of his conscience rejecting the defence of mitigating circumstances, he attempted to turn his mind to the matter of the Polsand murders. In a way, this added to his sense of guilt; adultery was bad enough, but to give way to sexual desires shortly after finding a woman with her throat cut seemed almost abnormal. Then there was the aspect that he had taken advantage of Helen whilst she was in shock. All in all, he despised himself. Eventually, he managed to force his concentration on to the Penny Deane murder. The logical next step would seem to be to familiarise himself with the wooded area around the estate. As he entered the woods the sky in the east was glowing red and somewhere in the recesses of his mind he remembered hearing during his stay in England the doggerel weather forecast, 'Red sky in the morning, shepherd's warning.' Shepherds and policemen, he thought, both in poor shape this morning.

The recent fine weather had left the ground under the trees reasonably firm and dry for which Odhiambo was grateful as he had no proper walking boots. He picked his way along, cursing occasionally as his foot snagged a trailing root, until ahead of him the trees thinned and he could see the sea. Cautiously he paused at the edge of the tree-line. As he expected, he was looking down at the wheel, now bereft of its bloody companion.

A movement caught Odhiambo's attention. Rising from behind a rock was the capped head of a policeman. After a moment's hesitation, Odhiambo scrambled cautiously down to the plateau containing the memorial. The policeman heard his approach, turned and came towards him.

'Sorry, sir, this area be closed for sightseers for now.'

'Good morning. It's OK, I won't disturb anything. Wouldn't matter if I did. I was here last night with Chief Inspector Pendham. I discovered the body.'

'Ah, the gentleman from Africa. I've heard talk of 'ee. Policeman too, I'm told. I'm just a Special, sir. You know, part-time volunteer like. Keeping an eye on the place. Bad business all round, I reckon.'

'Yes, that's certainly true. I was just exploring the woods. When I was here last night I didn't realise there was a path through the woods to the lodge.'

'Ah, riddled with paths, sir, hereabouts. Not only paths, neither. Shafts and such. Used to be a tin mine where we're standing backalong. Like two 'undred years or thereabouts. Squire at the manor ran it, see. Some say 'twere used for more than mining latterly. There's cave at bottom of cliff near where the lodge is with tracks cut in rocks so's they could push cart down to the boat and load the contraband. Nice sheltered little cave, y'see, no access except by boat.'

'When you say latterly, you don't mean recently, do you?'

'Ah no, sir. I'm talking backalong. Around the time this 'ere wheel were put up. When smuggling were common hereabouts. Not much of that these days, although there's still a bit of smuggling goes on – different sort of trade these days, mind.'

'What, drugs you mean?'

The special constable seemed to realise he was letting his tongue run away with him to a stranger.

'Well, there it is. Anyway, you'd better be 'eading back, sir. Be breakfast time soon. My relief'll be here soon; be looking forward to a bit of bacon myself after a night out here.'

Odhiambo took the hint and retraced his steps. As he approached the back of the lodge he paused to detach a bramble from his trouser leg and scan the lodge itself. There was no sign of life, but that was deceptive.

'Boo!'

Odhiambo was startled at the unexpected sound. He turned to see the smiling figure of the younger lodge resident, Nigel. He was dressed in slacks and a pullover and carried a rolled-up towel under his arm.

'Couldn't resist making you jump. Aren't I naughty? How are you this morning, dear African cousin? None the worse for eating Alex's fish, I hope. What an attractive lady you were with. I'm surprised to find you out and about alone. But I suppose your evening got ruined, didn't it?'

'I like a morning walk and it's very beautiful around here.'

'Oh, very. But don't tell me you're just enjoying the morning air. You're looking into that dreadful thing that happened yesterday. Poor dear. Penny, I mean. No woman is safe these days, Inspector. Aren't men horrible?' The young man gave a theatrical shiver.

'When did you hear about Mrs Deane?'

'Last night. All the comings and goings along the road. I left Alex to potter about closing his place and when I saw all the cars I naturally went to see what was happening.'

'Did you see her at any time yesterday? Walking past the lodge, perhaps?'

'No, no, I didn't. You think she walked to her place of doom? I wondered if she'd been murdered somewhere else and dumped there. I mean, can you imagine someone doing that in broad daylight where he could be seen?'

Odhiambo avoided being side-tracked.

'You didn't walk past the memorial at any time yesterday? On your way to the restaurant for instance?'

'Oh dear! Are we all suspects, then? Account for your movements and all that. I'm afraid you're a bit late, dear cousin. Our local constabulary beat you to it last night. No, I didn't come this way. Actually, I joined Alex at his restaurant, having spent the afternoon walking on the cliffs, but the other side of Penleith.' Nigel giggled, causing Odhiambo to wince. 'I wouldn't call this the most exciting place on earth, would you, my good black brother? I mean, there's not a lot to do except walk and swim. Unless like Alex you like watching people eat fish which were unlucky enough to fall foul of Menherian.'

'Menherian is one of the local fishermen, is he? I think I met him in the pub. Didn't seem to like those of us from Polsand very much.'

Odhiambo was surprised at the reaction. Nigel's face darkened and he spoke with venom.

'Menherian, that's him all right. He does some fishing for Alex. Crab, lobster and this and that. But he doesn't exactly endear himself, does he? Not to be trusted, I've discovered.'

'You're not local yourself, are you? How long have you been living here?'

'No. We were in India for a while. Alex is a water engineer. He was working on one of the dam projects in Utter Pradesh. We came here three years ago. I have to confess to you, dear friend, that I would favour a return to civilisation. Cornwall is a bit like Uttar Pradesh, if you ask me.'

'Mr Bastian is retired then? I mean, from his engineering career?'

'Yes. At least for the time being. You know what middle-aged men are, Inspector. Male menopause and all that. Alex fancies himself as a gentleman of leisure cum restaurateur. I say to him, "Alex," I say, "let's be real about this. What are we doing in this dreary place?" But I suppose I'll have to sit it out until the fad passes. Now, talking about Alex, I must go and prepare his breakfast otherwise he'll be very cross with me – and we wouldn't want that, would we?'

'Just before you go – did you know Mr Mahendra in India?'

'Oh, you're being a policeman again. Just as we were having a nice chat. Actually, Alex did know him. He came to visit the dam. Just a casual business acquaintance, you might say.'

'And you met him again here?'

'Yes. I suppose he must have heard about us from Deane when he visited the Centre. He dropped in to see Alex about six months ago. Now, I really must be off. Toodle-oo, Inspector.'

Odhiambo watched the young man descend the slope to the rear wall of the lodge garden and hop over it. Nigel's wet hair, damp towel and a wet band-aid peeling off the underside of his wrist confirmed he had come from an early morning swim; presumably another who was not deterred by the reputed dangers of the lake.

Odhiambo resumed his walk back to the Centre. The wind was rising and beginning to disturb the branches of the trees. The weather seemed to be changing; heavy clouds were building up over the sea and rain seemed probable. As he neared the Centre Odhiambo's mind returned to his other preoccupation, his guilt over his hours with Helen and his betrayal of his wife. But he was not destined to be allowed to brood for, as he emerged from the trees and the Centre came in view, a scene of considerable activity met his eyes. Three police cars were parked in the front drive and a number of figures were emerging from the house amid a scene of some bustle. Before Odhiambo could identify individuals, one of the police cars departed in a slamming of doors and scattering of gravel. As he got nearer, Odhiambo saw Gregson gesticulating at a policeman whom, a moment later, he identified as Sergeant Trewin. Gregson was clearly agitated and his voice carried across the lawn as Odhiambo crossed it.

'It's placing us in an impossible situation. A house full of people from all over the Commonwealth, can't send them home, and now you take away the staff.' He caught sight of Odhiambo and turned towards him. 'This is too much, Odhiambo. They've taken Deane in for questioning and say no one can leave. What the hell are we supposed to do?'

Odhiambo looked questioningly at the policeman, who grinned sardonically. He didn't seem too upset at inconveniencing Gregson. He addressed Odhiambo.

'Mr Deane has been taken to the station. Actually, Mr Pendham was looking for you, you're wanted there too. Perhaps you'd care to come with me.'

'Are you taking me in for questioning, too? I mean, are you detaining me? Or is this an informal request?'

Trewin looked momentarily nonplussed.

'No, no, it's not like that. More of a request, like. Obviously a policeman like yourself realises we need a full statement as you were the one finding the body and all.'

Gregson was looking apoplectic.

'This is becoming a nightmare. There's no hope of running classes in this atmosphere. We've just got people kicking their heels. And they're frightened. I mean to say, two deaths in two days. And I understand the weather is worsening. At least at the moment they can walk around the grounds.'

'Don't worry, Mr Gregson, we'll get something organised while Mr Deane is away. I think the best thing is to sit everybody down for a good breakfast.'

The voice was cool, composed and confident. Odhiambo turned his head. Helen had come up on his blind side. Her appearance was consistent with the voice. Smart suit and blouse, red hair demurely tied back. She didn't look at Odhiambo but smiled at the sergeant and laid her hand on Gregson's arm.

'Right, my dear, lead on. Glad to see someone's on top of things.'

As they moved towards the door, Helen did turn to look at

Odhiambo. To his amazement and further confusion she winked. He felt almost weak-kneed with conflicting emotions. God, what am I doing here, he thought. This is no place for a simple Luo. And Cari, what was he going to say to her? What a fool. He was brought back to the present by Trewin.

'Strange sort of chap, that. Seems more nervy than you'd think he should be, given he's not involved other than seeing that Indian chap drown. Or near enough.'

Yes, Gregson's behaviour was becoming agitated, thought Odhiambo. He had a feeling that this might be something to do with his wife, Muriel, but he held his own counsel.

'What about Mr Deane? Do you and Pendham suspect him or what? Have you got something to tie him in to Mrs Deane's murder?'

But this time it was the sergeant's turn to stay mum. Grumbling about being deprived of his breakfast, Odhiambo allowed himself to be directed to the second of the police cars. He had a feeling that this day, having started badly, with his oppressive feeling of guilt, was going to worsen.

Superintendent Stephens looked at Pendham speculatively. They were sitting in Stephens' office in the main Redbourne police station with Pendham impatient to get to work interviewing his suspect.

'You reckon you've got the man then, Bill, do you? Jealous husband deal, is it?'

'Seems so, Super, seems so. We know Deane was not where he said he was when the Indian was drowned. We've got a witness to say that Mahendra and Mrs Deane were in Mahendra's bedroom together for some time earlier in the evening. My guess is he wanted to catch them pants down as it were after their moonlight swim but somehow or other things got out of hand and the Indian was drowned. But that still made his wife a fornicator with our friend from the East and Deane didn't like it. So yesterday he made her pay too.'

'But the MO, man. Cutting her throat and fixing her to a ship's wheel; that's the act of a weirdo, Bill.'

'Well, perhaps he is a weirdo. Perhaps he went that way worrying about his wife screwing all the multicoloured talent arriving at the house. Or he was trying to divert suspicion. That's what I'm about to find out.'

'OK, Bill, get on with it. But be careful, you hear me. This has the potential for a big stink. All these foreigners and diplomatics mixed up in it. Everything's got to be according to Hoyle with this one, my lad. Which brings me to another thing – we don't want any charge of racism to make matters worse. That's why I want to see this chap, what's his name?' Stephens glanced at his notepad on the desk in front of him. 'Od-iam-bo. That's it. From Kenya, isn't he? Kid gloves, Bill, that's the word. Friendly Commonwealth colleague. Hail fellow, well met. As long as he's not mixed up in it, of course.'

'That's the point, isn't it? Don't expect me to do him any favours. Always about when the bodies surface. To be fair, I'm not saying he's mixed up with Deane, or whatever, but he's one of those who think they're superior to us rural policemen. Blimey, we were solving crimes when he was still in the trees.'

'That will do, Pendham.' His listener smiled; Christian names were suddenly going out of fashion. 'That's just what I mean. Racist remarks. Say that to his face or let the press boys get a sniff of it and we're in front of the Foreign Office or the bloody Equal Opportunities lot. Watch your tongue, you hear me?'

But Pendham's mind was back on the task in hand. He rose and, receiving a grunt from his superior, made his way out of the office.

Stephens pondered awhile. He could do without double murders with diplomatic complications. He had no further ambitions, Super was fine; what he wanted now was a quiet life as he made his way gracefully over the last steps to his pension and ample time for the golf course. Pendham was good, but dangerously tactless. He'd have to keep a close eye on this whole business. The announcement of the arrival of the African policeman heralded step one of his intended supervision. Smooth this chap down and remove one potential source of complication was the task, and Stephens knew he was good at the massaging of egos.

'Chief Inspector Odhiambo, welcome to Cornwall and to Redbourne police station. I'm sorry that it's because of this unfortunate business at Penleith that I got to hear of you. Sit down, please.'

Certainly the African was an impressive figure, Stephens thought: a big handsome man who entered the room and now sat at Stephens' invitation with the wariness of a panther.

'Good morning. Your sergeant brought me in, I think the phrase is. Although I expected Pendham. I hadn't heard about your involvement.'

'Not really involved. Bill Pendham is in charge. He's interviewing a suspect now, or, rather, interviewing someone who we believe can help us in our enquiries. You know the form. I don't know if you have to be so careful in your country? What with the press and the civil liberties lobby here one has to guard one's tongue pretty carefully.'

'It's a little different in Kenya. The pressures come from other directions, but I know what you mean.'

Odhiambo had now summed up the situation. This was to be the good cop of the good cop–bad cop paired interviews. After the abrasiveness of Pendham this was the soothing oil. Stephens fitted the part well: a tall man, slim, greying hair expensively cut and shaped and wearing a suit a long way in cut and price from the crumpled version favoured by Pendham.

'Tell me, Inspector. How do you see the situation at that Centre place? Always glad to have a professional opinion.'

Odhiambo considered a moment before making a decision. OK, he thought, why not? If Stephens wanted the old pals approach what reason was there for not going along?

'I don't have access to the results of Pendham's enquiries, obviously. So I can only give you my impressions as a temporary resident there. Clearly, the murders are linked. Mrs Deane was almost certainly in the vicinity when Mahendra was drowned, but I'm not sure she was the person Mahendra was supposed to be meeting for a swim. I may be wrong on that. Anyway, she saw something or was involved in some way or another in Mahendra's death and she was killed because of that. The two deaths would indicate a disturbed mind. There's a sick aspect to both deaths in terms of the way they were done. Also a recklessness. The second carried a very high risk of being seen.'

Stephens was paying attention now. This chap seemed cooperative enough, despite what Pendham said. Just showed. Have to know how to handle people. Particularly foreigners.

'That's precisely my view, Inspector. The MO is strange. We're dealing with a psycho. Worrying, that. Need to get him quick.'

'Psychopath yes, but not a random killer. There's a motive behind the acts.'

'I gather you reported a row you overheard just before the chap was drowned. But you're not sure if he was involved.'

'That's right. Although, equally, even if it was him there it doesn't mean it's connected with his death.'

Stephens rose and looked out of his window with his back to his visitor. Then he turned and looked down on the seated man.

'You say the Indian might have been meeting someone other than Mrs Deane. A lady friend, perhaps? Who?'

'I don't know. After all, I only met him for the first time a few hours before he died.'

Stephens' voice sharpened in intensity.

'Pendham tells me that the Admin Officer there is an attractive woman. The sort to catch his eye. What's your view on her?'

Odhiambo cursed to himself. Stephens was beginning to move away from the diplomatic posture towards his, no doubt, more familiar role of the inquisitor.

'I think you can forget her. By an odd chance, I knew her in connection with another case in Kenya. She had no more than a casual acquaintance with Mahendra. I can vouch for her presence at the Centre, the house I mean, all afternoon and then she was kind enough to introduce me to a restaurant in Penleith for dinner.'

'Yes, Pendham said you seemed to know her well. Strange, the arm of fate, isn't it? Just by chance, you say?'

Odhiambo ignored the inference, and after a few desultory exchanges he took his leave. Stephens escorted him to the door and shook his visitor's hand with a parting remark.

'I suppose you'll be leaving with the others as soon as Pendham can give the all-clear to let you all disperse. I'm sorry for any inconvenience.'

'No problem. I understand. I'm sorry if Pendham sees me as getting in the way. Not intended. Just the way events panned out.'

'Oh, silly of me, I nearly forgot. Got to go through the paperwork stage, I'm afraid. Bill Pendham would like you to get your statement down. I'll get someone to look after you while you handle that, if you would. And I expect you could do with a cup of something.'

Helen Shropshire sat back in the chair in her office and sighed. The last two hours had been hectic. All pretence of running the seminar had been abandoned – two murders and the removal of the Centre's Director by the police had created a tension impossible to overcome. She had managed to organise participants and staff through breakfast and then explained the peculiar circumstances they all found themselves in. Some of the participants accepted the situation with patience. The Tanzanian, Matembe, continued to suspect some neo-colonial plot and Asuna regarded the affair as a deliberate tactic to keep him in this 'dead end' away from the minimum amenities of life such as night-clubs. Some were frightened and demanding to be allowed to go away from this place of killings. Helen did her best to assure them that everything was being done to look after their security in the Centre and its immediate environs. She warned them not to go wandering alone in the woods. She hoped she could contain the situation until the police let them go.

Her physical activity in organising the Centre's continued operation had prevented her from worrying about the two matters of greatest personal concern, but now as she sat for a minute's respite these concerns returned.

The horror of the previous evening with Penny Deane dead on the cliff top made her shiver anew. Then there was Odhiambo. Strangely, she did not feel as guilty as she felt she should. OK, the tug of sexual attraction she had always felt for him had finally caused her to lose her self-control. The stress and shock of the evening had contributed, no doubt, but she had known what she was doing. It had been good, too; she had never felt such desire and such fulfilment. Nor, as she knew, did she need to fear any consequences in terms of pregnancy. Now it had happened it was over and done with and they must understand that. She was pretty sure, though, that James would be feeling enough guilt for both of them.

A tap on the door announced the renewed appearance of Gregson. A somewhat harassed-looking Gregson – almost a caricature, Helen thought, of a colonial administrator hearing the faint sounds of the drums heralding a native revolt.

'Ah, my dear, er, Helen. I've been in touch with London again. In view of the situation with Peter. Bit awkward; I mean, not knowing whether he's coming back or not. And, if so, under what circumstances. Not to say the loss of his wife. Anyway, the chaps there took my point. They're cancelling the next seminar and they'll keep the situation under review. Meanwhile they asked me to act as liaison with the local police to make sure our participants get out as soon as possible. And to assist you, of course, in running this place under difficult circumstances.'

That's all I need, thought Helen, having Gregson under my heels all day. She thought fast.

'There is one thing that would be a great help if you could organise it. We must do something with those here. They're going mad, stuck here with nothing to do. If we lay on our bus we could take them to see the local sights, Land's End, St Michael's Mount, stuff like that. The police won't mind that, will they?'

Gregson was grateful to be allocated a specific task.

'They'd better not. You leave them to me, my dear. You organise the transport. I'll see to the rest.'

Helen sighed and turned to the rapidly mounting pile of slips recording telephone calls. The press were on to the story and she was sure that soon they would be at her door.

12

Pendham left the interview room at Redbourne police station dissatisfied with his progress. Deane was saying very little. It was not a sullen silence, rather he appeared distraught and in a state of shock consistent with an innocent man who has just heard that his wife has been butchered. But Pendham knew when he was being lied to and Deane was lying. He admitted that the meeting he claimed to have attended in Penzance had not taken place. He claimed he had made a genuine mistake on dates and only discovered his mistake when he arrived at the museum. He was vague about his actions thereafter, going no further than saying he 'walked around'. He denied being with his wife in the woods the previous afternoon and claimed to have spent the afternoon and evening doing paperwork in his apartment, having vacated his office for the use of the police. For the rest he cried out to be left in peace to mourn his wife; to be taken home so he could make the necessary arrangements for a funeral; and what about the Centre, he was needed there.

Finally, Pendham had adjourned the interview, leaving Deane to make telephone calls to the Centre and to his solicitor. He had not wanted legal representation earlier, but now seemed to recognise that he was in need of it. Back in his office he scanned the messages that Sergeant Trewin had phoned in and a pathologist's report that with some equivocation indicated the likelihood that Mahendra's ankle had been gripped shortly before death by a hand. Impressions of what appeared to be fingernails were evident in the skin. Further forensic examination was in hand, the report said; presumably, Pendham thought sardonically, no pun intended. He looked at the messages again. What he needed was a witness who could place Deane inside the estate when he claimed to be in Penzance: but so far, it seemed, Trewin had drawn a blank on that score.

It was lunch-time and the Centre was beginning to reveal once more some signs of organised behaviour. Lunch was to be followed by the Gregson–Shropshire expedition. As Odhiambo entered he saw the purposeful drift of figures towards the dining-room. He sighed, but it was no use delaying the embarrassing encounter any longer. He moved determinedly towards the office of the Administrative Officer.

Helen Shropshire responded to the tap on the door with an invitation to enter. She was expecting the coach driver for they needed to agree on an itinerary, but when she looked up there stood Odhiambo looking, she thought, like a naughty overgrown schoolboy. She could almost feel the tremor in the hand on the door handle. Oh dear, she thought, I'd better do something about this.

'Ah, there you are, James. Free from Mr Pendham's clutches once more? Come in and shut the door, for heaven's sake.'

Odhiambo was relieved at the tone of voice and the demeanour of the woman at the desk. Damn it, she was attractive. But what have I done? He obeyed the instructions and attempted his rehearsed apology.

'I want to say, it was all my fault . . . last night. I mean, er, it was unforgivable, but, er . . .'

Helen interrupted the embarrassing stuttering.

'Right. Now look here. I'll say it once and that's all. What happened was both our responsibilities. I'm OK, in fact it was lovely. But I can understand your guilty feelings so it mustn't happen again. It was one of those things, I was frightened and there you were. Now it's behind us. But don't go creeping around the place looking like a guilty husband. I don't want everyone to know.'

Odhiambo stared at her. Thank God she was taking it well.

That left Cari to worry about. But still he found words hard to come by. Once again he was rescued.

'Now, I need to know what's going on. You can fill me in on what you think is happening and likely to happen. Is Peter going to be arrested? I don't think he could have done it – either of them, I mean, but particularly not Penny.'

The memory of the previous evening on that dreadful cliff came back to her once again and she shuddered. For some reason this overt sign of vulnerability settled Odhiambo.

'I don't know what's happening to Deane. I didn't even see Pendham, only his boss. Gave my statement to a constable.'

Helen interrupted.

'Peter called. From the station. He sounded as if he's in a terrible state. Poor man. They're keeping him there for more questioning. Apparently he's getting a solicitor.'

'I wonder what they've got to go on. Well, it's nothing to do with me.'

'You keep saying that.' Helen smiled. 'Now I've laid on a coach trip for you this afternoon. Take your mind off things. Go and get your lunch or you'll be late.'

Another knock heralded the awaited driver and Odhiambo found himself back in the hall. He needed a drink more than lunch and he didn't intend to go on the trip despite Helen's orders. Looking up, he saw the figure of Muriel Gregson at the top of the stairs, her padded coat and woolly hat indicating that she intended to brave the rising wind now carrying a dampness that hinted at worse to come. On impulse Odhiambo slipped out of the front door and headed down the drive, albeit slowly. Sure enough, he soon heard behind him the crunch of another's footsteps. He turned.

'Oh, good morning – Mrs Gregson, isn't it? Taking a pre-lunch walk?'

Mrs Gregson looked nervously at the large man in her path.

'Ah, yes, it's, it's . . . er . . . Mr Odhiambo isn't it?'

Odhiambo stood aside and then joined her as she came level. She was a handsome woman – Goya would have chosen her as a model, he thought, in preference to the models who now reigned so ubiquitously on billboard and magazine cover.

'You don't mind if I walk with you for a while?'

It would have taken a thicker skin than Odhiambo's not to notice that his companion did not seem overjoyed at the prospect, but she courteously made an effort to overcome her reluctance.

'Of course. I hope you don't think I'm in any danger in broad daylight. That poor woman. I didn't know her, of course; only spoke to her once, but so dreadful.' Then a sudden change of tack. 'Actually, I'm meeting someone. An old friend who lives near here.'

'Would that be Mrs Tamlyn?' Odhiambo smiled as his companion's head snapped sideways towards him. 'By a strange coincidence, I met her on the beach, or the Bar as they call it here. Yesterday. More or less bumped into her in the mist. She told me she knew you. You were with her, of course, the night Mahendra died.'

Muriel Gregson snorted. They were now on the road leading not to the lodge and bar but in the other direction, skirting the lake on their right. They had emerged from the shelter of the trees; the wind, roughing up the lake surface, seemed to take her expression of derision and send it sailing into the meadows on their left. Her hands went to the collar of her coat and she pulled it up around her neck.

'You're that African policeman, of course. Hugh said you were, what's the phrase, pursuing your own enquiries. Said the local police weren't too pleased.'

'Not really. I just seem to get in the wrong place at the wrong time. But Hugh's correct. Pendham and Trewin would sooner I was not among those present.'

'Hugh says they've arrested Peter Deane. Do you think he did it? Killed his wife, I mean. Or both murders, I suppose.'

'I don't know. It doesn't seem right, somehow. But I haven't any inside information from the police.'

'She was sleeping with Javi Mahendra, you know. Mrs Deane, I mean. He could have found out.'

'Are you saying Peter Deane drowned Mahendra and then cut his wife's throat?' Odhiambo spoke harshly; he wanted to shake the woman out of her withdrawn manner, as if she wasn't part of the community involved. 'Did you and Mrs Tamlyn see anything that night? Did you take a walk by the lake after dinner?'

They turned a corner and ahead of them at the water's edge was an old boatshed. Odhiambo remembered Deane mentioning that his wife sometimes came here. There was a bench seat along the front and Odhiambo could see a figure seated on it. His companion stopped and turned towards him.

'I think it would be better if you left it to Inspector Pendham, don't you?' She looked at him a moment and then turned back and hurried towards the figure, who had risen from the bench. 'Hello, Angela, here I am.'

Angela Tamlyn came to meet her, but as she neared Muriel Gregson her eyes were focused past the other woman on to Odhiambo.

'And with a companion, too, I see. Hello, Inspector, we meet again.'

Odhiambo gave a slight nod and then, as if reluctant to intrude, approached them. His apparent reluctance was feigned for, in truth, he felt an urge to know more about Angela Tamlyn and the relationship between the two women. Somehow, in some way, he believed Muriel Gregson to be involved with Mahendra and her alibi for the night of his death irritated him.

'Ah. The Lady in the Mist. I can see clearly now, as someone sang.'

Muriel Gregson looked from one to the other with irritation.

'Mr Odhiambo invited himself along. He's interested in our movements the night Mahendra drowned. He seems to have set himself up as a one-man alternative police force.'

But her irritation did not seem to be shared.

'Given the awful sequel yesterday, you can't blame him for being interested, Muriel. I gather you found the body of poor Mrs Deane, Mr Odhiambo.'

'News travels fast in these parts, it seems. I thought you lived in a lonely spot.'

'Yes, it does. The milkman cometh and brings the gossip with the cream. Muriel is coming back to lunch with me. Would you care to join us? It's a cold collation, more than enough for two women trying to watch their weight.'

Odhiambo noticed that the invitation was not well received by the other guest, whose irritation now led her to turn her back on them and gaze petulantly across the water.

'No, no, thank you very much – I must get back to the Centre. I've intruded on you ladies enough. But, as I've butted in, tell me one thing. Do you know Mr Deane, Peter Deane, the Centre's Director?'

'Slightly. Well, a little better than that, I suppose. He and I have a common interest in painters, local painters. We're members of a group that meets in Penzance. Once a month.'

'Ah, I see. I gather he was in Penzance two nights ago. But it wasn't your group, I suppose, as you were here with Mrs Gregson.'

Despite herself, Muriel Gregson had turned back to face the conversation and now intervened.

'But that's where he claims he was, so Hugh tells me. That's his alibi, attending a meeting that didn't take place.'

Angela Tamlyn was prepared to suspend judgement.

'Well, he was out by a week. He might have put it in his diary for the wrong Tuesday and gone there expecting a meeting. I remember poor Penny telling me once he'd done that before. There's an exhibition on at the moment, Inspector, of the most famous of the local schools of painters, the Newlyn School. You should take time and visit it. Give you a feel for life in these parts in the old days, a hundred years ago.'

'Was, or should I say will, the meeting be held where the exhibition is?'

'Yes. At the museum.'

Muriel Gregson saw her chance.

'And you could go this afternoon. Hugh has organised a trip. Get you from under the feet of the police.'

Angela Tamlyn laughed.

'Oh Muriel, don't be rude.' Then, turning to Odhiambo, 'But you should go, you'd enjoy it.'

After a few more pleasantries and after declining a repeated invitation, Odhiambo retraced his steps. The wind was still strengthening and was now at a level where walking into it required a deliberate effort. He reached the sanctuary of the hall and paused to regain his breath. As he stood there, Gregson appeared from the direction of the dining-room, heading for the offices. He saw Odhiambo, stopped and changed direction.

'Ah, Odhiambo. Thought I didn't see you breaking bread with the masses. Just going to see if everything's ready. You'll be joining us, I hope. See the sights, St Michael's Mount, that sort of thing, and then a spot of culture; take them to some local art exhibition. Keep them out of mischief, eh?'

Odhiambo could recognise fate.

'If you've got a spare seat. When are you leaving?'

'In about half an hour. Helen's going to stay behind and look after the place. One of the staff will act as our guide. Hope to have you on board.'

With that Gregson bustled on. Odhiambo needed a beer more than ever. There was no bar at the Centre but drinks were available with meals, so he made his way to the kitchen area via the rear passage, avoiding the route through the dining area. A friendly member of the staff supplied him with two cans of lager and a thick-cut sandwich which he took to his room. Feeling better he made his way to the front door. The coach was there and Helen was shepherding people aboard. She saw him and laughed.

'So you're going. Good. I had a feeling you were going to duck out.'

Odhiambo returned her smile.

'I can't resist a bit of culture. I gather we're going to see, what is it, the Newlyn School of painters.'

'Yes, I think that's right. What do you know about it?'

Odhiambo hesitated, but there was something about Helen that overcame his normal reticence. He had always liked to discuss his cases with his wife, but Cari was not available.

'Helen, I get instinctive impulses. Peter was supposed to have been at this museum Tuesday evening. That's his alibi for Mahendra's drowning. But the meeting he was supposed to be at is next Tuesday. Or so Angela Tamlyn tells me. She lives across the lake. She and Peter are on some committee or something to do with these paintings. The female Gregson made sure I was aware that his alibi was full of holes. And you arranged transport to take me to it. My instinct tells me when a coincidence like that happens I should go along for the ride.'

'But how will looking at the paintings help you? What's that got to do with anything?'

'Nothing that I can think of.' Odhiambo sounded and felt in good spirits. He didn't know why, but somehow his depression had lifted. 'But if Peter Deane isn't lying, then he was there on Tuesday.'

'I see, or I suppose I do.' Helen sounded doubtful and looked at Odhiambo as if she guessed he'd been drinking. 'I wish I could come, but I've got stacks to do here. And talking to you won't get it done.'

'OK. I'm sorry. I'll leave you in peace.'

'You know, James, it's strange. I should feel frightened, depressed or whatever. The horrible goings-on. Yet somehow I feel on top of things. It's a terrible thing to say, but I almost feel excited.'

Odhiambo had been turning to leave, but now turned back.

'It's not abnormal. First, you're a very able woman so you're responding to responsibility. Second, I know what you mean. The adrenalin starts to pump when you're involved and not just a bystander.'

Helen smiled to herself. At least he didn't claim the credit, she thought. She intervened once more as Odhiambo went to the door.

'No. Wait a minute. This woman you mentioned. Where does she come into it? And how do you know her?' Helen blushed as if realising that her last words could be misinterpreted as some kind of petty jealousy. 'I mean, how did you come to be discussing Peter with her?'

'The Lady in the Mist, you mean?' Odhiambo grinned. 'I ran into her in the mist one morning. Her relevance to this business is that she seems OK. No involvement, nothing odd about her, but she is Mrs Gregson's alibi. Old school friends who spent the evening together.'

A voice behind interrupted.

'Old school friends, you say. You mean my wife and Mrs Tamlyn? Someone told me they'd seen you with them.'

Gregson sounded about as friendly as his wife.

'We happened to run into each other. Is anything the matter, Hugh? Is there something worrying you?'

'No, no, of course not. Just wondered whether you were still checking things out. Wondered what it could be.'

'You know, if there's something worrying you I hope you've told the police. I tell you straight, Hugh, I think not coming clean was what did for Penny Deane.'

'Don't be ridiculous, man. What are you insinuating? It's as I said at the time. I heard a cry, went to recce, slipped in, that's it. Can't say more than that for there's nothing more to say.'

He moved away, urging latecomers on to the coach. Odhiambo winked at Helen and joined the passengers.

13

Odhiambo was the recipient of some envious looks from other passengers for his companion on the coach was the most attractive of the group – the pretty girl from Montserrat. His good fortune was not of his own making; he had sat himself in a vacant double seat, for the capacity of the coach well exceeded the number who boarded, only for the girl, belying her shy demeanour, to ask if she could sit beside him. She was more than pretty, Odhiambo thought; her face was flawless and, although modestly attired in slacks, blouse and cardigan, she had a model's figure, slim but beautifully proportioned.

The coach wended its way towards Penzance along a country road with occasional glimpses of the sea – glimpses that revealed the growing turbulence as the gathering wind whipped the tops off the rearing waves. Odhiambo contented himself with pleasantries, but he was not surprised when, after some time, the girl, whose name turned out to be Jacinda, turned to more substantive matters.

'Excuse me asking, but you're a policeman, aren't you? In Kenya, I mean.'

The voice was both hesitant yet determined. Odhiambo turned his head to establish eye contact.

'Yes, that's right. Why do you ask?'

'It's just, it's just, I don't know, but . . .' A pause, then a rush of words as she took the plunge: 'I wanted to ask your advice on something.'

Odhiambo noticed that his companion was keeping her voice low. Although feeling somewhat ridiculously conspiratorial, he too lowered his voice as he bent his head towards her. He noticed for the first time the aroma of her perfume. Like the wearer, discreet, pleasant, but not flamboyant.

'OK. Fire away.'

Again a pause for final doubts to be considered.

'It's just, just that I overheard someone talking. I didn't mean to. I wasn't spying or anything.' Odhiambo hastily nodded to indicate that this could be taken as accepted. 'I was looking at the pictures in the passage, you know, from the top of the stairs to the common room. It's dark along there and I was behind that statue thing, the head and shoulders of a man. They didn't see me. They went past talking and I couldn't help hearing a bit as they passed. I wasn't trying to listen or anything.' Jacinda paused and Odhiambo waited; any interruption was more likely to put her off than silence. She was like a nervous kitten, poised for flight. 'One said, "We've got to keep the story straight. If the police find out about Tuesday we could be in trouble." The other said there was nothing to worry about but his friend said, "Yes, there is. You saw how easy it was to get at that place. I hear it's brought in here. In boats. Suppose there's a tie-in. Drugs and murder go hand in hand." '

It was to Odhiambo merely a question of perfunctory confirmation, but he asked it anyway.

'Who were these men? I assume they were men.'

'Oh yes. It was Asuna and Adimojo, the two Nigerians.'

Odhiambo nodded.

'You remember the words exactly? I mean, is that precisely what was said?'

Jacinda blushed.

'I think so. I have good recall for conversation. Not books, unfortunately.'

'I see. And what advice are you asking me for?'

'Well, I'm not sure what to do. Should I tell the police? The English police, I mean. Then they'll get to know about it and they may be angry at me. They . . . they frighten me a bit. I don't know why, but they do.'

Odhiambo looked at the girl. Her lip trembled as she spoke and then looked away. He could imagine her thoughts. Alone in a foreign land, precipitated into a situation with a murderer on the loose and two burly bully-boys who could accuse her of telling tales. He allowed himself a chuckle. The girl turned sharply towards him, afraid she was being laughed at. Odhiambo laid a hand on her arm, protectively.

'Don't worry. I think our Nigerian friends are loud-mouthed, but I don't think they're going to trouble you. We have a saying in my land, "The hippo makes a fuss but the crocodile fills his belly." But, yes, the police must be told, just in case it is important. At the very least these two know something relevant to the investigation of Mrs Deane's murder. I tell you what – I'll tell the police, if you like, and try to keep you out of it. If the Nigerians are implicated you'll have to confirm your story, but if they're not they needn't know of your involvement.'

The girl made vague noises of not wanting to concern him, but quickly showed her real relief at the offer and thanked him. Odhiambo continued to make reassuring noises, but his mind was considering the Nigerians. He wasn't surprised. That local fisherman had guided them to a place that night where there was more available than beer. He remembered the locals' reaction to the mention of Mahendra. Had he known something about drug smuggling in this area? Was that what he was going to tell Odhiambo about?

The touring party spent an hour at St Michael's Mount, the strange castle-like dwelling perched on an atoll in the bay, accessible by foot along a causeway that was under water during high tides. After that they were driven through a couple of attractive villages with quaint harbours. Now they were at the Penzance Museum of Victorian Art and Crafts, being shown around by one of the staff. The exhibition of paintings by the Newlyn School artists was the main feature and Odhiambo was impressed by the ability of the leading exponents to capture the sense and feeling of fishing life in the late nineteenth century. The sense of life hanging by a thread, both economically and physically, as portrayed by painters such as Walter Langley reminded Odhiambo of the life-style of many of his kinsmen in Western Kenya at the present time, and he found the relationship strangely moving. Most of the paintings were on loan from major museums and art galleries; clearly the best of the Newlyn School were of considerable value. One water-colour of medium size portrayed a young woman leaning against a sea wall gazing out to sea with a look of utter desolation. The background was dark and ominous; clearly the woman had lost a loved one in a storm. It was an impressive painting. Odhiambo noticed that a small note beside it indicated it was loaned from the private collection of Mrs A. Tamlyn.

Odhiambo's main interest lay elsewhere and, detaching himself from the group, he found his way to an office area. An attractive woman, blonde, in her early thirties, was bending over a catalogue. Odhiambo asked if there was anyone available who could tell him about local groups who took an interest in Cornish paintings. The woman looked surprised.

'Yes, of course, Mr er . . .'

'Odhiambo. I know I don't look local and I'm not, but I'm staying here at the moment.'

'Mr Odhiambo. Yes, Derek here can help you.' She raised her voice to address a man seated at a desk. 'Derek. There's a gentleman here interested in joining a local group.'

Odhiambo moved over to the short, stocky, nondescript man who rose, shook his hand and waved him to a chair.

'How can I help you? Wilcock is my name. And you're Mr . . .?'

'Odhiambo. I'm at the Polsand Centre with Peter Deane. He told me about his interest in the Newlyn School and encouraged me to take an interest. I know it must seem odd as I'm not Cornish or even English. But I've enjoyed seeing them this afternoon. Wondered if I could join something to learn more? I think Peter said he's a member of a group.'

Wilcock looked for a moment as if he found Odhiambo's tale suspicious. Odhiambo supposed that not many Africans came seeking to join local art study groups. Then his innate politeness took over.

'Of course I know Peter well. Any friend of his and so forth. Yes, there is a group, Peter is a very keen member. He could bring you along next Tuesday; introduce you and so forth. Glad you're taken with our old boys in Newlyn.'

'Ah, next Tuesday, fine. Is it weekly, then? Peter told me he was coming here last Tuesday. That's when he first mentioned the Newlyn School to me.'

'No, no, you must be mistaken. The group meets approximately monthly. There was no meeting last Tuesday. In fact the museum was shut in the evening. We were preparing for this exhibition.'

A few desultory remarks later Odhiambo took his leave of the obliging Mr Wilcock. When he had mentioned Peter Deane's comment he had seen out of the corner of his eye the reaction of the blonde woman. She was startled, her hand going to her mouth. A moment or two later she moved away through the door leading back to the main exhibition area. Having escaped from Mr Wilcock, Odhiambo followed her but a quick scan of the public area revealed no blonde. Playing a hunch, Odhiambo left the gallery, which faced the promenade separating it from the sea. There against a rail, looking at the sea, was his quarry. Her hair blew viciously around her face in the gathering wind. He crossed the road and approached her.

'Excuse me butting in again, but I'm a little worried, you see.'

The woman turned, startled and, yes, frightened.

'What do you want? Why are you following me? Didn't you get what you wanted from Derek?'

'Please. You see, we had a death at Polsand on Tuesday evening. You must have heard.' It was clear she had. 'I'm worried that the police are questioning Mr Deane and he says he was here. I wondered if you could help me confirm he came here.'

'You're lying. You're deceiving us, aren't you? You're not interested in the painters, are you? You're trying to get evidence against Peter.'

'The reverse is true. Don't you see, if someone saw him here he's in the clear.'

The woman's face told Odhiambo what he wanted to know. It

revealed uncertainty about her inquisitor, yes, but also awareness of his point, and guilt that she was about to lie.

'I don't know anything about it. You must leave me alone.'

She turned and hurried away. Right, thought Odhiambo, that seems clear enough. Deane had a girlfriend in Penzance. He could have been with her on Tuesday – whether admiring the paintings together in a deserted gallery or engaged in alternative pursuits, he neither knew nor cared. It would be up to the police to track down the woman and check it out. Odhiambo set off to find his group of fellow travellers; rounding the corner he saw them mounting the steps of the coach, clutching their hats and coats to them as the wind funnelled its way up the narrow street.

The art exhibition had been the penultimate call and the last in terms of local culture, unless culture was rather generously defined. Gregson or Helen had decided to include a drink at the Crab's Claw in Penleith in the itinerary and there the party arrived in the early evening. The sky over the sea looked angry as dark clouds built up, multi-layered and shifting with uneven contours. The wind was now at gale force and the forecast storm seemed close at hand. Entering the bar, Odhiambo saw, almost with a sense of inevitability, the figure of the fisherman he had encountered during his previous visit, Menherian. No sign of recognition crossed Menherian's face, but Odhiambo was sure he had been seen and recognised.

After a few minutes, lager in hand, Odhiambo worked his way over to where Menherian was sitting.

'Good evening. It's Mr Menherian, isn't it? We met on Tuesday evening. I was with the group from the Polsand Centre.'

The fisherman had been surveying the new entrants into the pub with a jaundiced eye. He had studiously avoided catching Odhiambo's eye. Now it seemed an age before he turned his head slowly to face Odhiambo.

'Don't remember seeing ye. But then I 'ave difficulty telling you lot apart.'

'Yes, I was here. But you left with two of my colleagues – from Nigeria. I'm from Kenya myself. Wondered if I'd missed something. They said something about going on somewhere.'

Menherian focused on Odhiambo more carefully. Odhiambo got the impression of a sharp mind at work behind the unprepossessing features.

'Ah. I've got ye now. You're the nosy bugger. I've heard tell of a blackie going round asking questions. Think we don't have no police 'ere, do 'e?'

'You heard about me from Mr Bastian perhaps? I'm told he gets his fish from you. Very good too. If I may say so.'

Menherian did not take up the matter of his informants. He scowled at Odhiambo.

'I hear you've lost another one up there at the house. Not another wog like that Indian but Mrs Deane, more's the pity. Weren't nothing wrong with her. Good sort, I've always found.'

'Yes, a terrible thing to happen. And it's not nice knowing there's a murderer loose among us.'

'Bain't surprised at anything with the mixed lot of you up there at the house. 'Tain't natural.'

'You knew Mrs Deane, then?'

'To say "morning" to, that's all. Didn't mix with us in village much. Her nor him. Unlike you lot. Soon sniff the women out, you buggers from Africa.'

Odhiambo attracted the attention of the barmaid and gestured towards Menherian's glass.

'You'll have one with me?' There was no gracious response, but the girl, no doubt used to his surliness, whisked the glass under a tap to refill. 'You know Mrs Deane was found hanging on that wheel near the cliff top? I didn't know that wheel was there. They say it's set to be seen from the sea. But nobody saw her body. At least nobody reported it.'

'Way I heard it, you found 'er; up there with your bit of stuff.'

Menherian drank from the brimming glass. Still no acknowledgement to his benefactor.

'But nobody on a boat noticed her.'

'Weren't that many around last even. Those well out in bay wouldn't notice. Got better things to do when yer in boat than peering at bloody land.'

Menherian sounded as if his suspicions were rising. His scowl deepened and he took another deep sup of beer. Odhiambo waited; eventually Menherian continued.

'And there'll be no bugger out tonight. Going to be a bad do an' all. You'll learn some'in' 'bout this coast this night, mister. Going to be a beaut, innit, Alf?' Another weatherbeaten local salt had eased his way to the bar. 'Got these foreigners around, Alf. Don't know their ass from their elbow when it comes to a sea, do 'ey, boy?'

Alf grinned at Menherian and gave a doubtful sidelong look at Odhiambo.

'Ay. 'Tis going to blow tonight alreet. Straight from the west. 'E'll keep ye awake later on, will this.'

'It's a pity.' Odhiambo addressed Menherian directly. 'I was going to ask you if you could take me on a trip along the coast tomorrow. You know, close in. I'd like to see it from the sea – the cliffs, I mean, and so on. Do you do any hire work?'

Menherian looked at the large African with closer attention, but it was Alf who got in first, prefacing his words with a sardonic laugh.

'Oh, Daniel here'll take anyone out if the price is right. Could show you more than cliffs if 'e 'ad a mind to. Isn'at right, Dan?' Then, more reflectively, 'Shoun't rule out tomorrow. After a really big storm it blows itself right out. Could be real still come morrow afternoon.'

'I ain't intending to take this bugger no place. Nosy enough now. You go back where you come from, mister, and leave us be. Us don't want you blacks down here and that's a fact. Giving it to you straight, like.'

Odhiambo forced a smile.

'I don't find you strange, Menherian. There's plenty like you where I come from. Fishermen on the coast suspicious of outsiders. Mind you, they're black, but you could be blood brothers.'

Menherian started to get up from his stool.

'Don't you go comparing me to no black bugger. Ain't no half-breed 'bout me.'

His friend put a restraining hand on Menherian's arm.

'Don't you fret now, Daniel. Reckon you asked for that. No need for aggravation.'

But Menherian had stopped, his mind obviously working. Then he poked a large and deeply seamed finger at Odhiambo's chest.

'OK, mister. See how it is after dinner tomorrow. Maybe I will take 'ee out to see the sights. Long as you're a good sailor.'

Odhiambo was not confident of his sea-legs. He didn't like setting sail on Lake Victoria, let alone on the rough Cornish sea. He wished he hadn't raised the subject, although he had a curiosity about the caves the special constable had mentioned that morning. What was more intriguing now was the question of why Menherian had suddenly changed his mind. Given his racial prejudices and what seemed a personal animosity to Odhiambo, his change of tack was more than surprising.

Gregson now arrived at his elbow wanting his herd, including Odhiambo, to come together to be shepherded back to the coach. Whilst the coach made its last short journey, Odhiambo thought his afternoon had not been wasted. Now for the evening and the night's storm.

14

Odhiambo's anticipation of the storm grossly underestimated the reality. He was accustomed to tropical storms, rain of cloudburst density, lightning over Lake Victoria that forked down with an intensity that stunned the retina; but nothing in his experience matched the winds of that dreadful night.

The old manor house, facing south-east with the wooded slope behind it, was protected from the full force of a westerly gale. Even so, as the evening wore on the noise, or rather noises, grew to a frightening level. There was the almost monotonous moan of the wind as it thrust through the trees around the house to beat against the large sash windows, a sound like the beating of a million wings, and this was overlaid, with ever-increasing frequency, by a higher-pitched pulsating note of the wind around the chimneys as if the gods were playing a giant set of pan-pipes. For some time the rain held off but then it, too, added its contribution to the demonic noise as it splattered on to the windows in frenetic bursts.

Some of the residents watched the television in the lounge after dinner, but Odhiambo, Hugh Gregson and Helen Shropshire took their coffee in Helen's office. Muriel Gregson had excused herself, complaining of a headache. The news was relayed to them from the lounge that the weather forecasters were now predicting winds of severe storm strength gusting to hurricane force, reaching their worst for the westerly approaches at midnight. The three formed an unofficial administrative team, for the police had confirmed by phone that Peter Deane was being detained overnight.

It was Odhiambo who had spoken to the police. He had succeeded before dinner in getting through to Pendham after a couple of abortive calls when Pendham was 'engaged in interviews'. Their conversation followed the now well-set routine, each bridling at intended or unintended slights. Pendham's temper was, in any case, poor given his lack of progress with his number one suspect.

Odhiambo conveyed the essentials of what the Montserrat girl had told him. Pendham seemed sceptical.

'What's this then, a new spirit of co-operation? Shopping a couple of your fellow Africans?'

'I've told you, Pendham, I've about as much clan affinity with those two as you do with a couple of Greeks or Turks. But as always you pick on the irrelevancies. While you're wasting your time with Deane there's more useful interviewing you could be doing.'

'Don't worry, we'll get on to your Nigerian pair. Although you haven't given us much to go on.'

'God Almighty, Pendham, what do you need? Surely you can take it from there?'

A grunt from the other end was the only acknowledgement. Odhiambo waited, forcing Pendham to maintain the conversation.

'That's it then, is it? The Cornwall and Devon Constabulary thanks you for your co-operation. We will act accordingly.'

Odhiambo cut across Pendham's parody of a formal acknowledgement.

'No, that's not it. I don't know why I'm doing all your leg work, but I can give you something to follow up that has a bearing on Deane's alibi for Tuesday night.'

Odhiambo smiled as he caught the muttered expletive. He went on to relate his encounter with the museum employee. Pendham clutched his hair in frustration as he listened. Finally, he managed to speak with careful control.

'OK. We'll look into that also. But tell me, Odhiambo, you say you've only been down here a couple of days – how do you account for your extensive list of contacts? You seem to be better connected than the local mayor.'

Odhiambo grinned.

'It's called keeping your eyes and ears open, Pendham. And being receptive. You should learn from it. I suppose it's too much to ask if you're going to release Peter Deane?'

Pendham assured him that his assumption was correct, it was too much to ask, but as they ended the call he contradicted himself at least to the point of confirming that Deane would not be home that night. So here they now were, a troika taking charge. At least Helen and Hugh had some claim to power, Odhiambo thought; he was self-elected, even if it was clear Helen was glad to have his support.

Helen took the gloomy but realistic view that the mains electricity would soon become victim to a fallen line, so Odhiambo and one of the Centre's maintenance staff went to check the readiness of the stand-by generator. This, it transpired, was intended to supply power to the kitchens for the freezers and refrigerators and to a minimum number of lights in the administrative, service, hall and stairway areas. Helen organised a check of rooms to ensure that candles and matches were available, bringing home to the temporary residents that this might become their sole source of light to retire by. This served to encourage most to leave for their rooms early whilst full lighting was still available. At ten o'clock Helen's fear was realised: the lights flickered for a second or two and then died. Unheard within the general noise level the generator duly came on duty, aiding the departure of the remaining television watchers, faced now with a blank screen.

'Well,' said Helen, 'I don't know what can happen next. No one can say that life is not eventful here at Polsand.'

'Fortunately,' said Gregson, reaching for the brandy bottle on Helen's table and adding a generous tot to his coffee, 'the house itself was built to withstand storms. And it seems in sound condition.'

As if to give him the lie, the noise of tiles hitting the ground outside the window was loud enough to be distinct from the general cacophony. Helen managed a smile.

'Peter said it was time to think about retiling. But the cost of local slate tiles for a roof this size is astronomical. And we're a listed building, so no cheap substitutes allowed.'

'So now you can put the onus on the insurance company.' Gregson saw the silver lining in an otherwise pretty dark cloud. 'Better this way than get a storm like this just after you've finished the job. I think we'd better make a check of the doors and windows. See if everything is holding up.'

Odhiambo was amused by Gregson's reaction to a mini-crisis. This morning he had been a twittering old fool, but now, faced with responsibility, if only *de facto*, for maintaining order he showed himself to be a true descendant of a long line of colonial administrators. Nothing stiffened their spine more, thought Odhiambo, than to be in an ill-equipped outpost with a few faithful retainers and faced with a native uprising. Odhiambo and Helen were cast as the retainers and, thought Odhiambo, I, at least, am even the right colour.

Once more Gregson's words seemed to provoke an immediate response. His mention of doors was followed by the sound of someone hammering on the rear door between Helen's office and the kitchen area. Odhiambo made his way to it and with the light from the room he had just left he could see the large old-fashioned key in the lock. Opening the door revealed a figure in oilskins who, once inside and bereft of his head covering, turned out to be the manager of the estate, responsible for the maintenance of the woods, lake and incidental pastures. He operated independently of the Centre and lived in one of the converted stables behind the walled garden, but Odhiambo had met him at one of the meals earlier in the week.

Quickly enough, as he dripped water on to Helen's carpet, the new arrival imparted his news.

'They've launched the Penleith lifeboat. It seems one of those transatlantic solo sailors is out there in the bay and heading for the bar. They got me on the short-wave. I'll get the tractor out and head down there, just in case.'

'Oh, my God,' said Helen, 'I asked what could happen next. There's no end to it.' Then her practical self resurfaced. 'We need a couple of men to go with you. I'll get Jones – he's inside somewhere tidying up. And who else?'

Odhiambo grinned. He felt almost light-headed at the way fate seemed to be pulling him along.

'If you can rustle up some gear for me to wear, I'll go. I'm strong in the arm if thick in the head.'

Helen looked doubtful.

'But you're not local, James. You don't know the sea and what it can do. It's dangerous.'

'Neither are you, young lady. And I certainly don't intend to challenge the sea. A pair of arms if we need to clear branches off the track or whatever, that's going to be my only contribution.'

Gregson, fortified by brandy and the tradition of colonial District Commissioners, resolutely added himself to the number. Helen, ordered to stay and hold the home fort, reluctantly complied and went to the storage cupboards to fetch some oilskins while the estate manager – who, Odhiambo discovered, was called Morgan – went ahead to fetch the tractor from its shed.

Suitably draped, Odhiambo, Gregson and Jones went out into the night. Shutting the rear door behind them was in itself a matter requiring substantial effort. The darkness outside was intense; the single remaining outside light did almost nothing to penetrate it. The rain had stopped, at least temporarily, but the wind was howling around the house in such gusts that Odhiambo and his two companions clutched on to each other to avoid being bowled over; Gregson also held on to a large torch.

The tractor had a closed cab into which Gregson was able to squeeze alongside Morgan while Odhiambo and Jones hung on at the back, their arms locked around the tractor's cross-bar, cowering as best they could in the lee of the cab to avoid being pulled away. Once they were away from the house and on to the path between the trees, the wind force was much reduced, although the shrieking of the trees above them, overriding the noise of the tractor, was a reminder of what they could expect when they reached the unprotected cliff. As expected, progress was delayed by branches across the road, some of which required manhandling aside. When they were within a few hundred yards of Bastian's lodge the damage intensified: across the road lay an enormous trunk with another just beyond. Morgan, after a reconnoitre by the others, was able to manoeuvre the tractor into the trees and bypass the blockage. Odhiambo could sense the danger around him as he moved cautiously ahead, searching in the pale headlight for hidden problems underfoot that would trap the tractor. The trees were *in extremis*. The noise of their tortured bending was awesome and any of them could at any moment follow the two already down. Well, thought Odhiambo, this would be some way to go after all the hazards of policing in Kenya, under a falling oak in some benighted English wood.

Eventually they reached the lodge, which, not unexpectedly, was in darkness. Here the full force of the wind battered the tractor as they crouched against its side. The wind noise was deafening, but even above that there was added now a new and equally awe-inspiring sound – that of gigantic waves dissipating their incredible force on the huge sand-bar below where they stood. So dark was it that little could be seen except the slightly luminous streaks of the wave tops as they reared on to the sand. The total effect was such as to numb the mind. There was a sense of physical forces at work that would brook no interference by man or land. Their quixotic journey seemed suddenly to be one of total uselessness. Indeed, the tractor itself, far from being a source of protection, was now a threat: as it caught the full force of the wind it was in imminent danger of overturning. Odhiambo, Gregson and Jones crouched under a hedge as Morgan backed the tractor into the trees.

And then as they paused, huddled against the poor protection of the hedge, a great change occurred. The wind noise dropped away, imperceptibly at first, with gusts that convinced that no lessening was in prospect, and then more dramatically until it seemed almost still.

Verbal communication had been impossible, but now Morgan's voice came in their ear so loudly that Odhiambo felt an irrational urge to tell him there was no need to shout.

'We must be in the eye of the storm. It'll be quiet for a time at least.'

Quiet was still an exaggeration, for though the wind noise had gone the sound of the waves filled the vacancy in the background. And then the rain started again, straighter now, but in great volume, as if there were breaking waves above as well as below.

Cautiously the men edged their way on to the path leading down to the sand. Gregson's torch gave them but a limited view through the curtain of rain. While still well above the great sand-bar they were drenched in spray hurtling up from the maelstrom below. Morgan and Odhiambo moved a little further on foot and were soon enveloped in water as a wave broke on the top of the bar, sending a wall of water over into the lake beyond. They fell on all fours gasping and choking, clinging on to each other and the stony edge of the path to avoid being pulled down to the sea itself. Regaining their feet they beat a hurried retreat. It was obvious that no man or machine could make it on to the bar.

As they gazed helplessly into the darkness, it was split first by a searchlight from overhead and then by another from sea level, coming into their view as it passed from the obstruction of the cliff top which blocked their sight-line to the west. With the overhead light came the noise, intermittently audible, of propellers; a helicopter was hovering off the sand-bar, although Odhiambo found it incredible that such a machine could have become airborne and stayed airborne in the winds that had only just subsided. The two searchlights fluttered this way and that but occasionally met and the silent watchers caught at such times glimpses of a solid object.

Jones, whose eyesight seemed to be the keenest, informed the others, 'It must be the yacht. It's overturned. That's the keel we can see. Wonder if they got the poor bugger off it in time.'

As they watched they saw in the searchlight from the helicopter a small object emerge and fall slowly towards the other light.

'They're winching someone down,' said Morgan. 'On to the lifeboat, it seems. Perhaps that means they got the chap. They'll winch him up and fly him to the hospital.'

'Ah,' said Jones. 'If anyone can fish someone off a boat in a sea like this it's Menherian. Wily ol' bugger he is. No one knows the sea round here better than Menherian.'

Odhiambo was startled. Somehow he hadn't thought about who would be crewing the lifeboat.

'Is Menherian the captain of the lifeboat then?'

His question produced a snort from the local, Jones.

'Don't call them cap'n, sir. Cox, he be. Coxswain, that is. Ay, all volunteers, you see. Always answer the call. But shouldn't think they've been out in many worse than this.'

The wind was beginning to pick up again; the eye had passed and now would come the back end of the storm.

'Well, we're doing no good here.' Morgan wiped the water off his eyes and tried unsuccessfully to focus on his companions, whose faint images were distorted by the rain. 'I reckon that boat will finish up as matchwood on the bar, but we can't get to it. As long as the lifeboat doesn't follow it.'

As they watched, the helicopter completed the winching and the lights separated, the helicopter heading over them and disappearing with a clatter inland. The watchers waited a little longer until the light from the lifeboat also disappeared from view, indicating it was under power and on its way back to Penleith. Then they commenced their cautious retreat up the slope to the tractor in the shelter of the trees.

Odhiambo found himself speculating on Menherian. He had formed a pretty unflattering opinion of the fisherman and here he was engaged in a death-defying mission to save a fellow sailor. His recent experiences in Kenya had given Odhiambo a cynical view of his fellow men. The bad, in his view, were rotten to the core, and it was the bad that were all too prevalent in his path. Menherian he had firmly placed in this category, so selfless acts of heroism did not fit his theory of mutually exclusive sets; bad men were not heroes, heroes were not bad men.

The bedraggled party reached the gate leading to the lodge. Light from an oil-lamp was shining through the front entrance. They looked at it in puzzlement – nobody would leave their door open with the rain pouring in. Then they saw the shadowy figure crouched outside the door. Leaving Jones and Morgan to retrieve the tractor, Odhiambo and Gregson grappled with the gate latch then hurried up the drive. The figure stirred as they touched him. Prompted by Gregson's hand under his arm, he rose and allowed himself to be shepherded into the comparative shelter of the hall. Once inside the man's conscious mind seemed to return and he gazed at his visitors with what Odhiambo recognised with a shock was a look of desperation and despair.

'Mr Bastian, what has happened? What's the matter?'

His question sounded faintly ridiculous to Odhiambo's own ears. To ask someone what the matter was on a night like this seemed somewhat naïve. Bastian focused on the black man in front of him and a faint nod indicated recognition.

'It's Nigel. You must help me. He's down there. On the rocks. Half-way down the cliff. I can't get to him. You must try.' Bastian wiped his sleeve across his face. 'The sea might wash him away. Hurry.'

Odhiambo realised, with a renewed shock, that it wasn't just rain-water staining Bastian's face; he was crying.

'Listen, Mr Bastian. We'll help, but take your time and tell us what you mean.'

At this point Jones and Morgan, having brought the tractor to the gate, slopped their way in, shutting the front door behind them.

Bastian made an effort to collect himself.

'Nigel went out earlier in the evening. Just for a walk. He didn't return. I became worried and went to look for him in case he'd been in an accident with this wind. I got to the point where the road bends, two hundred yards from here. Just then a helicopter went over the cliff. I didn't know then that it was looking for something else. I caught sight of something white as the light passed over. I shone my torch down. It's just possible to see his sweater. Nigel is there, half-way down the cliff.'

'Right,' said Odhiambo, 'now let's see what can be done. Is the telephone working? If so, Jones, can you get that helicopter back? Morgan and I will go and have a look. Hugh, can you co-ordinate from here and look after Mr Bastian?'

Getting nods all round, Odhiambo led Morgan out of the lodge. The wind had strengthened further in the last few minutes and the rain still fell like a giant waterfall. The two men made their way to the cliff top and on to the corner. Odhiambo had appropriated Bastian's torch which was a powerful one, better than their own now carried by Morgan. There seemed little danger of falling over the cliff, for the wind coming in from the sea was attempting to blow them off the path in the other direction – although leaning hard into the wind left them stumbling towards the edge when the momentary lulls occurred between gusts. They reached the corner and Odhiambo cautiously lay down and pulled his head over the cliff edge with Morgan sitting on his legs. At this point the top of the cliff consisted of heather and grass with a foot or so of soil. Below that the granite rocks seemed solid enough. Odhiambo shone Bastian's torch downwards. It was difficult to see anything with the rain lashing into his eyes, but after a sweep of the torch slowly from side to side he saw nothing. He moved a few yards down the path and repeated the process. This time the second pass of the torch caught a patch of white. He held the torch steady; yes, it did look like a sweater of the type Nigel wore, and he thought he could just make out the shape of an arm. He eased back from the edge and Morgan helped him to his feet.

'He's there, I think, half-way down as Bastian said. God alone knows if he's still alive, but I suppose we'd better try and add to that number by finding out.'

The wind was in one of its quieter lulls so the two men could communicate in an almost conversational level of voice. Morgan sounded doubtful.

'Go down, you mean? Bloody dangerous at the best of times, let alone on a night like this. We could wait for the helicopter.'

'Yeah. Don't know, though. We ought to try and see if he's alive and secure him better if he is. Suppose he fell the rest of the way while we're looking on.'

The wind was picking up yet one more time and Morgan had to raise his voice to a shout.

'If we bring the tractor down there's a long chain on the back. I brought it in case there was something we could do on the Bar.'

Odhiambo found a large stone and placed it on the path to mark the spot and then the two men, grabbing hold of each other for support, returned to the lodge and the tractor. Odhiambo slipped into the lodge while Morgan manoeuvred the tractor. Gregson confirmed they had contacted the air station and a helicopter would be overhead soon. Bastian was sunk in a chair clutching what looked like a large brandy. He seemed to have withdrawn from his surroundings.

Odhiambo, accompanied now by Jones, caught up with the tractor which, out in the open once more, was again in danger of being toppled by the wind. Back at the spot Odhiambo had marked, Morgan eased the tractor broadside across the path with its rear facing the cliff edge. At least this meant it was pointing directly away from the wind and was, therefore, somewhat more stable. Jones started to uncoil the linked cable. Odhiambo hesitated, but, hell, it was his idea. As Morgan emerged from the cab with a piece of rope, Odhiambo took it, passed it through the end link of the cable and then wrapped it around his waist. Morgan looked at him through the rain and mouthed a query which Odhiambo did not hear and did not react to. He gestured at his waist. Morgan shrugged and then, acquiescing, bent to ensure that the rope around the other man's waist was securely and tightly fastened.

A few minutes later Odhiambo descended the cliff, lowered gingerly by the two men on the top. Odhiambo clutched the better of the two torches with one hand and hung grimly on to the chain with the other. Strangely enough, here against the cliff face the force of the wind was not as strong nor in the direction he had expected. He had assumed he would be battered against the rocks, but the wind seemed to come from below him, almost lifting him back up the cliff, and close to the cliff face itself there seemed to be almost a vacuum as the wind swirled up and over the jutting edge at the top. Once he had overcome his initial feeling of terror, Odhiambo summoned the will to shine the torch down and strain his eyes along the beam. On his third attempt he saw what he was looking for; below and to his right was the body he presumed was that of Nigel. As he drew level, Odhiambo's feet encountered the ledge of rock that had arrested Nigel's fall. A ledge with a rock protruding upwards from it. The body was held in the fork of the ledge and the protuberance of rock. Odhiambo flashed his torch in the agreed signal to indicate that the men above should stop lowering him. He braced his feet on the ledge and inched his way closer to the body. Reaching it, he was able to grab hold of the protruding rock and bend forward towards the body. He shone his torch on to the face, which was sheltered inside the rock fork. He felt a frisson of horror. It was Nigel Bastian, or whatever his surname really was, and although clearly terribly injured, his body rigid at an unnatural angle, he was alive. His face was bloody, but the eyes that stared into the beam blinked. It was his eyes that shook Odhiambo. They were eyes that had seen the gates of hell opening.

As far as Odhiambo could tell, Nigel was firmly held by the rock. Any attempt to move him would increase the danger. He bent closer to the man's face. The eyes flickered. Odhiambo was sure that what he saw in those eyes was fear rather than pain.

'Can you hear me? Just got to hold on. The helicopter is coming any minute.'

It seemed almost quiet in the lee of the rock and against the cliff face. Nigel's head did not move, but his mouth opened. Odhiambo bent closer with his ear next to the man's face.

'. . . God help . . . can't feel my legs . . . nothing . . . need to be quick . . .'

Before starting down the cliff, Morgan had thrust upon Odhiambo his own rain jacket, securing it to the cable around Odhiambo's waist. Carefully he managed now to free it from the cable and wrap it around the wet rigid body. He continued to mutter more useless words of comfort and encouragement, but the injured man seemed to have slipped into unconsciousness. Minutes passed and then Odhiambo heard the sound that he was praying for. Above the noise of the wind, which he believed was now definitely waning, came the chopping noise of a helicopter's rotary blades. Glancing up, he was soon caught in the beam of a searchlight. As if, again, the light was the stimulus, Nigel's face took on animation once more. The terror was itself terrible to behold. Odhiambo leaned over him again.

'Soon be OK now. Soon have you out of here.'

He listened. Nigel was clearly trying hard to communicate.

'. . . not my fault . . . sick . . . sick . . . don't want to die . . .'

'Take it easy. You're going to be OK.'

'No . . . didn't mean to . . . felt strange . . . my head.'

'You mean you felt dizzy and fell.'

The eyes told Odhiambo he had misinterpreted the anguished message.

'No. I meant before . . . I was sick . . . This was 'cos . . . I was seeing men . . . he knew . . . threw me over . . .'

Odhiambo was unable to prevent his voice rising to a shout.

'Who? Who threw you over?'

The battered face twisted with effort, but it was a final one. All Odhiambo heard was '. . . bas . . . that bas . . .' and then the mouth went slack, the face stilled and the dread in the eyes faded into an eternal void.

'Oh God!' Odhiambo cried out aloud. 'Why now, when he'd lasted all this time?' He was conscious of something close above him. Looking up, he could see a basket-like contraption at the end of a cable containing the reinforcement to assist him in the rescue. 'You're too late!' Odhiambo screamed as his own mind gave way to the stress of the night. 'And I'm not sure what he was trying to tell me.'

15

Odhiambo woke in his own bed. He was grateful for that, as memory returned, for there had been some effort the previous night to take him to hospital on the grounds of exposure. Odhiambo had succeeded in claiming that a hot shower was all that was required. The helicopter had departed for the hospital, although that too was hopeless; there was no doubt that Nigel, whose body it was transporting, was dead. Odhiambo and his fellow rescuers had broken the news to Alex Bastian and left him in the hands of Gregson while they returned to the manor house. There Odhiambo departed for his shower, while the indefatigable Morgan brought Helen Shropshire up to date, before leaving for his own bed with a coffee and brandy warm inside him.

Odhiambo had eventually got to bed about three and a glance at his watch told him it was now half-past seven. He felt alive and well despite both the short night's sleep – his third in succession – and the nightmare that had troubled him, causing him to wake. He had seen Nigel battered and moving in an aimless way, as if he was drifting in a void, crying out to Odhiambo with his arms outstretched in supplication: 'Save me from damnation. I was sick . . . sick.' It was the eyes that woke Odhiambo in a sweat, but they were no worse in his dream than his remembrance of the reality.

Odhiambo sighed, got out of bed, pulled on his dressing-gown and went to the window. Yes, his senses had noted the absence of sound and the brightness of the morning light. The storm had gone as if it had never existed, the air was still with a well-washed clarity and softness. There was a promise of a beautiful day. Gone the storm might be, but it had certainly left a wreck behind. As he looked across to the woods, Odhiambo could see the broken branches and one giant elm leaning at an acute angle against its neighbours. On the lawn and meadow was the detritus of the night, branches, leaves, one dustbin and assorted roof tiles.

As he showered, shaved and dressed, Odhiambo reviewed the past night's events in the context of all that had happened since his arrival at the Centre. He had a feeling that affairs were reaching a climax. Not before time, he thought; we have three corpses already and a murderer still on the loose. But his instinct told him he was approaching the heart of the matter. Side issues there were, whose resolution would be of some interest, but the core issue that was turning Polsand into a charnel house needed to be identified and focused on. Well, he thought, sighing again, his first opportunity to exchange views on that issue was not likely to be long delayed. If he was lucky he might be able to enjoy a good English breakfast before the arrival of Chief Inspector Pendham.

Early risers were already in evidence in the dining-room with muted but excited-sounding conversations about the night just past. Odhiambo wondered whether the news of the drama on the bar and the second one on the cliff had yet commenced circulation and embellishment. From the way conversation seemed to stop momentarily as he entered the room, it seemed that the gossip was well advanced. Over in a corner Odhiambo saw Gregson. He looked exhausted and somehow still bedraggled, although he had clearly changed his clothes. Odhiambo filled his tray as he passed along the counter and then crossed to join him.

'Good morning, Hugh. You're back, I see. You didn't spend the night with Bastian?'

'Oh, good morning, James. What a bloody night. Don't want another like that for a while. Yes, I stayed with him for some time. He got the call confirming the boy was dead. Seemed to lose interest after that. Lowered the brandy bottle a bit and finally fell asleep in the chair. So did I, as a matter of fact. Woke up, stiff to the marrow, just before dawn. Bastian woke as I was moving about. Seemed to want me out of the way. Bloody rude, as a matter of fact. Still, shows he was back to normal, I thought.

So I toddled on home, if you can call this place home. Seem to have been here for ever.'

Gregson spoke in a fast, staccato delivery, as if anxious to get his version on record before anyone questioned it. This nervousness where no nervousness seemed indicated was puzzling Odhiambo. Although Gregson seemed to be on the fringe of things, his manner kept indicating to Odhiambo that he expected to find himself in the middle.

Odhiambo looked at the other man for some time, his knife poised over his toast.

'Hugh, I'll tell you what's bugging me. Mahendra made some cryptic allusion the night he died, when I first met him. Asked me to keep my eyes open around the place. The estate rather than inside the house. Then I heard him at Bastian's place on my way back from the pub. Or rather, I heard Bastian telling him to go to hell. And he went, if you see what I mean. In your ODA capacity were there, are there, any concerns about something here, other than the actual running of the Centre?'

The relief was evident. Whatever Gregson was worried about, it was clearly not Mahendra's relationship with Bastian. Odhiambo was more convinced than ever that what was eating away in Gregson's mind was his wife's relationship with Mahendra. But her alibi was solid, so it was presumably not murder that was worrying him but his wife's possible infidelity. Unless of course Gregson himself jumped in the lake and drowned the suspected lover. But to do that fully clothed seemed bizarre.

Gregson chose his words carefully; when he spoke his voice was relaxed and the tension lines disappeared around his mouth.

'I can't help you there directly, old boy. But you may be on to something. Strange that Mahendra should be at the lodge. What would he have in common with that pair? You think that young fellow's death was tied in with Mahendra in some way?'

But Odhiambo was not going to divulge any more of his thinking. He was spared a reply by the arrival of Mrs Gregson.

'Good morning, Mr Odhiambo. I'll just have my usual, please, Hugh, if you would.'

As she seated herself, and her husband dutifully made his way to the service counter, Odhiambo assessed this woman whom in some nagging way he regarded as a woman of mystery. She seemed more self-assured this morning and was clad in a bright blouse and tan trousers, both of which, even to Odhiambo's novice eye, spoke of designer quality and designer price. He greeted her gracefully and she eyed him with less antagonism than during their last encounter.

'It's a wretched business, this whole affair. And what a night. And now Hugh tells me some other young man is dead.'

'Yes. Hugh and I and others were out and about and we came across the owner of the lodge looking for his son.' Odhiambo's description of the relationship produced an arched eyebrow in his listener. 'We got to him, but too late, I'm afraid.'

'Yes. Hugh said you were very brave, going down the cliff in that storm. Well done. We must be sure your courage is recognised. I'm sure Hugh will be reporting it. But he said you found the fall had killed him.'

Odhiambo looked at the woman. She seemed almost thrilled at the escapade of the previous night, even though a man was dead. He thought for a moment and then said in a throwaway tone, 'Well, not exactly. It did, I mean, kill him, the fall, but he was still just alive when I reached him. He said a few words.'

Hugh Gregson had just returned with cereal and coffee on a tray; Odhiambo's words, if he heard them, left him unmoved, but the effect on his wife was dramatic. The assured, supercilious air gave way to a startled look of concern. Her mouth actually fell open.

'What? He was still alive?' She pulled herself together. 'Hugh, you didn't tell me that boy was still alive when Mr Odhiambo got to him.'

'Didn't I, my dear?' Gregson arranged the items in front of his wife. 'Not sure if I realised it myself.'

Odhiambo waited and his wait was rewarded. Muriel Gregson returned her attention to him.

'What did he say? Did he explain how it happened? I mean, what was he doing out there on the cliff?'

Odhiambo waited, watching his interlocutor; but now she was composed. The demeanour of the memsahib addressing the servant had returned.

'Nothing of consequence, I'm afraid. At least, nothing that seemed to make any sense. Not yet, at any rate. Not surprising, of course. The boy was close to death. He was afraid of dying.'

Superintendent Stephens arrived at the station in querulous mood. He had received a telephone call from the Assistant Chief

Constable which in turn led him to listen to the local news on the radio. The storm and its consequent damage dominated the airwaves, even nationally, but included in the 'on-the-spot' reports was an account of another death on the cliffs of Penleith and a rescue in which an African visitor at the Polsand Centre was closely involved. Stephens' question as to whether Chief Inspector Pendham was in was answered in the affirmative; a summons to his superior's presence was quickly dispatched to him.

Pendham, in fact, had been at work for some time. He too was worried, but for a different reason – indeed, he was blissfully unaware of the night's happenings at Penleith. No, Pendham's problem was that he had got nowhere with Peter Deane and, meanwhile, other evidence garnered during interviews in Penleith by Trewin and his men, plus last night's information passed on by that African policeman, were threatening to complicate matters. The call to Stephens' office he regarded as a minor irritant.

'Morning, Super. Got in OK after the storm, then?' Pendham knew that Stephens lived on the north coast, and regarded that as placing him in the toffee-nosed, effete brigade. Pendham himself lived in a somewhat run-down street in Redbourne, attended Redbourne Rugby Club matches and was proud of his urban, mining ancestry. Coastal resorts and tourists were alien to him.

'Morning, Bill. Yes, quite a bit of damage in my area, and trees down everywhere. But the telephone still works – at least the Assistant Chief Constable got through all right. This Penleith business is becoming too prominent, Bill. We need to get a grip on it.'

Pendham stared at his superior in surprise.

'What's agitating the ACC?'

Stephens groaned.

'You're not keeping up with the news. I'm talking about last night. Our friend Odhiambo making the headlines trying to save the fellow on the cliff. And the fellow dying anyway. And he turns out to live on the Polsand estate.'

Pendham stared again, this time goggle-eyed.

'What are you talking about? I don't know anything about this. Don't tell me that African copper has found another body. I don't believe it.'

It took a few minutes for the two policemen to brief each other in the areas of their individual lack of information and to issue calls for up-to-date briefings and a summons for Odhiambo. Stephens was adamant.

'I don't care, Bill, you'll like it or lump it. We need a good heart-to-heart with this chap. We need to put our heads together and make sure we're on the same wavelength.' In times of stress, Pendham had noted on several occasions, Stephens was inclined to resort to a string of clichés. 'Think, man, what it's going to look like – here's this African chappie on the ball, finding the bodies, going down cliffs in a storm to save a possible witness or whatever, and where are we? Sitting here interviewing a suspect who probably has nothing to do with it. Supposing he solved it, Bill, have you thought of that? We'd have egg on our faces then and no mistake.'

'You mean, refugee from Black and White Minstrels solves murder mystery.' Pendham felt the bile rising in his throat. 'OK, let's see this black Hercule Poirot or whatever. But I tell you, Super, he hasn't been playing the game with us. I mean to say, the coincidences are beginning to pile up. Every time a body turns up around Penleith there's our African friend bending over it saying, "Hello, what have we here?" Come on!'

A policeman knocked and entered, bearing a message.

'We got through to Polsand, sir. We spoke to . . .' he glanced down at the note in his hand, 'a Mrs Shropshire, the Admin Officer it seems. She said she'd get the message to the African gentleman, sir.' The policeman didn't trust his tongue around the syllables of Odhiambo. 'She said he was hiding from the press and TV people who were arriving. Said he'd be glad to escape to see us. I've sent a car, sir.'

Stephens acknowledged the message, and turned to his subordinate.

'Where's the local sergeant, Trewin?'

'Interviewing people in Penleith, as far as I know. Someone must have seen something up on that cliff with that woman draped over that bloody wheel.'

Stephens waved the constable away.

'You see, Bill – TV star in the making. "Interviewed today, Chief Inspector Odhiambo, a visitor from darkest Africa, said he hoped the local police would soon be able to stop the daily deaths occurring all around him!" '

Pendham did not reply. He sat visualising Odhiambo dangling over a cliff on a rope, with himself at the top brandishing a pair of garden shears.

Odhiambo was not the only source of interest to the media as news spread of the previous night's events on the coast off Penleith. Menherian, too, was featuring as the daring coxswain who had managed to rescue the lone yachtsman just before the yacht became matchwood on the famous and notorious Polsand Bar. The exploit of bringing the lifeboat so close to the bar in such a sea without disaster was being hailed as a great feat of seamanship. Menherian was waiting for the pub to open – at least then he could get the reporters to buy him a pint in exchange for an answer to a question. At the moment, however, he was being interviewed on the local radio station by an earnest young male reporter.

'They say you were more out of breath getting on the boat than when you got off. Did you feel as cool as your men say you were?'

'Well, that's fair do, isn't it? I had to run to the 'arbour like, when the siren went off. 'Taint using up much breath standing on a boat now, is it?'

'Where were you when the call came?'

'Oh round and about. In the pub, I reckon. It's a tidy step from there down to quay. Specially when you got a pint or two inside yer.'

'Do you ever get frightened, Mr Menherian? Does it ever get worse than last night?'

'Ah, gesson with ye. It were a tidy blow, mind, but I've been out in a few in me own boat let alone a lifeboat. Take a lot to sink 'er. Frightened? 'Tisna any good being frightened. I said to Jack once, I says, he's one of the lifeboatmen, I says, "If your number's up it's up, no use worrying about it," but he says, right enough mind, "What if your number's up and I be out there with 'ee." '

Menherian laughed a great bellow of a laugh. The interviewer raised a chuckle before changing the subject.

'Mr Menherian, have you heard about the man on the cliff? While you were rescuing one man, another was falling to his death.'

'Ay. Terrible business. What's more, I knew 'ee. Young fellow lived at Polsand Lodge with his father, Mr Bastian. I've had some business with both of 'em. Tragedy, 'twas. Nice enough young fellow.'

'I see, so he was a friend of yours. Do you think he was on the cliff trying to observe your efforts? Encouraging you, in a way.'

'No. No point in fancying the business up. He were over the

cliff before we got there. Before we got started, most like. Pity 'twas so dark, we might have seen 'im stuck there. Get someone to 'im bit faster like.'

To some of his listeners who knew him it seemed that Menherian's Cornish accent was growing more prominent as he developed his media persona. He was enjoying playing the part of a Cornish seaman for a large audience.

'Ol' Menherian'll be getting free drinks for weeks after this lot,' said one habitué of the Crab's Claw to Sergeant Trewin. 'Story will get bigger as the days go by, including the fancy bits. Running from the pub indeed. I seen him run to the pub many a time but I never saw him run away from 'im. Anyway, here's your cup of tea. Nice and strong. I likes me tea strong.'

Sergeant Trewin thanked his host; he was glad of a hospitable cup.

'Now, never mind Menherian and his exploits. Do you mind if we turn that radio off? I want to go over with you what you told me you saw yesterday afternoon.'

'I told you already. I do a bit of gardening for Mr Bastian. Just an afternoon a week. Went up there yesterday. He were in the back with a bonfire. Didn't seem pleased to see me. Forgotten it were me day, he said. Told me to forget it. Some cock-and-bull story about storm coming so no point in tidying up. Came with me to the gate and gave me my money. Strange carrying-on.'

'But you saw what was on the fire?'

'Well, some of it, like. Apart from the rubbish. There were a pair of trousers and gym shoes, you know, those fancy ones they wear nowadays. And he'd put a fair drop of petrol on 'un. Going up a treat, it were.'

Trewin tried to conceal his excitement. Good job he'd run into Fred in the street before he blabbed his story all over the Crab's Claw – if he hadn't done so already. He'd better get hold of the Chief forthwith. He drained his cup and proceeded to warn his witness about keeping his mouth shut.

16

For the second time in two days Odhiambo walked into the police station at Redbourne, and, as before, he was shown into

Stephens' office. Stephens rose to greet him, affability to the fore, instructing the constable who ushered Odhiambo in to tell Pendham he was awaited.

'Thought we'd have a good pow-wow. Put our heads together, see if we can't work out what's behind all this business at Polsand. Glad if you could help us out.'

He waved Odhiambo to a chair. Odhiambo in return grunted his willingness to participate in the great 'pow-wow'. Stephens continued.

'While we're waiting for Bill Pendham, let me congratulate you on your feat of derring-do last night. Going down a cliff in that storm, goodness, that takes a bit of doing.'

'Wasn't that bad, actually. Pity was we didn't save him. Apart from saving his life, I think he could have been of help in solving this affair.'

Stephens thought to himself that Pendham was right, the coincidences were growing too fast.

'You mean a potential witness goes and falls over a cliff? I mean, what's going on out there?'

Odhiambo smiled, a humourless smile, almost a grimace.

'If he fell. Supposing he was pushed? By the murderer.'

Stephens felt his head spinning and made a conscious effort not to clutch his desk. His discomfiture was covered by the arrival of his Chief Inspector. Odhiambo and Pendham nodded at each other like a pair of wary bulls. Stephens rose to foster the matey relationship that he was determined to bring about.

'It's about lunch-time. I suggest we go and have a pint and a sandwich. The Blue Hart. Know the landlord, he'll give us a snug to ourselves so we can talk in peace.'

The journey to the Blue Hart was completed without any significant exchanges. Pendham made a point of sitting in front and talking to the driver about the forthcoming local rugby game. On arrival, Stephens ordered a round, having ascertained that Odhiambo knew what English beer was, but preferred lager. Once the glasses were in front of them and sandwiches ordered, Stephens set about his task.

'Right. Now, Mr Odhiambo, as I said before, we're delighted to have you visit Cornwall and only sorry your visit has been soured by all these unfortunate events. However, Bill and I want to have a good heart-to-heart with you to make sure we're missing nothing. You being so close to the scene and . . . er . . . finding one of the victims and so on. Lucky for us to have a professional on the spot. Got to take advantage of it.'

Odhiambo took a sip of his lager and nodded.

'Fine by me. I think it's time to make sense of this seemingly senseless affair. What's happening about Peter Deane, by the way?'

Pendham looked from Odhiambo to Stephens. What he was about to say would be news to his superior.

'Our investigations and follow-up interviews are being hampered by the consequences of the storm. But I have just heard from the Penzance station that they have been in contact with the lady you mentioned to me last night. Although she is, apparently, proving somewhat reticent, it does appear that she will claim Deane was with her sometime Tuesday evening.'

Stephens raised his eyebrows.

'Alibi involving a lady, Bill? You mean Deane's refusal to co-operate is based on some notion of chivalry; don't drag ladies into embarrassing revelations – that kind of thing?'

Pendham reluctantly nodded his confirmation.

'Yes, looks a bit that way. So we're about to let Deane go. For the time being anyway. Of course, he's still no alibi for his wife's murder and that's what we're after him on chiefly.'

Odhiambo put down his glass.

'This is a better lager than I've had down here. Nearly as good as ours back home.' His companions looked sceptical that good beer of any description was available in Odhiambo's land. Odhiambo grinned and continued. 'What about the Nigerians?'

Again, Stephens looked puzzled and Pendham hastened to explain.

'There's some reason, Super, for believing Mr Odhiambo's fellow Africans are mixed up with some unsavoury locals, including girls. Trewin is following up, but again the storm damage and the drain it's causing on our resources are delaying things a bit.'

Stephens felt it was time to demonstrate that he was in the middle of things.

'Meanwhile, forensics are pressing on, they are making progress, fibres and suchlike on Mrs Deane's clothing. So, it seems that mutual co-operation is working, Mr Odhiambo. That's very pleasing.'

Pendham was not willing to allow Odhiambo to be elevated to the status of equality in the investigation.

'Meanwhile, Mr Odhiambo continues to be closely involved, including physical presence, in these matters. Too closely involved. Much too closely involved.'

'Bill, let's remember, open exchange is the keynote.'

'It's OK, Superintendent. Mr Pendham is correct. I take his point. Like it or not, I've got a bit too close to this case.'

Pendham looked as if he was examining each word, looking for the trap. Once again, it was his superior who took the initiative.

'Not your fault exactly, is it? Claustrophobic circumstances, all of you on the estate. So, Mr Odhiambo, tell us how you see things at Polsand in the light of events since we met yesterday. We'd be grateful for your assessment.'

Pendham managed this time to pick up his cue and mutter with as much grace as he could muster a supportive, 'Quite so.'

Odhiambo looked around as he took another drink. The pub was outside the town and was set in its own grounds – probably once a substantial private house, he thought. There were a good number of customers around the bar and neighbouring tables. A restaurant lay through a door on the other side of the bar from where the policemen were sitting. As anticipated, Stephens had secured a quiet corner that was not closely overlooked or, rather, overheard. Odhiambo wondered what arrangement Stephens had with the publican. When he spoke he kept his voice low.

'OK. It looks to me as if Deane is innocent. His behaviour is due to the fact he didn't want to reveal the existence of his girlfriend. Plus, I think he suspected his wife was having an affair with Mahendra.'

'And when he found out she'd killed him, he killed her in a jealous rage.'

Pendham's suggestion was made more to provoke him to rebuttal, Odhiambo thought, than from conviction.

'I don't think so. The new twist is the death of Nigel Bastian, or whatever his name was. From what he told me before he died, he was pushed or thrown over. At least, he believed that, but of course a man *in extremis*, as he was, might have been delirious.'

There was a silence which seemed to extend in time and space. This time it was Stephens who broke it.

'And what exactly did that young man say to you?'

'It's difficult to be sure what he was saying. He used the phrase "threw me over", but he also mentioned seeing men, men unspecified that is, so I suppose he could mean one of his boyfriends threw him over in the personal relationship sense. I asked him who threw him over and all I got before he died was something that sounded like "bas". Funnily enough, in Swahili that means "enough" but as I don't suppose he spoke Swahili he could have been trying to say "that bastard".' Here Odhiambo paused, the actor wanting to keep his audience on edge coming to the fore. 'Or he might have been trying to say Bastian.'

Pendham sounded doubtful.

'It's not much to go on. As you admit, what he said could mean anything, not necessarily murder. It's like Mahendra, you keep jumping to conclusions as soon as you see a body.' He chuckled ghoulishly. 'Even one that's still warm as with poor Nigel.'

'But I was right about Mahendra. And even you don't think Penny Deane committed suicide.'

Stephens stepped in quickly as the men on either side of him bristled once more with latent antagonism.

'Let's assume for the minute this young fellow was pushed. It's too much to assume we've got two murderers wandering about out there on the cliffs. So if there are three deaths they're all connected, right?'

Odhiambo nodded.

'Without revealing any confidences, can you give me any indication whether Mahendra might have known something serious about the elder Bastian? He looks the sort of guy who one could easily think was up to something, but that doesn't prove anything.'

Stephens looked at Pendham and gave a small nod. There was a further delay now as their sandwiches arrived, laid out on a plate surrounded by potato crisps. Pendham took one in his large hand, took a bite, chewed for a while and then reluctantly took the plunge.

'They've looked at Bastian in the past with reference to drugs. Nothing came of it.'

Stephens decided to amplify Pendham's admission.

'We know there's a sizeable quantity of hard stuff being brought in somewhere along the coast. Probably transhipped from a cargo boat to a small boat that can land in one of the coves. We've caught one or two over the years using that trick. The big boat drops it overboard with a float that holds it underwater some way and a fishing boat or similar drags it in. The two boats never have to meet. Coastguard unable to spot anything and so it goes.'

'One of your reserve men guarding the Penny Deane site told me there's a cave somewhere under Bastian's place and an old mine shaft.'

Pendham nodded and helped himself to another sandwich.

'True. But that's not so unusual around these parts. Can't arrest everyone with access to an old mine shaft. Where we are now is riddled with old mines.'

All three men chewed slowly and looked at each other. Odhiambo looked at the others in turn before breaking the silence.

'A local fisherman was able to guide our Nigerian friends to some place where they could get a snort or whatever. The same fisherman spoke ill of Mahendra's interference. And the same fisherman works for Bastian. At least he sells him his fish. Suppose Bastian is a drug importer. Menherian is your man on the fishing boat. Mahendra discovers what's going on and threatens Bastian so he has to be disposed of. Penny Deane sees something so she's next. And Nigel suspects the old man so he goes over the cliff.'

Stephens gazed at the African open-mouthed, his glass poised half-way to his mouth. Pendham smiled.

'You can sure come up with some fancy tales. Actually, Bastian merits looking into.' He proceeded to inform his superior of Trewin's news of the bonfire at the lodge. Stephens showed signs of growing excitement.

'My God, we may be on to something. Have you told Trewin to pick up Bastian?'

Pendham shook his head.

'Not yet, Chief. We haven't got any evidence. Not unless our hero here can state that Nigel claimed he pushed him over. We're examining the remains of the bonfire, of course.'

'What about the fisherman chappie?'

'It's the first I've heard of him. Our friend here likes to keep things up his sleeve for a while.'

Odhiambo smiled.

'He's almost untouchable today. The local hero. He took the lifeboat out in that storm and rescued a sailor. There's something else you should know. Alex Bastian was in a hell of a state last night. Worried about Nigel. He wanted him rescued off the cliff. Why would he tell us where Nigel was if there was a chance he was still alive and could finger Bastian as the guy who threw him over?'

Pendham growled his reply.

'Well, we'll find out. There's a lot of scenarios. Nigel's death may have been the result of a row between a couple of poofters. But with Mahendra and the Deane woman, I come back to the sexual angle. It depends on what we can find in Bastian's home and garden.' He looked quizzically at Odhiambo. 'And I don't think you've come straight with us now. I think you've got other ideas inside that big head of yours. You're sure you and your fellow Africans aren't setting up some sort of drug business yourselves? Funny how it all happens after you arrive.'

'Black people are automatically suspect – is that it, Pendham?'

Stephens choked on the last of his beer.

'No, no. Misunderstanding. Trouble with us who haven't travelled much. Don't know enough about Africa.'

Odhiambo posed another question.

'Coming back to Deane – what state is he in? Apart from you grilling him, I mean. Is he distraught or what?'

Pendham scowled.

'You can ask him yourself. We'll send him back with you. No, I wouldn't describe him in your fancy words. He's climbed into himself. Withdrawn. Probably wondering whether his alibi will stick.'

Stephens was busy signing the bill that had arrived after they had refused the offer of coffee. Didn't go too badly, he thought. He couldn't be faulted for handling Odhiambo with courtesy. And Pendham might be close to cracking the case. He was aware that, despite his best efforts, Pendham and Odhiambo were never likely to warm to each other, but as long as he kept them apart all should be well.

Odhiambo, as he left, was full of unease. He had shared his thoughts, as he had told himself he must, but every instinct in his body told him he'd got it wrong. Most of the elements he was mixing were necessary, but the chemical compound resulting from the mix was unstable. He'd not got the right formula, he was sure of it, but unsure why he was sure.

17

The journey in a police car back to the Centre was a strained one. Pendham sat next to the driver with Odhiambo and the released

Peter Deane in the back. Small talk was minimal. Pendham and Odhiambo kept each other metaphorically at arm's length; Deane was reticent with Pendham and his reticence extended also to Odhiambo. Odhiambo assumed Deane resented the fact that he had revealed the existence of the potential alibi witness in Penzance. Odhiambo stammered his condolences concerning Penny Deane, spoke of the storm and the damage at Polsand, said that all was well at the Centre or as well as could be expected, but no response was triggered except the barest of monosyllabic replies. They were close to the Centre when Deane suddenly burst out as if he could contain the bottled-up words no longer.

'Tell me, Odhiambo. Why? Why did Penny die? And who did it? Damn it – nobody will tell me anything. Only questions, questions. Stupid questions. What did she do to deserve this? Nobody deserves to die like that, particularly not Penny. Why, man, why?'

Strange, thought Odhiambo, that the 'why' seemed to worry him more than the "who". He saw Pendham's head turn slightly, making sure his ear was tuned to the back of the car. He could visualise the sardonic cast of his lips.

'We don't know, Peter, that's the truth of it. It's all speculation at the moment. At least we've no idea who. Why? She must have seen something the night Mahendra drowned. Are you sure she didn't tell you what?'

'Don't you start with more questions. I've had enough from him,' gesturing angrily at the policeman in front. 'We hardly had time to talk before she disappeared. Damn Mahendra. Damn the bastard.'

An uncomfortable silence resumed and then the car drew up at the Centre, having managed to circumnavigate the branches that still littered the road inside the estate. Odhiambo and Deane got out and the car moved on; Pendham was heading for the cliffs and the lodge. As they slowly progressed down the stony path, Pendham turned to the driver with a question that the driver was wise enough to sense needed no answer.

'What do you think of a husband who asks why his wife was killed rather than who killed her, and curses another victim rather than his wife's murderer? Makes you think, son.'

Several press reporters were camped around the entrance to the Centre. Murders, storms of the decade, sea and cliff rescues –

the brew was aromatic and had attracted the worker ants. Odhiambo and Deane had some difficulty in running the gauntlet. Deane stopped to abuse them: a tactical error, as he was quickly surrounded. Helen Shropshire appeared to rescue him and Odhiambo took his chance and slipped away. He had scarcely gained the sanctuary of his room before a knock on the door heralded the entrance of Gregson.

'I heard you and Deane were back. Thank God for that.' Odhiambo wondered if Gregson really believed Deane was in a condition to take up the reins of Director. 'Now, Odhiambo, James, I've got an invitation for you. Muriel's old friend, Angela Tamlyn. She would like you to come to dinner; Muriel and me, as well. Do us all good to get out of this place. Even the food's beginning to get on my nerves.'

Odhiambo's first reaction was to refuse, but he hesitated. Why not? No point in moping around here. Why did his mind suddenly conjure up an image of Helen Shropshire? And Angela Tamlyn intrigued him. He sighed.

'Well, I don't know, Hugh. Do you think it looks odd? Going out to dinner, I mean, with Mrs Deane and the others dead.'

Gregson was on home ground here. Diplomatic niceties were his forte.

'You scarcely knew them, man. Applies more to me, really. Knew Mahendra and so forth. But not a public function. Quiet dinner party. Do you good. Take your mind off things.'

'Wonder why she invited me?'

Gregson grinned.

'You must have made an impression, old man. Damned attractive woman. Lonely widow and all that.'

'Don't be ridiculous. If I thought that was true, I'd certainly say no. Oh, all right; I suppose I might as well.'

'Good man. She doesn't need confirmation or anything. Said to bring you if we could. Seven thirty. Press boys and girls will have had to go and file their copy by then. We could walk around the lake, I suppose. Weather's good enough now. Could borrow a car from here if necessary. Any objection to a walk? No? Good.'

Gregson proceeded to probe Odhiambo for news of the murder investigations and the current status of Peter Deane as a suspect. Odhiambo pleaded ignorance. Just as he was wondering how to get rid of his visitor, another knock on the door interrupted another Gregson question. Odhiambo crossed to the door and opened it: there, looking composed, was Helen Shropshire.

'Hello, James. I've got Peter to his flat. I thought I'd better check if you made it to yours.' Odhiambo opened the door wider so that Gregson was in Helen's line of sight. 'Oh, hello, Hugh. I'm sorry to interrupt, but I've . . .'

Odhiambo interrupted her.

'No trouble. Come on in. Hugh was saying he had to leave, isn't that right, Hugh?'

Gregson had risen from the chair by the window at the arrival of a lady.

'What? Oh, yes, must be getting on. Yes, come in, please. I'm just on my way . . . Er, right, James, will . . . er . . . see you later.'

He left, looking quizzically from one to the other as he passed.

'Oh dear, James,' said Helen, watching the closed door. 'You shouldn't have done that. Looks bad, getting rid of him when a woman arrives in your room.' Helen blushed. 'He's a bit of a gossip, I reckon.'

'I thought he'd settle himself here for good. Couldn't pass up a good excuse to ease him on his way. Now, what can I do for you?'

'I have to tell you, you're famous and a hero. We're fielding all sorts of calls. Anyway, the local television wants to do a joint interview with you and the coxswain of the lifeboat. The two heroes of the night. In Penleith. For the six o'clock news. You need to ring them back to confirm.'

Odhiambo laughed.

'You're joking. That's all I need. Appear on bloody TV. No thanks.'

Helen was unperturbed, but her tone became somewhat firmer.

'I knew you'd say that. But you're wrong. People are interested. That was the worst storm for yonks. Probably since the sea put the bar there in the first place. You're a visitor. You owe it to them.' She raised a hand as Odhiambo started to intervene. 'And even from your point of view, it's the best course. Do one and get it over with. Say it's your last statement on the matter; otherwise you'll have the media pestering you at every turn. They're camped out here at the Centre.'

'What do you mean, I owe them something? Who's "them"? And why do I owe them anything?'

'Look, you're from Africa. You were around when they found Mahendra; you found poor Penny; and you climb down a cliff in the worst storm people have seen. And you're a detective. People are curious. You're their guest in a sense. They want to know a bit about you. You should be proud. I'm proud to know you.'

'Aw, come on, Helen, spare me the hype. I'd be embarrassed.'

'They'll track you down one way or another. I'm going to confirm you'll be there. No arguments.'

'Jeez, what a woman. Here, wait a minute. This other so-called hero, that's Menherian, I suppose.'

'The coxswain, you mean? Yes, I think that's his name. Why?'

'I've met him a couple of times in the pub in Penleith. Actually, I had him pegged as a nasty bit of work. Pair of bright heroes we are!'

'Well, there you are. Shows you don't always get it right. Well, I must get back and try to keep the lid on this madhouse. Poor Peter, he's in no state to take over.'

'What's the general state of morale?'

'Rock bottom. We've got to get these people out of here or we'll have an insurrection. Also people in Penleith are getting agitated, I'm told. They're saying all the foreigners at the Centre are the cause of all these problems, including the storm as far as I can gather.'

'You can hardly blame them. This is a week out of hell.'

'Right, I'm off. Oh, by the way, enjoy your dinner party. I hear you made quite an impression on your hostess in the mist.'

With that Helen was off, leaving Odhiambo to curse his fate. In fact, however, the deciding influence in his agreeing to be interviewed was the realisation of Menherian's participation. He wanted to meet Menherian again. There was still the promised boat trip, assuming the waves had become as quiet as the wind.

The interviews were conducted on Penleith's pier, the sea providing a suitable back-drop. The sea, in fact, was still sullen, with a large swell, although the wind was no more than a sea breeze and the evening sun lit the scene with a kindly light, which made it difficult to remember how hostile the environment had been such a few hours ago.

Menherian was there, dressed for the part in classic fisherman's garb. Odhiambo could smell the beer on his breath and assumed he had been holding court in the Crab's Claw earlier in the day. Odhiambo had opted for slacks, blazer and a tie in the national colours of Kenya. Menherian was by far the more animated of the two. Whereas the boatman was clearly enjoying himself, Odhiambo felt acutely uncomfortable. There was a small crowd of spectators, fascinated as always by the sight of a television camera but also, according to the muttering that reached Odhiambo's ears, because of the presence of the foreigner who was linked to the spate of deaths.

Odhiambo, posing next to Menherian, observed his companion more closely than he had hitherto. Daniel Menherian was a thickset figure, his stockiness exaggerated by the thick seaman's jersey with a roll-top neck, of medium height but barrel-chested, with long simian arms ending in large hands that looked as if they were capable of hauling in an anchor cable without gloves, as indeed they had. Seamed, weather-bitten face and hands, the face less glowering now than during Odhiambo's previous encounters.

'And now we turn to . . . James Odhiambo, a visitor from Kenya, staying at the Polsand Centre, who shinned down a vertical cliff in a Force 10 storm to reach a young man who had fallen over. James, you've heard Daniel here say that he was never frightened on that storm-tossed sea – how about you? Were you frightened, dangling on that cliff?'

The interviewer was a woman in her thirties, clad in thick white sweater and jeans. Pleasant-looking and a harmless interviewer, Odhiambo had discovered. At least she had tossed a succession of soft balls to Menherian, which he had dispatched with enthusiasm.

'Yes. But in that bedlam of wind and rain the senses become numb. You just press on as best you can.'

'Mr Bastian was still alive when you got to him, I understand?'

'Yes, he was. But he died before we could get him up.'

'How long had he been there? When did he fall?'

'I don't know. But I think he'd been there for quite a time.'

'Did he say anything? Or was he unconscious?'

'He spoke, yes. He was trying to tell me something. But it was difficult to hear him. He was having difficulty speaking and then there was the wind.'

'Did you catch anything he said?'

'Nothing that means anything at the moment. Just a few disconnected words.'

The interviewer moved on to bring out Odhiambo's background. The fact that he was a policeman seemed to come as a surprise to her.

'So, you're on a police training course, is that right?'

'No, no. It's a Commonwealth seminar. Nothing to do with police work as such.'

'Of course. There have been two other deaths here in the last week, isn't that right?'

'Yes, that's right. The police are investigating them. I'm afraid I'm not able to answer any questions on those deaths. You must contact the police.'

'Yes, yes, I understand. But when you're at home, do you investigate murders?'

Odhiambo cursed. He should have evaded the question about his occupation.

'If required, yes. Same as your officers here.'

'So it's sort of strange, isn't it, that you arrive at sleepy Penleith and there's a series of mysterious deaths?'

'Well, I don't think Chief Inspector Pendham suspects me, if that's what you mean.'

Odhiambo was getting angry. His answer threw the interviewer off her stride. She stumbled through denials of any such intention and wrapped the session up with a eulogy to 'a pair of brave men, one from here, the other from exotic lands, both heroes who responded to the call in the most appalling conditions . . .' Odhiambo winced; turning to Menherian he noticed that he had lost his earlier exuberance. He looked as if he too was glad to see the camera move away.

'Well done, Menherian.' Odhiambo had not had the opportunity of speaking to his fellow interviewee before the event. 'I wouldn't have wanted to be out there last night, whatever the quality of the boat.' He was aware of being under scrutiny, a suspicious scrutiny; the previous night's feats of daring had done nothing, it seemed, to induce a warmth towards Odhiambo. 'I don't know how anything could stay afloat in that. Anyhow, well done.'

'Never you mind none about the lifeboat. What you were a saying just now. The chap on the cliff. He were talking, you say?'

'Well, muttering would be more like it, nothing very coherent. He was dying and he was scared.'

'Ay, but you told that there telly woman you hadn't made sense of it yet. Whadda you mean by that? You reckon it'll come to you, you mean?'

'Not really. Just getting by with the question. But why do you ask? Did you know him well?'

'No, not well, no. I mean, fair's fair. What would I 'ave in common with a pansy like 'im? But you seem to have an uncommon interest in 'im.'

'So, what's your interest in what he may have said to me?'

Menherian's eyes shifted left and then right; then he half turned to face the sea. Odhiambo had just decided he was to receive no reply when suddenly Menherian swung back and spoke.

'I do some work for the old man. Is 'na bad old chap in his way. Likes to 'ave 'is own way, mind. I were 'fraid maybe they'd fallen out or summat. I've 'eard 'em 'aving some terrible rows like.'

Odhiambo was listening carefully now, with ears and instincts turned up to full scan volume. It wasn't only what Menherian was saying; suddenly his tone was softer, friendlier, almost ingratiating.

'So you think he jumped over the edge after a lovers' tiff?'

'No, no. Say what you like about 'em as queers, I mean. Don't wish 'em no harm. Specially the old one. 'E's been fair to me. No, what I means is, you shouldn't take too much notice if Nigel were ranting on a bit. Nothing unusual, is what I'm telling you, after they'd rowed about summat. Wouldn't mean nothing.'

'So they wouldn't be likely to have a fight on the cliff? Real fight, I mean.'

Menherian snorted and wiped a hand across his face with the sound effect of dried leather being dragged over sandpaper.

'Course not. Queers don't fight like that, do they?' Menherian paused. 'Although I got to say, now you mention it, I did see 'em have a go once. The young 'un tried to scratch old Bastian's eyes out, but the old man gave him a straight right like. That 'ad 'im going backwards, I'll tell 'ee.'

'What would they fight over? Business?'

'What business? Bastian's place, you mean? Nah. What d'you think they'd be fighting over, a pair like that? You can't be that daft.'

Odhiambo glanced at his watch; it was time to go if he was to make his dinner date.

'Yes, well, it's not my concern anyway. So, I must be off.'

'Thought you wanted a boat ride? Sea's settling down nice. Be fine the morrow. I'll take 'ee out around the bay. Or has the storm scared you off?'

How right you are, thought Odhiambo. Somehow the boat trip no longer seemed such a good idea. He wasn't sure why he had bothered. Still, Menherian's attitude interested him. Menherian suddenly wanted to foster their relationship, it seemed. Had he something more to say?

'Not at all. When would you be free to take me?'

'Tide'll be good after dinner, say half-past two down across there.' Menherian pointed to where several boats were at rest inside the inner harbour, protected from heavy seas by the massive harbour walls between which was a gap that could be plugged, as it had been the previous night, by great wooden planks dropped on one another into iron slots set in the stone. 'That's where my boat's to.'

Odhiambo had been around long enough to know that dinner meant lunch, so half-past two made sense enough. He agreed to the assignation and left the fisherman, cogitating, as he walked, on Menherian's behaviour.

Pendham was tolerably satisfied. There was no sign of Alex Bastian when he called at the lodge and he did not yet have a search warrant. This did not prevent him from visiting the back garden. The remains of the bonfire were visible and at first sight there was nothing to see but ash; Bastian had made a good job of burning whatever it was he had wanted burnt. The bonfire area was sunk into the ground, open only at the front with an access aperture at the bottom over a grid to provide the means of setting the fire going and the required draught. The ash was congealed and wet but Pendham, undeterred, poked away through the aperture with a stick and quickly struck lucky. His stick snared a piece of fused metal that was still recognisable as part of a zip – the sort of zip that might have belonged to a pair of men's trousers. He summoned expert assistance and arranged for someone to guard the bonfire and watch out for Bastian.

He then joined Trewin in interviewing the two Nigerians in the local police station. He regarded the chance of his warming to the presence of Odhiambo as slight, but if anything could endear him to Pendham it would be the comparison he made with this pair of beauties. Asuna and Adimojo were uncooperative and surly. Also well versed in what Pendham regarded as barrack-room law, demanding access variously to their High Commissioner, a solicitor, a United Nations Human Rights representative and, pretty soon Pendham assumed, Amnesty International. Pendham enjoyed breaking through this veneer of bluster. Eventually the story seemed clear enough: the local fisherman had introduced them to Joe Pengelly's place where they had little difficulty in finding the congenial company of girls and a little powder.

They had heard some talk from the girls of how the stuff was brought in locally, but they had nothing specific to contribute and Pendham lost interest after enjoying putting the fear of God into a now chastened pair.

Good news then arrived from the forensic boys. They had found traces of skin under the nails of one of Penny Deane's hands. Her killer was probably carrying a scratch which by the nature of things was likely to be on hand or face. Bastian, old son, thought Pendham, turn up with a scratch and we've got you. Then another thought occurred to him; he rang forensic again and sent them on their way back to the mortuary. Yes, things were progressing; he had a feeling he was getting there.

18

The walk from the Polsand Centre to Angela Tamlyn's house took them past the boat-house where Odhiambo had last seen her, along the path to the most inland corner of the lake, across a footbridge spanning the marshy area where the surface water ended and back along the side of the lake into the newest and densest part of the woods. The trees here were mainly sea oaks, still on their way to maturity but old and large enough to provide an extensive canopy. The path they walked on was flanked by strips of grass and wild flowers and weeds. Odhiambo knew the names of none, but the miscellany provided a colourful picture. This side of the lake seemed somehow less stark, less inhospitable than the other, as if the prevailing winds from the west, having traversed the calmer waters of the lake, had lost some of the force that twisted the branches and chilled the earth. The evening was pleasant and the walk attractive. The only problem was the occasional need to manoeuvre around the scattering of debris, reminding the walker of the storm and the speed with which nature could change its demeanour. For Odhiambo and his companions, used to tropical storms followed by a rapid return to Equatorial sunshine, this was well within their experience and unworthy of comment. But very little seemed worthy of comment. Odhiambo found the atmosphere reminiscent of his recent car ride with Deane and Pendham. The Gregsons seemed to have had a disagreement for there was no easy communication between them; Muriel Gregson had resumed her air of condescension towards Odhiambo and her husband seemed bereft of his usual chatty manner which had been so evident in Odhiambo's brief acquaintance with him.

Hugh Gregson was carrying a paper carrier advertising one of the local supermarkets in which, his wife informed Odhiambo when it was too late for him to emulate them, were shoes to change into when they arrived at their destination. The precaution was well advised for in places the path was muddy. Odhiambo tried to walk on the grass verges as often as was feasible, but nevertheless it was clear well before the walk was completed that he would be arriving in dirty shoes; a prospect that Muriel Gregson did not seem to find either displeasing or surprising.

The path bent away from the lake and uphill; as they turned a corner the tree-line came upon them abruptly and there, situated in a large expanse of well-tended lawn, was a bungalow with which Odhiambo could immediately feel an affinity. It was long and low with a verandah running alongside most of the length of the front supported by spaced posts, white with black sash windows behind providing a contrast, and a stone chimney rising above a grey slate roof. The overall design reminded Odhiambo of the expensive bungalows of the former white settlers in Kenya, well located within their farms in the Kenyan Highlands and always with a verandah on which the evening sundowner was taken while the owners and their guests surveyed their empire. The rear and sides of the property were flanked by hedges but the front consisted of a triple-terraced lawn that joined the path that skirted the property. Nothing in front hindered the view down through a gap in the trees to the Bar with the sea pounding on to one side and the still, dark lake restrained by it on the other.

As they ascended the steps dividing the lawn, Odhiambo could see that there were four guests already ensconced on the verandah, clutching what looked like glasses of champagne. As they gained their goal, their hostess appeared, floral apron over a dark dress with a flash of gold around her neck. Odhiambo felt two immediate emotions, one that Angela Tamlyn was a very attractive woman and two that he was underdressed in sports jacket, slacks and, now, muddy shoes.

'Muriel, Hugh, you made it through the wreckage from last night. And Mr Odhiambo – please, do you know, I don't know your first name. Remiss of me.'

'James. I'm afraid the path has taken its toll on my shoes.'

'James. Yes, you look like a James. It has a solid ring to it. Don't worry, that's a common problem with guests who walk to see me. I keep some very nice slippers for just such a reason. Oh, Muriel, you've decided to bring your own. Now, let me introduce you all.'

The other quartet, Odhiambo gathered, consisted of a local doctor and his wife and a man introduced vaguely as a business adviser with a young blonde who was not his wife. The doctor and wife were middle-aged, worthy and a little dull; the other male was heavily built, but overweight even for his considerable frame, with a domineering approach to conversation; the young blonde was what young blondes were meant to be by men such as her friend, decorative and subservient.

Sitting with a glass of champagne in hand, Odhiambo reflected that Angela Tamlyn was clearly a widow of means; large bungalow in a superb location, finely furnished from what he could see through the french windows, and business adviser in tow. To say nothing of paintings lent to important exhibitions.

'Isn't this a lovely spot?' The doctor's wife next to Odhiambo addressed him in the slightly loud voice of an Englishwoman who isn't sure that the natives understand English. 'Is this your first visit to Cornwall, Mr . . . er . . ?'

'Odhiambo. Please, call me James. Yes, it is. I mean, yes, it's my first visit and yes, it's a lovely spot. It all seems to have survived the storm without damage.'

'Wind's a funny thing.' This was the doctor. 'Can totally devastate one swath and leave another untouched.'

'But in this case, Jim,' his wife wanted exactitude, 'I believe it's those trees, they act as a good wind-break. Except when it's coming directly from the south-west up through the gap there.'

The business adviser, who had claimed the name of Jan, was not interested in wind effects.

'Tell me – Odhiambo, is it not? What area of Kenya are you from? I know Kenya. Not well, but I have paid visits there.'

Odhiambo guessed from the accent that the adviser was not English, at least not English-born. Possibly Dutch, he thought, with that name.

Conversation ebbed and flowed inconsequentially until, after a few minutes, Angela Tamlyn reappeared, having completed her meal preparations, and summoned them to the table.

Dinner was good. Odhiambo was no gourmet, he regarded

himself basically as a meat and *ugali* man, but his wife Cari had improved his range of culinary appreciation, and he could recognise high-quality food served with elegance. Angela Tamlyn may have been the main inspiration in the kitchen, but she had assistance that now enabled her to preside at her table whilst food came and went at leisurely intervals. The table itself was old and polished so that the fine wood positively shone, reflecting the wine glasses containing a fine claret. On wine, as on food, Odhiambo was no expert – in Kenya the tariffs on imported wine were such that even plonk was expensive – but he had seen the label on one of the bottles, Château Pichon Lalande, 1966.

All this served to heighten Odhiambo's interest in Angela Tamlyn. She was clearly a woman of means and taste, probably older than he had assessed at their first meeting, but retaining a smoothness of skin that could allow her to pass as ten years younger, attractive in the sense that a vibrant personality within an orthodox face and body is attractive, an attractiveness of cohesion of physical and non-physical attributes rather than reliance on sheer sensual allure. He was attracted to her, not in a sexual sense as he was to Helen Shropshire, but as a person whose mind he would like to get to know better. In terms of conveying superiority through quiet assurance and understatement she demonstrated a manner that Muriel Gregson had never managed to quite understand, let alone acquire. She was accompanied at her table by a generally nondescript lot, Odhiambo felt – a dull medical pair, a brash, bordering on rude, vulgarian with an empty-headed girlfriend, the ever so slightly stupid Gregsons and a colonial bumpkin – yet she conveyed the feeling that this was one of the great dinner tables of England, graced by intelligence and wit.

Conversation inevitably concentrated initially on the recent storm, and, equally inevitably, expanded to include the ongoing problems of Polsand.

'I must say,' said the doctor as he gazed in the approved manner at the deep colour of his wine, 'to paraphrase Lady Bracknell, to have one murder is unfortunate, to have two is careless.'

'And the young man from the lodge,' interjected his wife, Rose by name. 'Three deaths in as many days.' She looked disapprovingly at her companions; she associated them with the epicentre of these unfortunate happenings. 'We're not used to that sort of thing here. It may be different where you come from.' This last was directed at the savage just emerged from the jungle.

'We don't have many country house murders in Kenya.' Odhiambo smiled at the woman opposite. 'I had heard it was a favourite pastime of the British, but I didn't expect to encounter it personally.'

'Well, I never.' Rose was taken aback.

'Murder begets murder,' said Angela Tamlyn. 'In some ways it is like a virus, and becomes more virulent as it grows. That poor girl, Penny Deane. It's too dreadful to contemplate.'

'And then the storm on top of it all. It's too much.' Hugh Gregson was imbibing both food and wine with gusto. 'Too much.'

Jan had been frozen during these last exchanges, food half-way to mouth. Now he managed to force his way in.

'What young man from the lodge? The lodge by the bar, you mean?'

'Oh yes.' Rose regarded the question as addressed to her. 'That young man – is he the son of the owner, Mr Bastian, who runs the seafood restaurant in Penleith? He fell over the cliff last night. Someone tried to save him, but no good.'

Jan turned to his hostess.

'I didn't know . . .'

Angela Tamlyn intervened to apologise.

'I'm sorry, I'd forgotten you met him once when you were last here. We were walking on the bar, were we not? I'm afraid so. Terrible accident. But, Rose, I can tell you that the hero of the hour is opposite you. It was James who went down the cliff in the middle of that storm to try and save him.'

The doctor peered at Odhiambo as if considering him for a test of whether he was eccentric or insane, but both Rose and the blonde seemed impressed.

'Really? How good of you. I suppose you're good at climbing. I mean, one sees on films young lads running up coconut trees and so on.'

'Ooh, I say! How did you manage to cling on? That wind. You must be so strong.'

Odhiambo tried to cut this topic off before his embarrassment deepened. He could see his hostess looking at him with a kindly but amused smile.

'You mustn't make it out to be a big deal, er . . . Angela. All that happened was that Hugh and I and two others from the estate were out seeing what we could do and they lowered me down a little way on a chain. I gather the real hero, and skilful with it, was the man guiding the lifeboat in those seas, Menherian. I've never seen anything like those waves.'

The doctor was willing to be generous to Menherian.

'Ah, yes. Menherian. A rough diamond, but the jewel is there beneath the dross.'

Angela was more realistic.

'I don't know about a jewel, Jim, but no one ever doubted the old reprobate knows how to keep a boat afloat in rough seas.'

Jan, however, was still single-mindedly concerned with the fate of Nigel Bastian.

'You mean, he was blown over the cliff? Seems bloody funny to me.' He turned to Odhiambo. 'You reached him, did you? Was he dead?'

Odhiambo was prepared to let the question dangle in the hope that others would pick up on Menherian's contribution to the night's events, but Gregson was more inclined to keep Odhiambo in the spotlight.

'Oh, he got to him all right. Held him until the helicopter came. And he was conscious for a while, wasn't he, James? Able to speak for a while.'

Jan leaned forward, pointing his knife at Odhiambo.

'Did he know he was dying? What did he say?'

But Angela had had enough.

'No, Jan, we don't want to get morbid and I don't think James wants to dwell on the matter. Now, would anyone like a little more of the duck?'

Strange, Odhiambo thought, how everyone seemed interested in the last words of the unfortunate Nigel.

Muriel Gregson was back to the general problem of Polsand and the personal inconvenience it was causing.

'Well, I shall be glad to get away from this place – not from here, of course, Angela, my dear – it's a complete shambles. The police don't seem to be getting anywhere, with the help or otherwise of Mr Odhiambo here. It's quite intolerable.'

Angela Tamlyn persisted and steered the conversation onwards, but Odhiambo now felt himself the object of some attention from around the table, including the girlfriend, who looked at him speculatively with tongue passing over moist lips.

The evening stayed fine and the party took their coffee on the verandah. Inevitably the conversation drifted back once more to the question of the Polsand murders. Worse, because of Muriel

Gregson's remarks, it was now known that Odhiambo was a detective.

'So what do you really think?' The doctor's wife was addressing some point between Muriel Gregson and Odhiambo, who found themselves sitting side by side with the businessman on Odhiambo's other side. 'Is there some mad killer stalking the coast and the lake?'

'Of course he's mad.' Muriel Gregson was in no doubt. 'Of course he's mad. What other explanation can there be?'

'But who, then?' Rose was concerned. 'I mean, it's terrible, we're walking around with one of those, what do you call them, serial killers on the loose. Do you have someone around at night, Angela? I mean, no woman is safe.'

'I have Fred Redman and his wife in the cottage next door. I feel safe enough. Now . . .'

'Who? That's the question.' Muriel was not to be diverted. Hugh Gregson looked at his wife with some concern. She, too, had drunk well of the claret. 'And we're not getting the answer.'

'What about you?' The doctor addressed Odhiambo directly. 'You're a professional. What do you think?'

Before he could reply, the blonde, whose name Odhiambo had now discovered was Emma, gave her opinion.

'Perhaps it was the bloke who went over the cliff. Perhaps he did it and jumped off in remorse. Like in that play on telly – you remember, Jan.'

But the company was more interested in Odhiambo's views than Emma's. Odhiambo had been considering his position as he sipped his coffee. Inevitably his cue would come and an alternative option to evasion and stone-walling had become attractive to him. The alternative was to claim more knowledge than he had and see what reaction, if any, was produced. It was time to provoke something and if this was to be his tactic he might as well start now.

'I don't think we have a lone madman on the loose, except inasmuch as anyone taking life like this is mad. There is a sadistic and exhibitionist element to these murders certainly. But I think both were motivated by something the victim knew which the murderer could not afford to have become known. And although young Bastian's death may not be connected, I think he too knew something more than he'd told the police. Something he said to me, together with what else I've pieced together, leads me to think I'm close to knowing what it is that has led to all this.'

If he had wanted the attention of his audience, Odhiambo had succeeded.

'Shit!'

This was Gregson, who seemed genuinely shocked. His wife was more explicit.

'What on earth are you talking about?'

'How exciting', 'Tut-tut' and 'I see, I see' came from Emma, Rose and Jim, but Odhiambo, who was watching for Muriel Gregson's reaction, also saw an amused tweak in the corner of his hostess's mouth. When he turned his head the other way he could see that even Jan was looking at him in bemusement.

Hugh Gregson, with recovered composure, decided it was his duty to issue the reprimand.

'Yes, very interesting theories, I'm sure. But James, I must say I think you should pass anything you know to the police . . . the English police, I mean. This is not a matter for amateurs, and, forgive me, dear boy, but over here in these circumstances you are the outsider, the amateur.'

Muriel Gregson snorted.

'Don't be so mealy-mouthed, Hugh. Tell him straight. We don't take kindly over here to visitors from abroad thinking our police are fools and they can do better.'

Angela Tamlyn stood up.

'James, I wonder if you could help me. I need to percolate some more coffee, but the new tin has been put on a shelf I can't reach. You're tall enough to reach.'

Odhiambo smiled.

'Certainly. I'm coming.' And then to his accusers, 'I'm sorry. I was asked my opinion and I gave it. Loose-tongued, I'm afraid. It must be Angela's excellent wine. I'm not used to such old wine that has lain waiting all these years in order to induce me to be indiscreet.'

He rose and left the verandah, following his hostess. Behind him silence fell, broken by the contemplative Jan.

'He may have said sorry to you, but I note he didn't withdraw what he said. I wonder what he knows. How interesting.'

In the kitchen, Odhiambo found himself being scrutinised again, but in a friendlier way.

'James, you're quite a character, aren't you? You really dropped the other shoe out there. What were you trying to achieve?'

Odhiambo looked at the woman as she put the coffee into the percolator. She was clearly highly intelligent and, if only one stumbling block was removed from his mind, he felt he could trust her.

'Sometimes it's necessary to try and break things open. Disturb the status quo. I've heard my wife say, "Run it up the flagpole and see if anyone salutes it;" American marketing slang, I'm afraid.'

'Yes, I thought so, but it can be dangerous, you must know that. And you can't believe that any of that lot are involved, surely?'

'I'm going to be frank with you, Angela, if I can assume what I say is in strictest confidence?'

Angela Tamlyn looked at him wide-eyed.

'Of course, if you tell me something in confidence I shall keep it so. But whatever do you mean?'

'Your friend, Muriel. I know she was with you Tuesday night, when Mahendra was drowned. But I believe she was on intimate terms with Mahendra and that's why Hugh's nerves are showing. Someone had a date with Mahendra in that lake and I don't think it was Penny Deane. Am I stupid in thinking she might have made that date?'

No expression of surprise, incredulity or anger showed on his companion's face. She continued to look on Odhiambo with a look of almost maternal concern.

'But James, if she did, she did it knowing she wouldn't be there. She knew she was coming to spend the evening with me. Why would she do that?'

The question lay between them like a ticking bomb. Both knew the possible answer. Finally, Odhiambo spoke.

'To spite him, perhaps. He was missing with Penny Deane earlier.'

'And a murderer just happened to be waiting? That's ridiculous.'

Odhiambo shrugged.

'Yeah. OK. Anyway, this is between us. Maybe I'm off the beam.'

'I'm sure you are, James. If he was having an affair with Mrs Deane it must have been her he was meeting, surely? She's there, or somewhere on the way she sees something, and that seals her death warrant.' The woman paused. 'It has to be a man, you know that. The killing of Penny Deane wasn't by a woman's hand. For one thing it would require strength to lift a body in order to stick the arms through the top spokes of that wheel.' Angela Tamlyn shuddered at the thought. 'Oh, what a ghastly business.'

'One last question. Or rather two. How well do you know Hugh Gregson? And how well do you know Alex Bastian?'

Another warm, understanding smile.

'You are in inquisitorial mood, James, aren't you? I don't know Hugh at all, really. Muriel is an old school friend and I don't see very much of her. Hugh I've only met on a couple of occasions. Now, who else? Yes, Bastian. Again, only slightly. Strange couple, of course. Down here that sort of relationship is still regarded as eccentric, at best. I tell you frankly, he gives me the creeps, and not because he's a homosexual. But I don't know anything specific against him. Now we must get back to the others.'

Their arrival on the verandah was greeted with some jocularity by Jan and his girlfriend. The blonde made her major speech of the night.

'Ooh, you're back. We were just wondering what you two were up to, weren't we, Jan? A long time reaching the coffee, we said, didn't we?'

Odhiambo noticed that the merriment was not widespread. Rose looked slightly disapproving, Hugh's thoughts seemed to be elsewhere and Muriel was looking at them, not with any amusement, but with scarcely concealed suspicion.

An hour later the party broke up. The doctor, who had driven from Penleith, arriving at the Tamlyn bungalow down the access lane from the inland side, offered the Polsand Centre contingent a lift home. The Gregsons accepted, but Odhiambo insisted on walking, claiming the need for exercise to counteract the food, the wine and brandy. In fact, he felt a desperate need for solitude and a time for thought. He was bluffing when he spoke on the verandah of being close to a breakthrough, but essentially he did feel he had enough of the pieces to fit together to be able to deduce the picture. Returning the slippers to his hostess, he put on his muddy shoes; a farewell peck on the cheek to Angela and he was on his way. Their last remarks indicated their expectation not to meet again.

'Goodbye, James. I'm glad I met you on the bar. I wish you luck.'

'Thanks, Angela. I shall always remember the Lady in the Mist.'

Approaching the boatshed, Odhiambo decided to pause and summarise his thoughts. His walk had done the trick in more ways than one. His head felt clearer and his pieces were just beginning to reveal a shape; a shape which he could scarcely believe. He left the path and approached the side of the shed. His heart skipped a beat as suddenly his solitude was removed.

'Who is it? Is someone there?'

The voice was frightened, half-way to a cry for help. No, surely not, Odhiambo thought, but it was.

'Helen? It's me, Odhiambo, James. Don't be frightened.'

It sounded trite, it was trite, but of course it worked. They met at the corner of the shed.

'Oh, James, you did frighten me. I didn't expect anyone at this hour. And what with the legends and all . . .'

'I'm sorry. Likewise, I didn't expect anyone to be here. I'm on my way back from the dinner party. Was about to sit in the moonlight and collect my breath and my thoughts.'

'Well, come on then – sit yourself down.' Helen's natural humour surfaced. She giggled. 'We must stop meeting like this.'

Odhiambo felt uncomfortable. The strange direction his thoughts had been taking had placed him in a state of some mental confusion, and now on top of this he found himself sitting by a lake in the moonlight with a woman whom he liked and who exerted a powerful sexual attraction on him. He struggled to collect himself.

'I've explained my presence. What brings you here? You shouldn't be out alone. I mean, it could be dangerous.'

Helen sighed.

'The house is becoming a hell-hole. Everyone irritable and anxious, and Peter's return has made matters worse. He's in a terrible state. I know how he feels, of course.' For a moment her personal tragedy hung like a brittle sheet between them. She sighed again. 'Once everything was done, I just needed some fresh air and a bit of peace. I didn't think beyond that, to tell you the truth.'

Also, like you, she thought, I wanted the chance to get things straight in my head, but she didn't tell him that. She could feel the tension in the body next to hers. I'm going to have to be careful here, she thought. No repeat performances – remember, you promised yourself.

'Yeah, I can understand that. It must be very difficult for you. The strain of all these events.'

Helen strove to keep things light.

'You're a star, do you know that? As well as a hero. Everyone saw you on the local news tonight. You were better looking than the lifeboatman.'

'God, that's all I need. What about the gossip? Any speculation as to what's going on?'

'The latest is that Asuna and his friend were taken away by Trewin. So that's fuelled the speculation. Asuna threatening diplomatic incidents, calling in the ambassador, charges of racism, you name it.'

Odhiambo closed his eyes. Things were beginning to spin out of control.

'And you? Any new ideas?'

Helen paused before delivering her surprise package.

'I was talking to Sergeant Trewin. He's a nice man, really. They carried out a major search at the lodge this evening. They found an access to an old mine shaft that goes right down to the sea in a sort of cave. He said they were surprised, it had been renovated as it were. Proper steps in the shaft and so on. And he hinted they found some evidence, but he wouldn't say of what.'

At last, thought Odhiambo, Pendham is getting to the Bastian connection. Well, that removed any need for him to go to sea with Menherian, although he thought he nevertheless would. Not to do so would be to lose face.

'They don't suspect Bastian of the murders, do they, James?'

'I don't know. Perhaps they do. I think he's certainly got some explaining to do. It's possible he's involved with drugs. But that's speculation on my part.'

'Drugs? How do you mean? Selling them?'

'Whatever. There's a tradition of smuggling around here, you know. But forget Bastian for a minute. There's another lead I'm pursuing. I can't say more about it now, but there's something you could do for me.'

'Say on, Mr Holmes, your Watson awaits.'

'You've got the wrong detective, Helen. It was Lord Wimsey who had a female accomplice.'

Helen noticed that he had now relaxed enough to have moved back to first name terms.

'OK, Lord Peter, what's afoot?'

'If you do it, you must just stick to the bare details – and in the house, and when I'm around. Then you stick to your office and to me. I don't want to put you at any risk. I've been through all that before.'

'I'm intrigued. But are you going to tell me or not?'

Odhiambo did. Helen listened and agreed to jeopardise her reputation for honesty. She listened again to his strictures.

'Oh, get on with you. Nothing's going to happen.'

They sat in companionable silence for a few minutes, watching the light reflecting off the water and listening to the gentle lap-lap of the water at the shore by their feet.

Helen sensed the electricity rising and the tension returning to the large man next to her. No, she was going to be firm.

'Right, James, come on, you can walk me home.'

She stood up and turned towards the house. Thanks to Helen's self-will nothing was to happen that night, but she was very wrong about the morrow.

19

The chance for Helen to put in hand the task assigned to her the previous night came earlier than she could have anticipated, and it came without her seeking an opportunity. She, like several at the Centre, had spent a fitful night, although no blame could be attached on this occasion to the fury of the elements outside. She rose and showered early and made her way to her office. She felt fatigue and nervous strain. It was surely enough to have to cope with murders without the complication of the storm as well. It seemed a long time since she had enjoyed a full night's sleep. Yesterday she had felt as if she had plenty of energy, exhibiting the delayed impetus of the adrenalin that survivors of a storm of that intensity experience. One had come through, the house around one was, more or less, intact, the wind having done its worst had faded and one felt, somehow, as if one had triumphed over nature. Today was different; all too obvious now were all the problems still to solve that arose from the incredible events of this week, including, not least, how to get the temporary residents of the Centre back to London before rebellion set in. And she felt tired, so very, very tired. Damn James Odhiambo, she thought, as she prepared some coffee in the outer office; wherever you are there's trouble. But as she conjured up the picture of the large earnest detective she couldn't resist a chuckle at his so obvious internal struggle to keep his hands off her last night.

The coffee was dripping through into the jug and beginning to spread a pleasant aroma when the door opened and in walked Muriel Gregson. She too looked as if the healing hand of sleep had passed her by. Tousled hair, face unmade-up and her frame enclosed in a woollen-looking track suit, she was a far cry from the well-presented wife of an ODA official that Helen had first met on her arrival – could it be only a few days ago?

'Ah, good morning, I thought I could hear noises. You're Mrs Shropshire aren't you? Admin and that.'

'Goodness, you're up early, Mrs Gregson. Would you care for a cup of coffee? I was just going to have one to wake myself up.'

'You look as if you need one, my dear girl. Whatever do you need to be about so early for? It's scarcely dawn.' And then, quickly, to ensure the offer was not overlooked, 'A cup of coffee would be nice, thank you.'

Helen poured coffee into two mugs and, having made the appropriate query, added the contents of a little plastic cup of cream to each. She passed one to the other woman, guided her into her office and waved towards a chair.

'Not much room, I'm afraid, but please sit down. Now, what brings you up so early? An early morning jog?'

'Good heavens no. Whatever do you take me for? No, I threw this on to go outside and get some fresh air. Couldn't sleep. How can one in this place? I mean, what on earth's going on? Here we are stuck in this house, police all over us, but never in the right place to stop another murder. It's too much.'

Helen could see what Odhiambo meant. There was a brittle falseness about Muriel Gregson; even her whinges didn't ring true.

'Yes, I know it's difficult. I'm hoping the police may relent today and let at least some of you go.'

Muriel Gregson sipped her coffee. She looked appraisingly at the younger woman. She was attractive in her way, she thought. If she took the trouble she could be very attractive. But even so, it surely couldn't be true what Hugh had told her.

'I believe you know that African who's here, the policeman. Odhiambo he's called.'

'Yes, I do. Well, I know everyone here more or less.'

This was waved aside dismissively.

'Yes, of course. But you know what I mean. Hugh tells me you knew him before. I mean, you know him to talk to.'

Helen waited.

'And you were with him when you found the body of Mrs Deane. You had been dining together, Hugh said.'

'That's right, but what do you want to know about him?' Helen allowed impatience to show in her voice. 'He's from Kenya, he's a policeman, he happened to have been on hand when the bodies were found, he risked his life to try to save someone during the storm, and . . . and he's a nice man. That's about it.'

My God, Hugh was right, thought Muriel Gregson. She is soft on him. Most inappropriate.

'The point is, my dear young lady, that Mr Odhiambo is becoming a nuisance. He is trying to show how clever he is by meddling in the investigation of these . . . er . . . unfortunate events. And in doing so he is impeding the proper police.' She raised an imperious hand to forestall an interruption. 'And he's proving rather stiff-necked about it. Won't listen to Hugh and others who try to advise him. If you know him well . . .' the emphasis on 'well' was subdued but unmistakable, 'it would be a service to him and us if you were to have a word with him.'

Helen's irritation died down; after all, she couldn't ask for a better lead into her own little fishing expedition.

'I know what you mean, Muriel – may I call you Muriel? I'm Helen, by the way. I know what you mean, but you see, I think he's on the verge of cracking it – the case, I mean. Naturally, he hasn't told me anything specific, I don't know him well enough for that, but he has some sort of evidence that someone lured Mahendra to the lake so that the murderer could follow him. I think he found a note that Mahendra scribbled earlier that evening.'

Helen could see that the bait had been taken by the fish. The other woman's face darkened with anger and, yes, Helen thought, probably fear. Her mouth opened, but for what seemed like a very long moment no voice emerged; then with a visible effort she closed her mouth and started again.

'Preposterous. Hugh checked his room the next morning. He would have seen it. That's exactly what I was referring to. The man is dabbling in things he knows nothing about and getting completely the wrong end of the stick. He has to be stopped.' As if she realised she was saying too much, Muriel Gregson rose and put her mug, still half full, on Helen's desk. 'But I must go. I've kept you from your work too long already. Thank you for the coffee.'

Helen watched her go. She hoped she'd played her part correctly and could give James an objective account of the episode. She wondered what Muriel Gregson was frightened of. It was impossible to believe she was mixed up in murder. And why had her husband searched Mahendra's room? He had not told Helen of his intention and she presumed the police would not be pleased to have him interfering with possible evidence. Getting the key would present little problem. Security at the Centre was pretty relaxed, or had been until Wednesday. My God, she thought, I think James guessed right. There had been a note or something tying Muriel in with Mahendra.

It was not only some of the inhabitants of the Polsand Centre who were up early. Chief Inspector Pendham was eating his breakfast in his kitchen with a fork in one hand and a cordless telephone in the other.

'Right, Sergeant, so there's a shaft and tunnel, all mod cons inserted, and you've got some residues for testing. Meanwhile we're waiting for the results of the bonfire contents. You told me the drug boys had looked at Bastian before; are they blind? They couldn't even find a bloody great shaft. What do you mean, they didn't have a search warrant? They should have got one. Anyhow, never mind them, or rather let's wait to see their faces when we break their case for them. Our problem is the murders. The likelihood is that Bastian is running the drug side; he was one of the last to see Mahendra; he was almost certainly burning bloodstained clothes after the Deane woman's throat was cut and he was on the cliff that his lover went over. It's an all-station call for friend Bastian. I want him in and I want him in fast.'

He listened but impatience soon broke through.

'I don't care how many press are camped there. You think I haven't got them bothering me? I'll issue a statement when I'm good and ready. I think the Super is organising a press conference so let him organise the press – our job is catching murderers.'

Pendham put down the phone and attacked the remains of his fried eggs and bacon with gusto. At last he saw the finishing line in sight, and even if it meant he had to give some grudging acknowledgement to Odhiambo, so what? Clear up the murders and close a drug-importing conduit at the same time. Can't be bad, he thought, as he mopped up the spilt yolk on his plate with the crust of his bread and butter.

The object of Chief Inspector Pendham's interest was at that moment sitting in the bedroom of a cheap hotel between Penleith and Penzance gazing blankly at the wall, reviewing his position and his options. Whichever way he came at it the situation remained bleak. Nigel was gone, one could grieve, but in the end it didn't change anything. The furore over the murders and the police activity they generated had left him in dangerous waters. His days at Penleith were at an end. He had been a damn fool. He should never have listened. Well, it was too late now. Luckily, in view of the pressures brought to bear on him, he had made his plans to move on. He had intended, of course, that Nigel would be with him. That wasn't going to be possible. And that was the point! Before going on to think about himself there was some action to take.

When he had recovered from the numbness that descended on him after Nigel's death he had decided it was time to vacate the lodge. The police would be upon him at any time. He had his retreat to his bolt-hole in Wales prepared, but while he did what he had to do in Penleith a temporary hideaway was needed. He had gone to his writing-desk in his study. This was his pride and joy. He had acquired it in India; it was beautifully made in mahogany, intricately carved by a local craftsman, and, in design, copied from a photograph in a Victorian journal. He pressed the head of one of the natives walking alongside the elephant in the carved scene of the tiger hunt, and the secret drawer opened. This had always appealed to him because of both a residual boyish enthusiasm for secret drawers and the masterly carving of the works that translated the button press to the sliding open of the aperture. He removed the sheath containing the knife, shuddering as he did each time he handled it or even thought about it. It was impossible to forget its last use. In fact, he retained enough of his sanity to be aware that it was the images of Wednesday night and the dreadful sequel of Thursday night that were destroying his sanity. He removed the knife from its sheath. It was clean, of course, he'd made sure of that, but he'd better sharpen it; its last use seemed to have blunted the normally razor-sharp long curved blade.

Now in his temporary bedroom he retrieved the knife once more and tucked it into his belt under his thick jersey.

Daniel Menherian walked up the steep street of the small market town that lay the other side of the Polsand estate from his home village of Penleith. He had got a lift in with a local farmer, and now he was on his way to the assigned meeting place. The phone call so early in the morning had perturbed him. Everyone was getting panicky and he had to admit that he shared in the feeling. Things were getting out of hand. If the police took an interest in Bastian, it wouldn't be long before they'd come sniffing round him.

He was passing the Eight Bells pub and was tempted to go in for a quick one. God knows he needed it. But of course it was too early. Not open yet. The pub was part of a row of eighteenth-century buildings in the main street, low doors, low-beamed rooms, and all in fair condition as they were part of a conservation area. Not that Menherian cared a whit about the age and architecture of the building – a drink was what he could do with. Still, he'd better get on. He reached a junction and turned left into an even narrower street that ran back down the hill he had just ascended. A hundred yards down was the small car-park and there, sure enough, he saw, as he approached, the grey foreign saloon.

As he bent to speak into the driver's window he was beaten to the spoken word.

'Get in, man, and quickly.'

Menherian crossed around the back of the car and eased himself into the front passenger seat. He had decided on the way that it would be necessary to assert himself from the beginning.

'What's all this about, then? Why do I have to come all the way here? What's the great mystery?'

'Shut up and listen.' The driver stared out over the steering-wheel, not looking at his passenger. 'We're not happy at the way things are going.'

Ignoring the requirement to be silent, Menherian burst out.

'You're unhappy. What do 'ee think I be, I'd like to know? Due to all this mess, not of my making mind, I'll be having the coppers round soon.'

'Will you listen, Menherian. Because of the killings we're going to have to close things down for a time. You must go out this afternoon, retrieve the residual goods and sink them much further out, sink them for good and all. OK? You got that?'

Menherian was shocked.

'You mean throw it away, like? What's wrong with leaving 'er be? No one's not going find nothin' there.'

'Just do as you're told, Menherian. Out deep, at least a mile, no float, nothing. Sink it where it will never be found. Then go home and forget you know anything about anything, right? If you're questioned you know nothing except you catch fish. Do as you're told and we'll all be all right.'

Menherian suddenly remembered an appointment.

'Here, I've got that black copper coming out with me after dinner. I tell you, I'm worried about that bugger. Think he knows more'n he's letting on. I were a thinking he might be due for an accident. Clumsy bugger. Can't help it if he falls overboard tripping over his great feet. Were only showing him around.'

This time the driver did look at Menherian, and then gave a short chuckle.

'You're a genius, Menherian. Fancy you having agreed to take Mr Odhiambo for a trip. Couldn't be better. Don't put him off. Take him. Kill two birds with one stone.'

'How can I fish up the doings if I've got that blackie aboard? You're talking daft.'

'Menherian, don't ruin my new impression of you as a strategist. Here's what you're going to do. Listen carefully and then go and do it without screwing up.'

Menherian listened and felt, despite himself, a shudder of distaste. It was true he was harbouring ill thoughts about Odhiambo and in the heat of the moment on the boat he was capable of anything, but it was the cold, calculating, emotionless style of the speaker that put him off. He waited until his companion finished.

'Right. Can do that, I think. But again it be me running the risk. What extra's in it for me?'

For once, Menherian found the negotiations for money relatively easy. His companion's interest in that aspect seemed slight, which was, in Menherian's experience, unusual.

'That's it, then. Now go – and keep sober, mind. I'll tell you what, you can go and have just a couple. Here's something on account.' Some notes were dropped on to Menherian's lap. 'I'll have a taxi waiting for you at one. Take you to Penleith. Now remember. Do everything exactly as I've said and everything will be all right. Have you got that?'

Menherian nodded.

'Yes, yes – I said so, dinna I? OK. I'm on me way, but Jeez, you're a cold bastard. Anyone tell 'ee that? No wonder you and that Nigel got on so well. Pair of beauts, you are.'

The driver watched Menherian walk back up the street. It was risky, of course, but given the coincidence that Menherian and Odhiambo would be together it seemed a heaven-sent opportunity. He left the car and walked over to a public telephone across the road from the car-park. He found some coins, dialled the number and spoke without identifying himself.

'The boat will sail sometime after two. You're set up, are you? The coast will be clear till after one. Yes, in the case. And you know where to put it, right? Right.'

20

Odhiambo had slept poorly. As with Helen Shropshire and several other residents of the Polsand Centre, the combination of murders, storms and nights with little sleep was beginning to take its toll and a good night's sleep would have been beneficial, but it was not to be. A nightmare disturbed him and then recurred to disturb him again. In it he was drowning in a storm-tossed sea; every time his head broke surface a great wave would engulf him and drive him under until he felt himself slipping irrevocably down into the depths. As he gazed into the abyss he saw the bloated body of Mahendra floating past and then below that the wreck of an old ship, rotting planks, barnacle-encrusted cannon and on the bridge a wheel where stood a jerseyed figure, who when it turned its head towards the drowning man was recognisable as Menherian, but Menherian with a ghastly wound across his throat that dyed the sea around him red. And as the reddened water eddied out into the wider ocean it became flaming tendrils that suddenly came together into the red locks around the face of Helen Shropshire.

After the second episode Odhiambo lay awake, far from sleep, with the events of the previous days racing through his mind. At times he felt he was close to seeing the truth, but each time as he sought to focus the blurred picture it slipped away. Finally, his mind rested stubbornly on the scene at the cliff face as he watched over Nigel's tormented last minutes. His words ran over and over in Odhiambo's mind, until the repetition lulled him at last back into sleep. This time he slept well and woke late, and when he sat up with a start at the sunlight streaming through his window he realised that one more elusive answer had been provided by his subconscious as his conscious mind slept. The last words of the man on the cliff took on a new meaning. He remembered too his appointment that afternoon. A mirthless smile was reflected in the mirror over the wash-basin as he ran water over his toothbrush. He would be daft to go to sea with Menherian, but he knew he was going to do it; his instincts told him matters were reaching a climax and his sense of fatalism inherited from his Luo forebears as they struggled in a troubled land would lead him to his destiny. Oddly, once he reached this point he felt lifted in spirit, depression falling away. He had experienced this before. It was uncertainty about which path to take that troubled him; once he was committed, for good or ill, the tensions lessened.

Downstairs Odhiambo avoided the dining-room, going instead to find his accomplice. He was thwarted at first, finding only Helen's assistant, Jane, in the office. Helen, it seemed, was paying a call on Peter Deane to check his mental state – which, by all accounts, was not good. Jane had two hot news items. Pendham had telephoned to say that the participants at the aborted seminar could now depart, although there were three exceptions: the Nigerians and Odhiambo himself, required to stay to render 'further assistance to the police'. The Gregsons' presence was also required. The second item was that a substitute for Peter Deane was arriving to take over as from Monday with Deane himself put on compassionate leave. Jane was also able to supply Odhiambo with a coffee and a sticky doughnut.

On Helen's return they retired into Deane's office where Helen brought him up to date with events, particularly her rapid completion of her mission agreed the previous night.

'She's not very pleased with you, James. But I suppose that was the idea. And worse, her husband's not very pleased with you either.'

'Why, have you seen him too?'

Helen allowed herself an impish smile.

'No, Lord Peter, I exceeded my instructions slightly. I told the girl manning the telephone exchange to let me know of any calls made by the Gregsons. Well, Hugh called London shortly after I had my chat with Muriel. I didn't tell her to listen, of course.' Helen attempted a virtuous look of innocence. 'But she too exceeded her instructions. Hugh is getting the ODA to liaise with the local police and have you removed from here. Obstructing the course of justice.'

'Ah, so Pendham wanting me to stay may be overtaken by instructions to Stephens to get me away. You've done great, Helen. Now, in view of all this I'm going to make myself scarce so Pendham can't pick me up. Remember what I said – I don't want you going for a walk in the woods or anything. Stay here and stay with people around. I know it sounds daft, but it's a precaution.' He hesitated for a moment, then decided she deserved to be kept in the picture. 'I've got a sea trip lined up for this afternoon. With Menherian on his boat. Local heroes go sightseeing. So I'll keep out of the way until then. But don't let anyone know I'm going with Menherian until it's too late for them to stop me. OK?'

Helen stared at him. He seemed to have an infinite capacity for leaving her bewildered.

'OK. But why are you going joy-riding with Menherian? I thought you thought things were coming to a head?'

Odhiambo laid a hand on her arm, but she noticed that any sexual tension was missing this morning. His mind's on other things, she thought.

'They are. They are. And instinct tells me the boat trip is part of that. Can't explain why now. But I'm going to leave a letter for Pendham. Just in case. You know I can't swim.'

But Helen was not deceived by the lightness of tone.

'Oh James, no. You're putting yourself at risk again, aren't you? You don't have to go out there. Maybe Hugh is right; you need to be taken away from here. I won't let you go.'

Odhiambo's grip tightened.

'Listen, Helen. There's a ruthless and vicious mind behind all this and it has to be stopped. Think of that poor woman on the wheel. No, I'm sorry, I'm insensitive, I know. Don't upset yourself. But you know what I mean. I must go on. I need to find just one or two more pieces of the jigsaw then Pendham and Trewin can put it all together. I'll be OK. I'm a big Kenya boy.'

' "And thick in the head." ' Helen finished the saw for him. 'And that's what you are, James Odhiambo. Thick in the bloody head. If you come rolling in on the next tide it'll serve you right.'

She turned away to hide the tears welling up in her eyes.

'Helen, please, I'm . . .'

'Oh go away. Go on. Play your games, damn you. Leave me in peace.'

And with that Helen went to the door and left him to his thoughts.

Pendham gazed at his superior speculatively.

'So someone wants him removed from the scene, eh? Interfering with the course of justice. Ha! I could tell them a thing or two about that. I agree, get the bugger out of the way, but when someone tells me to do it, I tell you, Super, I smell a rat.'

'Yes, well, maybe, Bill. But we don't want any diplomatic incidents. Have him in for one last interview, get his address and ship him back to London. That's the scenario.'

Pendham, to his own amazement, found himself defending the African.

'Suppose he doesn't want to go? It's a free country, at least so they say. He's helping us with our enquiries and he hasn't done anything yet to give me an excuse to run him out of town.'

Stephens sighed, placed his elbows on the desk, put fingertips together and explained the facts of life to his awkward subordinate.

'Listen, Bill, his hosts in the British government want him back in London. He's in this country under their auspices so they're entitled to say "go and he goeth, come and he cometh". The only thing preventing them doing that is us saying he can't leave yet awhile. So we lift our restriction on him leaving and, hey presto, our Kenya friend is on the train.'

Pendham did not have a reputation for stubbornness for nothing.

'Remember that Arab who shot a policewoman? Iranian Embassy, wasn't it, or Libyan, one of those Arab ones. Foreign Office let him take a walk. Suppose Odhiambo is mixed up in these murders. Let him off the leash now and we won't see him again. By the way, there's another line. I had another look at the younger Bastian. His face is scratched all over, falling over the cliff and that, but I'm getting forensic to check a sample of his skin.'

Stephens looked puzzled and was about to ask his junior what he was on about when a knock at his door produced a constable with a note for Pendham. Stephens watched while Pendham glanced at the paper, his face darkening.

'Bloody hell. The bastard's done a runner.'

Stephens enquired querulously what Pendham was talking about.

'Sorry, Super. It's Bastian. The guy at the lodge, right? The one we were talking about. He's not there and according to Trewin it looks as if he's scarpered. He didn't return last night and Trewin thinks there's signs of a hurried packing. It looks as if he's our man, so we need to find him.'

'So you think it may all be put down to him?'

'If he's done a runner that shortens the odds for a start. I'd better arrange to have Odhiambo picked up too. Before he decides to scarper as well.'

The two men laughed briefly. They didn't anticipate that Odhiambo would have gone far. They wouldn't have laughed if they could have foretold the next message from Trewin, confirming that Odhiambo too had joined the missing list. 'Gone out,' Trewin was told at the Centre, and 'I don't know where.' Helen kept her fingers crossed behind her back as she lied to the long-suffering sergeant.

Odhiambo had spent a pleasant hour or two with the estate manager, Morgan. He had met him when he left the house and entered the woods rather than walking down the road to the lodge and on into Penleith. He had time to kill and it was better if he avoided the direct routes where he might well run into the local constabulary bent on shipping him out. Morgan greeted him warmly; the events of the night of the storm had created a bond between them. Odhiambo quickly accepted an invitation to accompany Morgan on his walking tour of the woods, checking on the planting programme already in being arising from earlier storms and enumerating the damage caused by the recent one.

At one point they were close enough to the lodge to catch sight of it through the trees. Odhiambo used the sighting as a cue.

'Tell me, what do you know about that man Bastian? Seems an odd sort of character.'

Morgan looked at him appraisingly.

'I presume you know that he and the boy you tried to rescue weren't father and son?' Odhiambo nodded. 'I used to run into the younger one more often round and about. The old man kept himself to himself. Didn't see him out very often. Used to go from his place to his restaurant and back and that was about it.'

'I keep hearing rumours about him and drug smuggling. There's supposed to be a smugglers' cave right under his property.'

'Ay. There be that. Now the young one, I reckon he took something and the word in the village is he supplied some of the stuff used by the young tearaways. But I don't know about Bastian.

Certainly he could bring it in from the sea to the cave and up the shaft as long as he kept the shaft clear. It's commonly believed you can access the shaft from inside the lodge.'

'And do you know Daniel Menherian?'

Morgan snorted.

'Ah. He's bad news, that one. Wouldn't put anything past him.'

'But he's in charge of the lifeboat. And I'm told that's a voluntary job. He risks his life and doesn't get paid for it. I mean, he acted like a hero the other night.'

They paused as they came to two fallen trees, one still leaning at an angle where the top branches of the falling tree had lodged against the branches of another. Morgan surveyed the damage and made a note on his clipboard. Then he turned to Odhiambo.

'There's more than one sort of courage. There's what I call proper courage and there's the wrong sort. Menherian has contempt for the sea. He dares it to do its worst. There's a character in a famous book we got to read at school. Captain Ahab.' Odhiambo nodded as an indication he knew of Melville's *Moby Dick*. 'Menherian's a bit like him. He'll go out in the worst of seas cursing it and defying it out of a personal obsession. I suppose it's courage of a sort, but I don't respect it.'

A little later Odhiambo took his leave of the estate manager and found his way through to the cliff top and the wheel, intended to commemorate the drowned sailors, now likely to be for ever identified with Penny Deane. He watched from the shelter of the trees as several couples and trios walked around the monument. This was to be expected, he supposed. The curious would be bound to make their way to see the place where a woman had met her dreadful end draped against a ship's wheel.

Being close once again to the scene seemed to bring him into contact with the dead woman. He could feel her presence inside his mind. So intense was the mental image that it became a physical one. He could see once more Penny Deane as she was when he first met her, pretty, friendly, enjoying life. Why hadn't he been more insistent with her the morning after Mahendra's death? He was convinced now that it was not Penny that Mahendra was meeting in the lake. She was spying on her lover who had left their love-making to meet another woman. She must have heard the splashing, sending a dagger into her heart, and then a more sinister splashing. Puzzled, she went closer and saw . . . Well, that was it, saw what? He was certain now in the presence of the woman's spirit that his surmise was correct, but what had she seen? Tell me, he cried out, but only in his mind, tell me what you saw. But as he asked he felt Penny Deane leave his presence for ever.

As he watched and allowed his mind to dwell on that dreadful scene of a few nights ago, he wondered why he intended to go ahead with meeting Menherian. He was putting himself in danger, of that there was no doubt. What's more, he was allowing Menherian to be literally in his element, a boat and the sea beneath, whereas for Odhiambo the situation would be an alien one. Yet he was convinced that alone with Menherian on his boat he would find his way to the truth. The problem was, having got the truth, to come back with it. He had confidence in his ability to handle Menherian physically. If Menherian armed himself with some shipboard implement it might be a different story, but Odhiambo had taken some precautions not to be defenceless in such an eventuality. Below his thick pullover, tucked into his belt was a heavy-handled dagger he had purloined from a suit of armour that stood at the head of the staircase in the Centre. But ultimately, Odhiambo relied on his conviction that his destiny lay in Kenya. When he had left his country he had had an insight akin to religious conviction that he was destined to return to face the unsolved issues including, at a personal level, his unfinished business with a certain sinister white man whom he despised. His African heritage, with the insight into the unknown it provided, gave him confidence that he would not die in a Cornish sea. He turned back into the wood to approach Penleith from the least visible route. What a fool I am, he thought, pitting my Luo instincts against the Cornish legends of doom awaiting the hapless sailor on this coast.

21

Alex Bastian approached Menherian's boat, tied to bollards in the inner harbour. From a distance he had seen a police car parked outside his restaurant. So the hounds were closing in. Perhaps his chance of getting away to Wales was slipping away. If they had linked him with the murders it would be difficult to elude them for long. No matter, for him there was an essential task to perform whatever the consequences. A fisherman known to him by sight told him that Menherian was not around as yet, but the fisherman had heard him make arrangements the previous evening to take his boat out this afternoon 'with that African from the ol' manor house who tried to rescue your Nigel. Us are sorry 'bout that, of course, sir. Terrible business.'

But Bastian was not interested in condolences; nor did he feel any kindly thoughts towards Odhiambo, attempted rescue or no attempted rescue. He identified Odhiambo as one of the contributory causes of his problems. Him and that blasted Indian. If neither of them had come to the Centre in the first place there would have been no need for any of this. And Nigel would still be alive. But why would Menherian be taking that damned African policeman out in his boat? He knew Menherian harboured no more kindly feelings towards Odhiambo than did Bastian himself. It might be worth lying low and listening to them for a bit. Might find out what he was looking for. In any case he needed to duck out of sight before the police started to look for him in the village.

As he neared his objective, Bastian saw a figure appear from the cabin and jump ashore. For a second he thought Menherian was already *in situ*, then he realised it was a slimmer, younger man whom he remembered seeing crewing for Menherian in the past. This could be a complication, but the man, after giving what seemed to Bastian to be a furtive glance around him, hurried off. Bastian reached the boat and also engaged in a scan of his surroundings: there were few people near and none appeared to be taking any interest in him. He clambered aboard, went below, settled himself in a niche between the bunk and a cupboard and prepared to wait. He could feel the knife in its sheath pressing against his side and it comforted him. He knew that he was not thinking clearly any more; his mind seemed to have shrunk into a white-hot tube, focusing on one thing alone, the one issue that consumed him, the circumstances of Nigel's death.

Menherian was the next to arrive and Bastian heard him pottering about the deck, no doubt making ready for departure. He came below, apparently to check the engine. He did not enter the sleeping quarters and Bastian knew he was invisible unless Menherian came up to the bunk and peered over. He heard the sailor return to the deck-level cabin and he heard the chink of a bottle. No doubt Menherian was engaged in his favourite pastime. Bastian settled himself more snugly into his niche. He could feel himself stiffening up, but that was a minor matter.

Odhiambo reached the boat without incident, having sought confirmation from a quayside shopkeeper of the correct vessel. He caught sight of a police constable, but neither he nor any other person around seemed interested in the large black man walking along the quay. If the police were looking for him, presumably they were still expecting him at the Centre. As he came alongside the boat, Menherian appeared from the cabin clutching a beer bottle. He seemed in amiable mood, inviting Odhiambo in an exaggerated local dialect to come aboard and set sail.

Once on deck Odhiambo looked about him with interest. The boat was about thirty feet long, smaller than he had expected and certainly smaller than some of the other boats moored in the harbour. A cabin contained the means of steering and controlling the boat, and presumably there was some space below. Odhiambo assumed it was a boat intended for coastal fishing by one or two men rather than extended trips into deeper waters with full crew. The crab pots in the stern seemed to provide confirmation of the local nature of Menherian's ventures.

'So, me hearty, you'd like a little run up the coast? Perhaps see the bar from the sea and – well, shiver me timbers, perhaps see the cave under Mr Bastian's place. Old smugglers' cave, it were. Well, you're in luck, me black beauty. I've got a little job to do right at that very spot. Should suit you grand. Can help me haul in the pots.'

Odhiambo looked at the sailor carefully. He was not drunk; his movements were confident and his tongue unslurred. He seemed, in fact, to be in good spirits. He was clearly looking forward to forthcoming events and Odhiambo, despite himself, felt his skin crawl.

A few minutes later they cast off, Menherian manoeuvring the boat with consummate ease through the gap in the harbour wall and out into the sea. Odhiambo was not a confident sailor and, although the sea was probably what Menherian would describe as calm, he felt the boat rocking in the swell and occasionally riding up and down a wave to the extent that he was induced to hope his sea-legs would be up to the task. To be sick now would be to add a farcical element to the drama.

Once clear of Penleith harbour and pier, Menherian turned the boat towards the bar at Polsand, running parallel to the cliffs on a course totally familiar to him and one he had traversed in such different circumstances two nights earlier. Odhiambo stood beside him in the cabin, sheltered from the wind and salt spray caused by the prow cutting into and across the waves. Little was said until the bar appeared in sight and Menherian started to ease the boat in closer to the shore. Odhiambo could see the sea occasionally splitting as it hit a rock that was almost level with the surface, a potential disaster for an unwary sailor. He could not restrain a feeling of admiration for a man who had managed to manoeuvre a boat around this area in that storm. He shook his head at the contrast between the experience, skill and nerve that this burly fisherman could display and the crass, crude and possibly violent side of him that Odhiambo had encountered.

Looking upwards, Odhiambo could see Bastian's lodge, but as the ship nosed in closer it was blocked from view by the overhanging cliff. Now it was possible to see the dark gash in the bottom of the cliff, the cave of which Odhiambo had heard so much. It appeared that the sea lapped into its mouth, but then the rising slope of the cave floor provided a terminus for the sea's advance. At the moment the tide was receding and the whole entrance to the cave was exposed.

'There 'ee be, Mr African Policeman. There be the cave you be interested in. You reckon the old smuggling days be going on still? There's tracks in the rocks there leading into the cave. Cut they were in old days so that a cart could be trundled down to load the contraband and put 'im back into the cave.'

They were quite close now and Menherian throttled back the engine to a murmur; moving to the side, he prepared to lower an anchor. Odhiambo followed.

'But if this is as close as you can get, how would one use the cave today?' Odhiambo watched Menherian carefully, but the man seemed relaxed and unconcerned. 'Difficult to get anything in and out, it seems to me.'

Menherian laughed, a short derisive sound that echoed off the cliff wall.

'That's 'cos you don't know nothing about it, see. Coming from Africa. Don't 'ave no water there, do 'ee? Better ways today than there were. I'm going to show 'e sumpin'.'

Menherian now took a long pole with a hook on its end that was lying alongside the side of the ship. He leaned over the side and started to fish with the pole. A grunt of satisfaction greeted the snaring of his quarry, a rope attached to a small buoy. Soon Menherian was pulling in the rope; as it tautened, he gestured to Odhiambo to lend a hand. Together they pulled until, breaking the surface, a crab pot came into view. It was not strictly a pot at all, but a hand-made basket of thick woven strips of wood fashioned in such a way, with an inverted chimney leading into the basket, that a crab could crawl in but was unable to escape. As they pulled it on to the deck, Odhiambo realised that it in turn was linked by rope to what presumably was another still under the water. But the focal point of interest about the pot was that its intended entrance was sealed so no catch of crabs was possible – what the pot contained was a parcel with a waterproof oilskin outer layer.

'Now the next, there's three of these 'ere pots.'

They pulled together and retrieved the full set. Each revealed the same, a sealed pot containing, not crabs, but a sizeable water-proofed parcel. Odhiambo watched Menherian closely. It was easy to make an informed guess about the contents of the parcels, and the blatant exposure of them to Odhiambo confirmed another of Odhiambo's suppositions: Menherian would not be likely to engage in these dramatics if he thought that Odhiambo would be reporting to the police on his return.

Menherian turned his own gaze to meet Odhiambo's.

'There 'ee be. That's it, see. T'other end of rope, or rather chain as it becomes, is inside cave, so they're snug and safe under water until needed when they're pulled in. Keep the chain under the stones away from quizzy eyes like yours and all's well.' He laughed derisively. 'Are you clear in your mind now, mister? I know you darkies are a bit slow on the uptake, like.' Odhiambo felt the metal under his jumper and his hand on that side of his body rested on his hip. Menherian seemed content to taunt and enjoy the situation he'd created, but at some point he must make his move.

'What now, then, Menherian? I take it you're confessing your part in drug smuggling and, by handing over the evidence, looking for consideration in court?'

Menherian laughed once more, the derision still apparent.

'Ah, you're a beauty, you be.' He considered for a moment then smiled before continuing. 'No. I'll tell ye what us'll do. We don't want these here parcels to get in the wrong hands. No good you telling me to hand 'em over to Trewin. One do hear funny tales about how stuff the police do lay their hands on 'as a funny habit of getting about again. Now that you and me have come upon these things we'll do the safest thing, take 'em further out an' sink 'em proper.

'Now, make yourself useful again and haul in our anchor. We need to get away from here; tide be going out.'

Odhiambo did as he was bid and then watched as the boat was expertly turned and headed out to sea. He crossed the deck to join Menherian once more. He raised his voice and shouted in the fisherman's ear.

'Turn back to Penleith, Menherian. Turn this stuff in and it could go well for you. If you don't you'll be in deep trouble – you know that. I'm irrelevant in a way. Chief Inspector Pendham knows what's going on as well as I do. You think Bastian will keep quiet now his boyfriend's dead?'

Menherian did not reply; only the sardonic grin reappeared and stayed as he gazed steadily ahead through the cabin window. Odhiambo wondered whether the moment had come to overpower Menherian. If he really intended to dispose of the evidence in the parcels Odhiambo would have to stop him. But it was Menherian's confidence that intrigued Odhiambo. He seemed unconcerned by the presence of the larger man with him. Was he armed? He was wearing a seaman's thick jersey and a pair of waterproof trousers. There was no evidence of a gun. Well, he decided, it was time to make a move. But as he reached this decision he was aware that Menherian's eyes were on him, and now the fisherman's Celtic insight was revealed. The grin widened and suddenly Menherian swung the wheel over, turning the boat broadside into a wave that, in turn, rocked the boat on to its side. Odhiambo, taken by surprise and an inexperienced seaman, lost his balance and crashed awkwardly against the side of the cabin. He put his hands down to break his fall as his feet lost their grip on the wet wood. Out of the corner of his eye he saw Menherian move with surprisingly agile speed, the flash of his arm, the braced hand with fingers together, then he felt the blow on his neck and knew no more.

The coastguard put down his binoculars and turned to answer the query of Sergeant Trewin. They were standing inside an old World War II concrete pill-box that still remained embedded in the sloping grass of the cliff top some few hundred yards from Bastian's lodge on the road to Penleith. Trewin, having been frustrated all morning in his attempts to pick up first Bastian and then Odhiambo, had played a hunch. He had asked the local coastguard to keep an eye open for activity around Menherian's boat and to record arrivals. When the coastguard phoned to say that Menherian and two companions were on board and that the boat was leaving the harbour heading east along the coast, Trewin was minded to ask the coastguard to intercept it with the coastguard patrol boat. But it was the description of Menherian's crew that gave him pause. One was almost certainly Bastian, so Trewin's hunch had paid off. But the other was reported to be a large black man; could it be Odhiambo? What was going on? He and the coastguard drove up the track towards Polsand; they could see the boat make its way in the same direction. Leaving the car they went to the pill-box, which gave a view of the coastline whilst affording protection from being seen. They watched while Menherian and Odhiambo pulled in the pots. Trewin was puzzled until the coastguard focused his binoculars on the pots and reported the absence of crabs but the presence of bulky objects. They watched also as the boat set off towards deeper water. It was time, Trewin felt, to intercept. He checked again with the coastguard; yes one man had visited the boat and left again, then a man answering to the description of Bastian had arrived and was presumably still on board, although there had been no sight of him on the boat since Menherian and Odhiambo boarded it. Were they making a run for it to the Continent with the available drug supply? And if so, what on earth was Odhiambo doing mixed up in it? Trewin made his decision, but as he did so the coastguard, who had his binoculars raised once more, let out a cry of surprise.

'He's pulled her around. What's he up to now? The black guy seems to have fallen over.'

'Get on the radio.' Trewin's voice took on a new urgency. 'Get your boat out to intercept them. As fast as you can.'

The coastguard looked at him questioningly, but then left the pill-box and went to his car to follow Trewin's instruction. Trewin, left behind, picked up the binoculars and with some adjustment focused on the boat. They were good binoculars, he noticed. Yes, Menherian was fooling around with the crab pots they had retrieved earlier. Was he going to sink them again? And where was Odhiambo? Trewin had a nasty sinking feeling that playing his hunch could cost him his pension. If they slipped through his hands now, Pendham would be incandescent. Come on, he mentally urged the coastguard, get a move on.

Odhiambo came to. He was lying on the deck beside the cabin. God Almighty, he thought, as his senses unscrambled themselves, how many more miscalculations am I going to make about Menherian? Who would have thought he was a martial arts *fundi* – the blow that had paralysed him was delivered swiftly and expertly. Next came the realisation that his hands were behind his back, tethered together with a rope or cord pulled so tightly that it bit into his skin. The rope seemed to extend from behind his back to where Menherian was fiddling with something beside the bow of the boat. With a momentary stutter in his heart, Odhiambo saw that Menherian was securing the parcels of drugs, so recently retrieved, to the same rope that was attached to him: with sudden dread he understood what Menherian intended to do.

Menherian looked around and grinned.

'So you've come to, me black beauty. Thought for a minute I'd hit you too hard. Wouldn't want you to miss enjoying your dip, would we now?'

Odhiambo struggled to sit up: resting his head against the cabin, he managed to twist himself on to his knees. Menherian watched him with amusement and then, as Odhiambo balanced himself, he tugged the rope, pulling Odhiambo back over and catching his head a fearsome crack on the deck. Once more his senses swam and he rolled helplessly towards the ship's side, the rope entangling itself further around his body.

'There now, don't 'ee be trying to get up. Just rest easy till it be time for you to have a dip. A dip, get it?' The fisherman laughed. 'Bit cold, the water might be, mind. For someone like you, I mean. From Africa an' all. This ain't no tropical water here. Still, you won't have time to feel too cold.'

Menherian crossed to the cabin and made an adjustment to the engine speed and the wheel. They seemed to be making very slow way on some sort of automatic pilot. The ship was bouncing and rolling; only the greater fear kept Odhiambo from being seasick. He looked up at Menherian, who had emerged from the cabin and stood looking down at him, the sardonic grin twisting his lips.

'It's no good, Menherian. I know what Nigel was trying to tell me. And it's not just me. I told the police.'

Menherian's grin widened.

'Don't 'ee take me for a fool, mister. If you knew as much as you're saying, wild horses would'na 'ave brought you on this 'ere ship with me. Now you can't tell me I'm not right, can 'ee?'

'No, you're wrong. I pieced it together. What Nigel was trying to say, your concern when you knew I'd been down the cliff after him, and what I heard when we were interviewed. You arrived breathless at the harbour that night. But it wasn't the pub you came from, was it? It was the cliff top, where you'd been meeting Nigel.'

'You're too smart for your own good, let alone for a darkie. So what are you saying? Speak up now 'cos you ain't got much time.'

'He, Nigel that is, was trying to tell me something. I thought he said he was seeing men. I assumed he meant Bastian got to know and was jealous. If he was thrown over it was by Bastian. But why would he and Bastian be out on the cliff? They could have a row at home. Then I realised what he meant. He wasn't saying "men", he was trying to get your name out. He'd been seeing you, Menherian. He was trying to tell me you threw him over.'

While he spoke Odhiambo was trying to ease the rope around his wrists sufficiently to pull one hand through. He wasn't going to die. He knew his destiny awaited him. He knew it in his bones. There was to be more to his life than this. Wasn't there?

Menherian seemed to be mulling over Odhiambo's words. Just a shadow of doubt was entering his mind.

'Well, there you are then. Even if you're right, telling me don't help your situation none, do it?'

Odhiambo noticed how the Cornish accent was much less evident now in the other man's voice. He had stopped clowning now; the game was being played in deadly earnest.

'But I can help you, Menherian. You went to see Nigel because you knew something. You accosted him with what you knew. He got violent. A tussle. You were defending yourself.'

'Ah, they'd likely believe that, wouldn't they? They wouldn't believe a pansy like that could attack me.'

'But he wasn't quite that harmless, was he, Menherian? You may have contributed to the death of Nigel, but you didn't kill the others, did you?' Menherian was listening now. 'You were dealing with a killer, Menherian. Nigel murdered Mahendra and Mrs Deane, didn't he? And you knew it.'

'You are smarter than I thought, you know that? But you still haven't said anything that'll save your skin, mister.'

'Don't be a fool, man.' The rope was easing a bit but still his hands were trapped. 'Whatever your purpose in meeting Nigel, his death could be an accident or self-defence. But if you kill me too, Pendham will nail you for the lot. You and Bastian together.

If we take these drugs back and tell your story properly, you could walk free. Breaking a drug-importing ring run by the Bastians, tackling a psychopath. You could be a hero again. And I'll forget our little contretemps on this boat.'

Menherian laughed.

'Maybe you don't know as much as you think. No, mister, there's going to be an unfortunate accident. I took you on a sightseeing trip and you, being unaccustomed to seafaring like, fell overboard.'

Odhiambo was desperate to stall. Menherian looked as if he was tiring of conversation. He redoubled his efforts. He had to get his hand free.

'What about Nigel, Menherian? What did you have on him? Concerning the murders, I mean.'

'Ah. You see, the night we first met you and your pals, someone said that bloody Indian was nosing about again. I went up to the bar to pass the message like. But then I thought 'twould wait the morrow. So I sat down at the foot of the cliff and had a pipe. Must have dozed 'cos when I come to I saw that bastard Nigel coming across the bar carrying a wetsuit. "What's he been doing swimming in the pool this time of night?" I said to meself. Course, next day I put two and two together. I'd always thought he was a wrong 'un. Not just a pansy, I mean. There was a vicious streak to 'im. Then there was the woman. That was more than I could stomach. So I went to tell 'im. Give him a chance to deny it 'fore I turned him in.' To blackmail him more likely, thought Odhiambo. 'Do you know, he laughed. He told me how he did for the woman. He was relishing it. Turned me stomach, I'll tell ye. Then he tried to threaten me. Me! That bloodthirsty sodomite who enjoyed killing women tried to threaten me! I tossed him over the cliff. Should 'ave done it afore. Rid the world of the bugger.'

Menherian stopped as if he realised he was getting carried away. Odhiambo tried to get him to continue. Just a couple of minutes more.

'Go on. What about your association with Bastian? Were all three of you in the drug business?'

Menherian laughed.

'No more talking. It's time for your dip. Tell you the truth though – the old man's no better than the boy.'

Menherian bent to pick up the rope. Suddenly behind him in the cabin doorway Odhiambo caught a glimpse of a man's face.

A demented face. Then events became a blur. There was a rush accompanied by an inhuman scream. Menherian stumbled two steps forward then fell to his knees, clutching his chest. Odhiambo could see an ornamental handle sticking out from his back.

The seaman rocked on his knees for what seemed an eternity, his face distorted into a visual image of a primal scream, then blood gushed from his mouth and he fell forward on to Odhiambo's legs.

Odhiambo looked up at the figure of Bastian, who had now replaced Menherian in the cabin doorway. His hand was still held in front of him, arm half extended from the manic thrust that had driven a knife into Menherian's back. He was dressed in smart slacks and jumper, but looked dishevelled, his clothes creased. He must have been hidden below since before we set sail, thought Odhiambo, but hidden for what purpose – and why would he be on the boat at all?

Bastian looked down at his hand as if seeing it for the first time. Slowly he allowed it to drop to his side. His eyes had previously been focused with a terrible intensity on the body of Menherian, as if wanting to be certain he was dead. Now he looked from Menherian to his hand and then upwards again to Odhiambo's face. Slowly the madness seemed to dim just slightly from the eyes and the body posture became slightly less tense. Finally he spoke.

'He killed Nigel. I heard him. You heard him. He killed him. Threw him over the cliff. The bastard! The bastard! God rot him.'

Odhiambo forbore to add fuel to the man's anger by saying that his sentiments had been shared by Nigel, who died trying to impugn Menherian's parents. He had a nasty feeling that his troubles, although momentarily alleviated, were not over. He had finally worked one hand free; he frantically clenched and unclenched his fingers to bring feeling back in place of the numbness that precluded any attempt to grasp his knife and free the other hand from the main rope leading to the crab pots.

'Take it easy, Bastian. Stay cool. Yes, I did hear him. Now we've got to get this boat under control. Do you know how to drive it, or whatever you call steering a bloody boat?'

'I warned him. I told him he was getting in deep. I tried to stop him. But he wouldn't listen. Oh Nigel! Why? Why? Still, I've got him, Nigel. I've sent the bastard to hell.'

Odhiambo brought his hand round to his belt and fumbled under his pullover for the knife. Luckily it was still there. He felt the hilt and carefully he pulled it from the scabbard. Bastian seemed too far gone to notice.

'Go back in the cabin, Bastian. Steer this bloody thing back to land.'

Bastian seemed to refocus on the man on the deck before him. Odhiambo was now sawing behind his back at the rope to free his other hand.

'Ah, now hold on a minute. That bastard was right about one thing, you're as bad as any of them. Since you and that damned Mahendra started nosing about there's been nothing but trouble. You're as responsible as this.' He kicked Menherian's body contemptuously. 'Yes, you're responsible.'

'Get a grip on yourself, Bastian. If we don't get back no one will know you've revenged Nigel. You must do that for him.'

Bastian bent forward, braced against the rocking of the boat that was still heading out to sea, set on its automatic pilot by the hand that would steer no more.

'No. You don't understand. Least said the better. Nigel wasn't bad, not really.' As Odhiambo watched, tears started from the mad eyes and made their way down his cheeks. 'He was driven to it. That Indian was a nasty bastard.'

Hastily, Odhiambo tried to keep him talking.

'He found out about the drugs? He was threatening you?'

'He was a blackmailer. I'd had a bit of trouble in India. A building contract. Out there backhanders are part of the way of life. But Mahendra could make things difficult. It was my bad luck to meet him down here. It was me he was after, not Nigel. But then he must have got this . . .' Bastian kicked the body again, 'this fool talking so he was sniffing around Nigel as well.'

'Mahendra, perhaps, I can understand. But why the woman?'

'She saw Nigel in the water. Or rather she saw a head in a mask, reflecting in the moonlight. She wasn't sure who it was. So when she met him the silly bitch asked if he'd been there. Nigel thinks she thought that he and Mahendra were swimming together. How dare she! As if he would. Still, he shouldn't have done it. I thought he was acting strange. Then I noticed some earth that had been dug in the garden. The silly boy had buried the knife. This one here.' He pointed at the handle in Menherian's back. 'I knew he wouldn't have been planting seeds, he wasn't much of a gardener. I accused him and he laughed. Then I found his clothes.' Bastian shuddered at the memory. 'I was too late in trying to stop him. He was wrong. I told him he was crazy. He got angry, threatened me. Me! Who would die for him . . . Still, it's over now. Or nearly.'

Bastian bent down and tried to extract the knife from Menherian's back but it was firmly embedded in the corpse. Odhiambo knew he was faced by a madman. First, the night of the storm – cowering and weeping in the rain. Now this, intent on exacting revenge with his lover's own murder instrument. Bastian, unable to dislodge the knife, cursed and turned to find another weapon, a club to beat out Odhiambo's brains. Odhiambo, finally free from the restraining rope, tried to leap to his feet, but his legs too were lacking in their normal response time to his brain's urgent signals. He stumbled and this, combined with the motion of the boat, threw him for the third time to the deck where he rolled uncontrollably into the bow. This probably saved his life, for as Bastian started towards him the whole world seemed to disintegrate and he had a brief searing image of Bastian rising from the deck looking bemused and startled.

The coastguard vessel was bearing down on its target when suddenly an explosion engulfed the boat in a great sheet of flame. The air turbulence reached their faces as the coastguards gazed in amazement at the sight. The boat had been blown apart; pieces of wood splashed back into the waves and as the boat sank the flames seemed to come from the sea as if the water itself was on fire.

'Christ Almighty,' said one of the two watchers. 'The boat's blown up.'

His companion did not criticise the triteness of the remark.

'Let's get alongside. There might be somebody left alive but I doubt it.'

Back on the cliff Sergeant Trewin and his companion had seen the flash in the distance. Trewin swore with a range and crudeness that the coastguard found impressive.

22

Chief Inspector Pendham arrived at the hospital at ten on Sunday morning. He had kicked his heels overnight, for the hospital had been adamant – no visitors, not even official ones, until the next morning at the earliest. Meanwhile, Pendham had experienced one of the worst evenings of his life. The explosion on the fishing boat, more deaths, including that of a local hero, on top of the sequence of events of the past few days, had placed Penleith and the Polsand Centre firmly on to the front pages and the national television news. Whatever way one portrayed the story, it looked as if a normally sleepy Cornish village was now a more dangerous place than the down-town areas of New York or Washington. Bodies were piling up at a rapid rate and in relation to the size of the local population it was taking on the aspect of wholesale slaughter.

The Chief Constable had been blunt but far from short in his criticism of Stephens and Pendham. The departure of the Chief Constable enabled Stephens to repeat the charges, suitably embellished, but laying the blame entirely on Pendham. And all this in an atmosphere that was becoming a media circus. The only consolation Pendham was able to secure during the evening was to go out and kick the cat, in this case by giving Sergeant Trewin the worst hour of his life.

Not having been to bed during the night, Pendham had dozed fitfully in the back of the police car during the ninety-minute drive to the hospital in Plymouth. At first, Odhiambo had been taken to a much closer hospital in Truro, but had then been airlifted by helicopter to a specialist burns unit in the Plymouth hospital. As far as Pendham could gather, Odhiambo's injuries were such that he could have stayed in the local hospital, but his burns gave a reason and an excuse to move him away from the immediate vicinity and the growing battalion of reporters. Pendham saw the hand of the government in giving him a journey longer than it need have been.

As he made his way to the room where Odhiambo was housed – the private room, with a constable discreetly placed outside, confirming to him the need to keep the patient isolated for reasons other than medical – Pendham ran through what he knew once more. The facts were clear enough: the toings and froings of the boat with its ill-assorted crew, the retrieval of parcels containing, almost certainly, drugs, the apparent altercations on the boat, the explosion and the rescue of a semi-conscious Odhiambo, picked up clinging burnt and half-drowned to a plank from the sinking boat. Of the other two men there was no sign, but Trewin was supervising efforts to get divers or cameras or both down to the sea-bed. Explosives experts had been summoned to determine from the available wreckage the cause of the explosion, and to Pendham's ears had come the dread news that detectives from London had been asked in by the Chief Constable to assist. All in all a pig of a mess, and Pendham's thoughts towards Odhiambo were not kindly.

Nor when he entered the room did sympathy overtake him. Odhiambo was sitting up engaged, it seemed, in an argument with a nurse. Pendham caught the end of an Odhiambo submission.

'. . . if I can't see the lady who's waiting and I can't have a telephone, I've got to get up. I can't sit here waiting for . . . Ah, Pendham, talk of the devil! You've had a lie-in, have you, it being Sunday?'

The nurse turned and viewed the new arrival with an astringent eye as she spoke.

'Right, your approved visitors are here. Now you must behave yourself.' She nodded at Pendham. 'I take it you're the policemen from Cornwall? I'll leave you to it.'

As the nurse left, Pendham cast an eye over the patient. One arm was bandaged from elbow to fingertip; his chest also had a bandage, which seemed to be holding a dressing on his side.

'So, Odhiambo, you continue to supervise the raising of the body count. Pity one of them wasn't yours.'

Odhiambo was clearly agitated. If he was in pain it was overridden by a more pressing emotion.

'Look, Pendham, let's cut the crap. There are things to do to bring this mess to an end.'

'Yeah, and one of those things is a full and honest statement from you. Given your previous record that may take some time. But get it I will.' Pendham gestured at the sergeant with him to seat himself and be prepared for his stenographer role. 'Now, let's take it easy and start at the beginning.'

'Balls! There's no time.' Odhiambo forced himself to calm down. Antagonising Pendham further would not aid his cause. 'Look, the basic facts I assume you know. I can make a full statement later. I'll add a quick summary of what happened on that boat. I was there hoping to get a confession out of Menherian about Nigel's death. I got it, but he outsmarted me. Had me tied up ready to tip overboard. With a load of drugs he hauled in from close to the cliff and was going to dump. Then Bastian appeared from nowhere and knifed him. Revenge for Nigel. Bastian's mind seemed to have gone. God knows why he was on the boat – waiting for Menherian, I suppose. Then the whole bloody thing blew up. Did Bastian survive?'

'Whoa, whoa. Let's calm down. And I'll ask the questions. But, since you ask – no, we haven't found Bastian. Now what are you saying? Menherian was the killer?'

'Of Nigel, yes. He told me. And Nigel killed Mahendra and Penny Deane. Mahendra was blackmailing the Bastians. It started with some corruption Bastian was involved in in India. Penny saw something that incriminated Nigel for Mahendra's death so she had to go. Menherian saw something too, namely, Nigel walking away in a wetsuit, so he put two and two together as well. Probably tried a bit of blackmail. Nigel went for him but it was Nigel who went over the edge. He – Menherian, I mean – could probably have claimed self-defence.'

Pendham was intrigued but puzzled.

'But Menherian was on the lifeboat. You're saying he threw Nigel over first?'

'Yes. That's why he was out of breath when he got on the boat. He'd run not from the pub, but further, from the cliff, pushed along by the wind perhaps, but still a fair jog.'

Pendham glanced at the sergeant busily taking notes.

'Let's go over this trip of yours in more detail . . .'

Odhiambo's impatience resurfaced.

'Christ, no, Pendham. Listen to me. OK, we know now who killed who, and that Menherian and the Bastians were running drugs. But the main question remains, you must see that . . .'

'The explosion, you mean. Yes. What do you know about that?'

'That's it, nothing. It couldn't have been an accident, could it? If it wasn't, someone wanted to blow Menherian to kingdom come. He was the only one whoever did it could be sure was on the boat.'

'Unless Bastian, who you say was after Menherian and who had taken leave of his senses, decided to blow both of them to bits. Revenge for Nigel and off to join him in some poofters' Valhalla.'

'But he didn't, did he? He gutted Menherian with a knife. Why would he carry that if he intended to stow away, wait till they were at sea and set off his bomb?'

Pendham considered for a moment. Well, why not? It was clear Odhiambo had ideas and the best way to get them out of him was to go along with him, drawing him out.

'It's true that another man was seen leaving the boat before any of you went aboard. So your theory is possible, if bizarre.'

'That's it. Who? Who did they see? That's the key, Pendham.'

'We don't know. A local, we think, but we don't have much to go on.'

'You see what this means. Someone ordered Menherian to go and sink the drugs where they couldn't be found. Closing down the business at least temporarily while all the fuss is on. But, in fact, Menherian was being set up. They planted a bomb so he wouldn't live to tell the tale. Timed it so that he could retrieve the drugs first. Would have taken him some time to head out to sea, do the dumping and get back to Penleith, so the timing didn't have to be that accurate. Unless it was radio-detonated.'

'It could still have been Bastian. Perhaps he intended to get off the boat, but Menherian arrived too early, trapping him. Then he decided to go ahead anyway. Decided to join Nigel in hell, as I said.'

'There's one more thing, Pendham. Then you'll see why you've got to get on with things. After he killed Menherian, Bastian said a few things to me. I don't think Nigel and Menherian were working for him as such. If he was involved it was reluctantly, because Nigel was right in the middle of it. I got the impression he'd tried to get Nigel out of it and away from it. Somebody else is running the drug business.'

'I'll tell you what I think, Odhiambo. I think you're concussed. You're not thinking straight. You always want to complicate things so you can go on playing the great detective.' Pendham remembered the presence of the sergeant. 'Anyway, we'll look into it. Thanks for your suggestion. Now let's get back to you. Your reason for going on this trip doesn't ring true.'

Despite Odhiambo's protests, Pendham solidly took him through what Odhiambo considered to be old hat events. Only the explosion dominated Odhiambo's mind. Suddenly he remembered Helen Shropshire.

'Look, that's it for now, Pendham. I'm not saying any more. I need a rest. Damn it, I'm injured. And I have to see someone from the Centre who's waiting. I've got to make sure they did what I told them last night, about my wife. She's in America. They wouldn't let me see Mrs . . . the person that's waiting until I'd seen you first. Well, I've done that.'

Pendham grinned, sardonically.

'Don't tell me your lady friend Mrs Shropshire is here.' He

shook his head. 'I've got to hand it to you, Odhiambo – you Africans, no one can say you don't keep at it. How are you feeling anyway? Burns troubling you?'

'Nice of you to ask after my health, Pendham. Took you a while, though. I'm not so bad, thanks. I'm told I'm a miracle case getting away with it as lightly as I did. That's what good living does for you. Only some visitors are upsetting me.'

Pendham thought he'd got enough to be going on with. Despite himself, Odhiambo's theory of a yet-unmasked drug smuggler was beginning to take root in his mind. It was time he got hold of Trewin and stepped up the search for the earlier visitor to the boat. Time to get on with it before detectives from London were tramping all over his patch. He would have liked to have someone listen in to Odhiambo's conversation with the woman, but that was not feasible.

At the door Pendham turned back towards the bed.

'Your journey was unnecessary. We know Nigel was the killer: skin under Mrs Deane's fingernails matches his and one of his scratches was made before he hit the rocks.' Ah yes, thought Odhiambo, the band-aid on Bastian's wrist. He should have realised its potential.

On the way out Pendham checked that the constable was still sitting outside.

With some reluctance the duty nurse was persuaded to allow Odhiambo to see his waiting visitor. Helen Shropshire arrived a few minutes later. She had seen Odhiambo briefly the previous evening when the rescue vessel had brought him to Penleith. News of the explosion had taken her to the harbour where she waited, as fishermen's wives had waited through the centuries for the fishing boat that did not return. He had seen her and managed a minute or two with her before he was whisked away. She had driven to Plymouth at dawn and had been waiting since. She was relieved at his appearance. Despite the bandages he seemed much recovered.

'Golly, James, it's good to see you back in the land of the living. How are you? You were incredibly lucky, you know. The coastguard said he couldn't believe you were alive, let alone in one piece. More or less.' She crossed to his bed and held his uninjured hand. 'I've brought some of your clothes with me. The stuff you had on is not likely to be any good to you again.'

Odhiambo's heart rose at the sight of the worried-looking but still, to him, desirable woman. She was dressed in casual slacks and cardigan, her face unmade-up and red hair dishevelled, but her pleasure at seeing him was transparent and gave her a glow and vitality that caught his breath.

'Helen, it's good of you to come.' How trite can you get, he thought to himself. 'I'm OK. They're making more fuss than necessary. To tell you the truth, I think they want me out of the way.'

'Oh, James, stop looking for conspiracies. You're lucky to be alive.'

'Yeah, I am that. But I'll tell you all about it another time. No time at present.' He interrupted himself. 'But, Cari, my wife – did you tell Hugh I didn't want her contacted at present?'

'Yes, I did. So we've done nothing yet. Anyway, you'll be able to ring her by the look of you.'

'Thanks, Helen.' He felt embarrassed, talking of his wife to Helen. What a mess he was getting into. Still, no time for guilt either. 'Listen, Helen, I've got to get out of here; get back to Polsand. It's urgent. I think we're close to the end of this business.'

Helen reared back as if he had struck her.

'You're mad, you know that, you're mad. Pendham was just here, let him get on with it.'

Odhiambo hitched himself into a straighter position.

'I would, Helen. I've already told him most of it and even the facts he has difficulty swallowing. The rest is theory, but only I can put it to the test. With your help. I'm OK. I told you, they're trying to keep me out of the way.'

The argument continued, but against her better judgement Helen allowed herself once more to be the accomplice in one of Odhiambo's schemes. I must be mad myself, she thought. The trouble is I can't say no to him. And, given the terrible things that happened on the boat, I suppose he deserves to see it through.

A few minutes later Helen left, passed the policeman sitting patiently outside and gave him a winning smile. As she moved on she suddenly swayed and leaned against the wall. The constable was quickly at her side.

'I'll be all right. Just a bit dizzy, . . . No, I don't need help. If you could just help me to that little waiting-room alcove . . . I'll be fine, honest.'

The policeman did his Good Samaritan act and returned to his post. Some minutes later the duty nurse returned.

'Has the visitor left?'

The policeman nodded and the nurse entered the room, only to re-emerge immediately.

'He's gone. The patient's gone.'

Once across the Tamar Bridge, Odhiambo relaxed a little: the bridge into Cornwall would have been the obvious place for an interception. He was lucky, first, to have slipped away up the corridor without running into a nurse whilst Helen was distracting the policeman and, second, that his disappearance was not immediately noticed, giving Helen and himself time to reach her car and drive the few miles to the bridge. He assumed that Pendham would now take the obvious course, namely to wait for him to turn up at the Polsand Centre to finish his investigations. Helen's foresight in bringing a complete set of clothes had been the key. With her help he had got his shirt half on with his right arm in the sleeve but with his bandaged left arm inside the shirt which was buttoned lower down his chest to hold it in place. A pullover on top, which he found constricting because of the bandage around his chest, completed a reasonably normal appearance, his lower half being clad in a more orthodox manner.

Helen glanced across as they emerged from the Saltash tunnel.

'Well, so far so good, but I still say we're mad. Are you sure you're OK?'

'I'm fine. The burns aren't that bad. They wanted me out of the way, that's all.'

Helen looked doubtful. She had seen him the previous evening. His arm had looked pretty dreadful then.

'Chief Inspector Pendham is going to flip over this, you know. And he'll be waiting for you if we aren't picked up earlier.'

Odhiambo turned towards her and grinned.

'I'm not so sure. I don't think it was him who wanted me put away. It was Gregson and the ODA, is my guess. But sure, he'll be waiting so we need to have our plan. Give me five minutes to get the flesh on the skeleton and I'll fill you in.'

Helen grimaced. What on earth was she doing? And yet she felt more alive than she had for ages – certainly since she had left Nairobi, and even for some time before that, if she was honest with herself. Another glance across confirmed that her companion was sunk in thought. Ah well, he would come clean in due time, she hoped; meanwhile she concentrated on the driving.

Pendham was thirty miles ahead of Odhiambo when the news of

his 'escape' reached him on the radio. The sergeant glanced across at him apprehensively, but after a moment or two when he seemed to be muttering to himself the sergeant was surprised to see a grin cross his superior's face.

'Ah-ah, our African friend wants to be in at the kill, eh? Not content with all the bodies he's been tripping over since he came here. Right, we'll give him his head and see where he leads us.' Pendham turned his attention back to the radio and issued his instructions. 'Get me Trewin, we need to prepare our welcoming party.'

A few minutes later Sergeant Trewin found himself talking once more to the source of his earlier tongue-lashing.

'Yes, Chief. We think we know who it was seen leaving Menherian's boat. Local chap, Matthews by name. Bad lot. Been in trouble off and on. Trouble is, he's disappeared. We've got an alarm out on him.'

'Small fry, though, is he? Not likely to be the king-pin, if there is one?'

'That's right, Chief. Very small fry. Not known for his intelligence. Although a bit handy with electric wiring and such. Worked for a local electrician once.'

It figured, Pendham thought – the bomb-placer and time-setter, almost certainly. Now, who was calling the shots if it wasn't the late lamented Bastians? Maybe the reason for Deane's reaction to his wife's death was that he suspected the Bastians and they were supposed to be under his direction. Then Pendham remembered that Odhiambo had always been suspicious of the Gregsons. And there were the other permanent residents at the Centre and in Penleith itself. Assuming, of course, that the orders were coming from a local source. Well, Odhiambo had a theory, Pendham was sure of that, so let him put it to the test.

'Are you still there, Chief?'

'Yes, Trewin, I'm here. Where else do you think I'd be? Now listen. Our black friend has discharged himself from hospital with the help of his girlfriend, the Admin woman at the Centre. He'll be turning up at the estate or thereabouts. I want a full surveillance operation. But covert, you get me? I want him under observation even if he goes to the bog. But I don't want him to know it. I want to see what he does next. And remember, Trewin, he's a copper, a detective, himself. So don't screw up again, or there'll be early additions to the widows and orphans liabilities.

I'll be there in thirty minutes, but get the organisation under way. I'll speak to the Super.'

23

Helen stopped the car outside the post office, switched off the ignition and turned to Odhiambo. She could tell that, despite his brave front, he was in pain. The whole thing was crazy; she should get him back to a hospital.

'Now, look, James I don't think . . .'

She was interrupted as Odhiambo grasped her arm with his good hand and spoke with a fierce intensity.

'No. We've got to do it the way I've explained. I know it sounds a bit wild, but I think I'm right and this is the only way to prove it. Now, will you do your part, please, Helen?'

Helen bit her lip.

'Oh, God, James, it's not my part that's worrying me, it's you. You're in no fit state . . .'

Again the interruption.

'Do it, Helen. I'm OK. It's all going to be over in an hour or two if things go well. And if they don't, Pendham will have me back in hospital anyway – or in a cell.'

'But suppose you're right? What do you do then? It might be dangerous.'

'It's you that's doing the difficult bit – I don't like asking you to do it, but I can't think of any other way. And if Pendham or Trewin picks you up and stops you going through with it, tell them everything, OK?'

Reluctantly, Helen got out of the car, went to the telephone kiosk, inserted a coin and dialled the number. She asked for and quickly got her assistant.

'Jane? It's Helen . . . No, don't ask a lot of questions, there isn't time. I'll explain later. I'll be back in less than half an hour. Tell me, have you seen Mrs Gregson this morning? . . . She is? Good. Look, tell her I have to see her about what we were discussing yesterday morning, will you? Tell her it's urgent . . . Right . . . Now, Jane, one other thing. Is Sergeant Trewin about, or any of his men? . . . Earlier, but none you've seen lately? . . . Right, I'll be there and I'll explain everything, I promise. 'Bye.'

She returned to the car. Odhiambo had twisted the driver's interior mirror towards himself and was gazing into it. He turned to her as she ducked inside.

'How did it go?' At her nod, the face strained with pain broke into a wintry smile. 'Well done, Helen. You're great, you know that?'

'I'm a fool, that's what I am, James. Nearly as big a fool as you.' Her lip trembled. 'Anyway, let's get on with it.'

She eased the car away from the kerb. She saw that Odhiambo was again watching the rear view through the mirror. He gave a short mirthless laugh.

'I think Pendham is playing it smart. I think he's on to us, but as long as he lets us lead him to the right solution that's fine. We have a saying in my home area: "Let the pack eat their fill after the leader kills." It refers to jackals or whatever.'

'You mean we're being followed?'

'I don't know, but I have a feeling. Now, where are we? The turning must be here somewhere, we're nearly at the woods.'

'I see it.'

She turned the car on to an unmade track. Odhiambo winced as the bumps sent waves of pain through his chest.

'OK. Let me out just by that corner. Yes, there's a farm gate. You can reverse there.'

'I hope you've got every angle covered.' Superintendent Stephens was a worried man. 'If we lose that African now, we're deep in the mire.'

Pendham sighed, but only inwardly.

'It's our best chance of breaking this thing once and for all. I told you, Super, I think there is someone else involved. Odhiambo and I agree on that. And I think he knows something he hasn't let on about. Typical of his behaviour all through this case. But as soon as he moves we'll be there. Him and the Admin woman. She's on her way back to the Centre now, just about there by now; Trewin is covering that end. I'm on my way to join our Equatorial colleague.'

'Very well, Pendham, but be careful. This whole matter has got out of hand. I've got the government breathing down my neck, to say nothing of the Chief Constable.'

'Don't worry, sir. It'll all be tidied up before the assistance you've called in is needed. I'd better be off.'

'No need to be sarcastic, Pendham. You know that decision was taken over my head. Right, get on with it.'

Pendham left the station and entered his car. He and Stephens had moved to the small station in Helston close to Penleith. He gave instructions to his driver and then reached for the radio – it was time to get an up-date from both of the surveillance sites.

Helen did not have to look for her quarry. As she parked the car outside the house both Gregsons emerged from the front door, hurrying to intercept her.

'What is going on?' Hugh Gregson was visibly emotional. 'Mrs Shropshire, I must insist on an explanation. Including your movements and what has happened to Odhiambo.'

'Please, let's go somewhere where it's private.' Helen gestured to the wall of the inner garden. 'Let's go in there, shall we?'

They entered the garden and crossed to the bench seat, Helen feeling the tension inside her, Muriel Gregson looking sombre and sullen, her husband fretful and at an emotional pitch where he seemed about to explode.

'Now, I demand a full explanation. You are behaving oddly and I must remind you that I, with your assistance, am temporarily in charge here.'

'Shut up, Hugh, and let her speak.' There was a snap and bite to the woman's voice that Helen had not heard before. 'Now, speak up. You wanted to see me – here I am.'

'I really wanted to see you alone, Muriel. Woman to woman. Follow-up to our talk yesterday morning.'

Her listeners were impatient.

'There is nothing you can say to me that Hugh should not hear. We haven't got all afternoon – please get on with it.'

'All right. Here goes.' Despite her best efforts, Helen's voice trembled with the manifestation of her inner tension. To her listeners this served as evidence of her sincerity. 'Inspector Odhiambo, James – I picked him up from hospital and drove him back here. He told me to tell you that he knows and can prove that you, Muriel, arranged to meet Mahendra at the lake the night he drowned. He knows about your alibi, but said he was discussing it with Mrs Tamlyn and would then be giving his evidence to Chief Inspector Pendham.'

'This is outrageous.' Hugh Gregson spluttered in his rage.

'Outrageous. How dare you? How dare he? I take the most serious . . .'

'Shut up, Hugh.' Muriel's dominance was growing ever more evident. She turned back to Helen. 'Very well. You've delivered the message from your Kenyan boyfriend, now tell me this – where is he now?'

'I dropped him on the track leading to the farm on the other side of the lake from here. Also, where Mrs Tamlyn's house is, I believe.'

Hugh Gregson threw up his hands in a combination of rage and frustration, but his wife, faced with confirmation of her expectations, now moved with an air of one who considered the time for action was at hand.

'Right. Hugh, come with me. There's no more to be gained from talking to the messenger. It's past the time for an encounter with that interfering Odhiambo.' As she turned away, she glanced back at Helen for one parting shot. 'As a potential witness to conspiracy to interfere with the course of justice, you will stay here until you are seen by the proper police. I regard your behaviour as scandalous and no doubt Hugh will take the appropriate steps to consider your suitability for this position.'

'Come on, my dear, don't say too much at this stage. Let's get to the source of this nonsense.'

Helen watched them go and felt herself start to shake with a mixture of a post-tension muscular tic and fright at what she was doing. My God, I hope James knows what he's doing, she thought. She felt as if she'd thrown a lighted petrol-soaked rag into a box of fireworks whilst still standing over it. She pulled herself together and entered the house by the side door that Odhiambo had opened to admit Morgan the night of the storm. Even that seemed an age ago. She found Jane sitting at her chair by the filing cabinets, but looking strained.

'Oh, Helen. Thank goodness you've come. I did what you said, but now the police are everywhere. What's going on?'

'It's OK, Jane. Just a little longer and all will be clear.' Helen crossed the corridor to the small office housing the telephone exchange for the Centre. She opened the door: there was the duty telephonist and there too was a uniformed policewoman with a head-set, taking notes as Helen watched. Helen retreated. James was right; Pendham had cast his net around them and was waiting to haul them in. She shivered again, but curiously also felt a sense of relief.

Odhiambo was spotted as he approached the rear of the Tamlyn bungalow; by the time he reached the door it had opened, revealing Angela Tamlyn looking as always younger than her years, clad in a crisp blouse and smart skirt, the unlined skin of her face glowing with the healthy burnish provided by the Cornish sea-air. Odhiambo pictured her as he had first seen her, standing on the sand with the mist swirling around her – there was something intrinsically romantic about this figure. She seemed to have an affinity with her environment, and this impression stayed with her even in the more prosaic setting of her back porch.

'James, whatever are you doing? I heard you were in hospital. Come in. You look terrible.'

Odhiambo followed his hostess into the lounge and sank gratefully, at her signal, into an armchair. His arm and chest were throbbing now, the result of the journey and the time that had elapsed since his last painkillers.

'Hello, Angela. It's a long story, but the immediate thing is that I need to keep out of the hands of the police for a little longer, so I need shelter. Also, I need your help in thinking my way through things.'

'My dear man, of course, to both requests. But first, you look as if you need a drink. A nice cup of tea or something a bit stronger?'

'A beer, or rather a lager, would be good. Back home we believe a good glass of *pombe* has medicinal value.'

He watched as the woman retreated into the kitchen. He heard the slight hiss of the opening of a refrigerator door and then the sounds of a can being opened. After a short pause Angela Tamlyn reappeared with can and glass.

'Here you are. Now you must tell me what is going on. I heard about the fishing boat and that Bastian and the fisherman were dead and you injured. What happened and why are you hiding from the police?'

Odhiambo took a long swig of lager and felt a little better. He looked at his hostess appraisingly. She managed to show concern whilst retaining her cool demeanour of somehow being outside local events – the observer but not the participant. He recounted a brief and edited summary of the nightmare boat trip.

'So it was drugs behind it all? And Bastian and – what did you say his name was? – were bringing them in? So what's the problem now, James? I repeat – why are you needing to be hidden and what help can I give?'

Before Odhiambo could reply the telephone rang. He watched as Angela got up off the arm of a chair where she had been perched and picked up the receiver.

'Yes, it is . . . Yes, what's the problem? . . .' A glance over to Odhiambo. 'Why do you ask if he's here? . . . No, wait, I don't think that would be . . .' A pained expression came over her face as Odhiambo watched. Then she firmed up her voice. 'Stop. I understand you're worried. No, listen – stay where you are and wait to hear from me . . . I don't care if Trewin is there. Nothing can happen, do you hear me? Just sit tight . . . It won't be long. Now goodbye.'

Angela Tamlyn replaced the receiver slowly and returned to her chair arm. She looked at Odhiambo and he could see a reassessment was taking place. He managed a grin.

'Our mutual friend, Muriel Gregson?' A nod. 'She's starting to panic. She'll be ready to talk soon.'

'According to her, it's you that's causing her to panic. She says you claim she had the appointment with Mahendra. You're obsessed by that theory, James. She was with me. I provide her alibi.'

'Yes, sure. She was with you, I accept that. But she made the appointment and stood him up, as it were.'

'But why would she do that, knowing she was coming to me?'

'Because she was told to. Mahendra had to die and getting him to the lake alone at night was a convenient way of arranging it. Particularly with a killer who has a taste for the theatrical. We're talking about a man who slits a woman's throat and then spread-eagles her on a ship's wheel. As you told me on Friday night, it takes strength, but it also takes a twisted mind.'

'And the killer was . . .?'

'Was is correct. He's dead. Nigel killed Mahendra and then, because he was seen by Penny Deane, he killed her too. Unfortunately for him he was seen on the bar by Menherian, but when he tried to deal with him he met his match.'

'But why would Muriel enter into Nigel's scheme?'

'You're asking all the questions, Angela. But it's me who should be asking them. She didn't take orders from Nigel, he was just the hit man.'

'From whom, then? Alex Bastian?'

'No. Bastian and I had a few words on the boat before it blew up. He was only a minor and reluctant participant in the smuggling.'

Angela Tamlyn looked over Odhiambo's head through the french windows and out to the sea.

'So, stop beating about the bush, James. Who do you think is behind it, as you put it?'

Odhiambo smiled, but without mirth.

'You, Angela. You pulled the strings attached to Muriel and Nigel. You're running the drug racket, aren't you?'

The woman got to her feet. She looked and sounded incredulous.

'Are you mad, man? What on earth gives you these loony ideas?'

'You're still asking questions, Angela. I was hoping for some answers. OK, I'll tell you why I know it's you. First, once I realised it wasn't Bastian, it had to be someone else local. Second, it had to be someone with some influence over Muriel Gregson. And to be able to keep her quiet afterwards. What story did you tell her, Angela, both before and after Mahendra was drowned? Or is she in it with you? Third, Menherian told me he was on his way to see his boss when he saw Nigel on the bar. He'd already passed the lodge so where was he going? How many places are there within walking distance of the bar? He was coming to see you, then changed his mind. Next, you described to me on Friday how Penny Deane was placed on that wheel. The police didn't release that information, I didn't tell you, so who told you? Stories pass around fast in these parts, you said. Maybe, but you were getting them from the horse's mouth: Nigel himself.'

Odhiambo watched as the woman sank slowly back on to her favoured chair arm. He admired her poise. He could feel that he had struck home – but not from any physical reaction, only from a tangible electricity that passed between them as clear to him as a verbal confession. His ears, in fact, received a direct contradiction.

'Oh, James, you're incorrigible. You've built a fantasy story in your mind.' She got up again. 'I'm not even going to do you the favour of a detailed denial. You're injured and you're not thinking straight.'

For the first time Odhiambo lied.

'I told you, Angela – Bastian and I, we had a chance to talk before the boat blew up. He shopped you. He was furious with you all because of Nigel's death. And before that I had an even longer if uncomfortable conversation with Menherian.'

'You're lying, James. Bastian knew nothing.'

There at last the slip, the inadvertent give-away. Odhiambo laughed as the woman bit her lip in a strangely attractive feminine gesture. He stood up and looked down at her from the benefit of his superior height.

'The game's up, Angela. I know what you're going to say. My evidence is hearsay. Dead men don't talk. But I'm giving Pendham the story and he'll have enough to go on. He'll dig and dig and he'll get there in the end. There's the bomb, after all. They'll trace whoever planted it. And as I said earlier, Muriel is ready to crack. She can do for you, Angela. And I'll give evidence of our chat today with a little embellishment if necessary.'

Angela Tamlyn's face was changing. There was a dangerous animosity now in her eyes and her lips had clamped into a tight line. But when she spoke the voice was still light.

'Oh, poor James. You will go on so. I'll tell you, James, to put you out of your misery. Muriel told me about sending Mahendra a note fixing a date at the pool which she didn't want to keep. It was out of jealousy, of course – apparently he was playing around with Mrs Deane. When we heard Mahendra was dead I told her to confess to her silly husband and get him to retrieve the note. He knew or guessed anyway. I'm afraid Muriel is somewhat promiscuous.'

Odhiambo gazed down at her incredulously.

'And you expect me to believe that Mahendra goes to his non-existent date and a murderer just happens to be waiting in case he comes along? Do me a favour, Angela. Grant me a modicum of intelligence.'

The woman smiled.

'It's true, James. It's true.'

Odhiambo considered.

'OK, I get it. Muriel tells you of her little plot and you see a great opportunity to deal with a dangerous nuisance. You make a call from the phone in your kitchen while Muriel is on the verandah. A call to Nigel and off he goes to get his wetsuit.'

Angela Tamlyn stood up and held eye contact with the man in front of her.

'Why, James, why? What's driving you into this nonsense?'

Odhiambo was conscious of the pain in his arm and chest. He felt faint, but he allowed his real anger to surface.

'Penny Deane, Angela, Penny Deane. Any murder is bad enough, but that was too much. Don't forget I found her. And I don't like drug peddlers. Is that enough?'

'You've said yourself that was Nigel. He was a psychopath. You can't blame anyone else for that. Even if your theory was right – I'll imagine it is for a minute – I don't suppose anyone told Nigel to kill Mrs Deane. And when she was found, if Nigel was working for a smuggling gang they probably grilled him about it. But now he would believe himself to be infallible and be full of self-confidence. He probably boasted about it.'

'He was your tool, Angela. You started him with a taste for blood.' He felt now he wanted to bring things to an end. 'And who organised the bomb? Your friend Jan.'

Angela Tamlyn smiled, almost as if in acknowledgement of his deductive prowess or guesswork, whichever. But the answers came from behind him.

'Enough of this nonsense. Angela, what do we do with him?'

Odhiambo turned. There was the man called Jan. His hand was in his jacket pocket; whether he had a gun or not, Odhiambo knew he was in no state to take him on physically.

Angela's voice was now harder, with a harsher tone. 'This poor man is suffering delusions. He's probably still shocked from the explosion – concussed even. He got someone to drop him in the lane. Unfortunately as he tried to find his way here he wandered into the field. Probably he wasn't aware of what he was doing and of course he wasn't to know about that old mine shaft in the corner.' She turned to Odhiambo. 'It was one of the effects of the storm. The soil subsided with all that rain and opened up an old shaft. The council will have it capped no doubt; pity it'll be too late. Closing the shaft after the visitor has fallen, to change an old saying.'

It was a revolver Jan had in his pocket. Odhiambo now found himself looking at it.

'Your reasoning won't hold up if the body has a bullet in it. I'm leaving. Thanks for the warning about the shaft, but I'll return to the Centre through the woods.'

The trouble was, he hadn't worked out a suitable conclusion to the little staged scene. He had confirmed his hypothesis, but was now waiting for something to turn up. Jan was approaching him, the gun still much in evidence. Well, the time had come to try something. He reached down with his good arm, grabbed the small carved table that was beside the chair he had been sitting in and with one quick movement hurled it at the approaching man. He turned, got to the french windows, twisted the handle desperately and stumbled through the opening door. The woman grabbed his bandaged arm; bolts of pain shot into his system, making him feel both dizzy and nauseous. He tried to gather himself, but Jan, moving quickly for a heavily built man, had reached him. The stabbing pain in his arm and chest was blotted out by a momentary curtain of blazing pain as the gun sliced into his skull. His last thought as he fell was that his face was heading for a large shiny official-looking boot.

24

Vague moments of consciousness kept giving way to periods of blackness. There was a picture of leaves blowing with a bright light behind it. Periodically images of faces appeared, some distorted in a strange way. He tried to focus to find out why the faces were so strange, but his attempts caused them to fade – or rather float away: that was it, they were the faces of drowned or drowning people.

One face came into focus, undistorted by water. It was Helen, her red hair glowing, but the eyes unaccustomedly sad. He tried to reach out but Helen too faded. Suddenly a voice penetrated his mind, but it was not the voice of Helen.

'James. Come on, big guy, you're nearly there. Come on, come back to me.'

Odhiambo opened his eyes. Framed against the window behind her, the leaves still blowing across the panes, was Cari, his wife Cari. His mind desperately sought a frame of reference – where was he? Cari saw her husband's eyes open and felt her own eyes dampen over.

'James, James, it's me. You've won through, lover. You've been away a while.'

He tried to speak, but his tongue did not seem to obey his commands. He reached out with his hand and felt it clasped. This wasn't another fantasy image, Cari was there and Cari was real.

Another voice, also female.

'I think we shouldn't excite him too much, Mrs Odhiambo. It'll take a little while for him to gather himself and he'll probably sleep now – a proper sleep this time.'

The face he knew so well came closer and he felt her lips upon his cheek.

'Take it easy, James. There's no hurry. I'll be close by.'

His mind drifted and when he regained control and opened his eyes again, Cari's face was gone. With a mighty effort he tried to raise himself, but hands gently pushed him down. They were white hands. This time he managed to get the right message to his tongue.

'Cari. Where's Cari? She was here. Where am I?'

'Ssh. She's outside, but you must rest now.'

'But, where, where is this?'

'You're in hospital. In Truro. You've been unconscious a long time. Your wife came over from America. Now rest.'

The next morning he woke early and this time he felt he was fully back. Carefully he turned his head; it seemed to be encased, but he was able to scan his surroundings. He was alone in a room with all the appearance and appurtenances of a hospital ward. He lay there reassembling his memory. Fragmented at first, gradually the screen filled in with the bits and pieces until a picture emerged. And then he remembered the last partial awakening and Cari.

One arm seemed to be strapped down, but with his other hand he finally found a set of buttons beside the bed. He pressed speculatively and after a short interval a nurse appeared.

'I could use a drink. My mouth, it's – it's full of fur.'

The nurse helped him to sip from a glass. Nothing had tasted better. The nurse murmured encouraging, but also inconsequential words.

'Listen. I'm fine. I mean, I'm thinking clear. Where's my wife and what day is it?'

'All in good time.' The nurse was solidly built, mid-thirties, he thought, pleasant-faced. 'You've been out to the world for three days. Welcome back to Cornwall.'

'And Cari?'

'Your wife? She's sleeping, just down the corridor. She'll be here when you're ready for breakfast. She had a long journey to get here.'

He lay back, feeling content to obey instructions. The nurse pottered about, fussed with his sheet and left. He closed his eyes, but did not sleep. God, what a trip Cari must have had. Plane and train or car, not knowing what to expect probably. And then back into his mind came the other image. He supposed it was based on a real one; she had probably visited him before Cari arrived. And with the sad eyes of Helen came the final stage of his mental recovery, the feeling of guilt.

It was the afternoon of the next day when Pendham arrived. By then Odhiambo had gleaned the fact that if the brain scan was OK he might be out in a few days. His burns were healing well and his skull was intact, albeit containing a badly bruised brain. Cari was making arrangements for them to go to Virginia where her parents lived.

'Recuperate quietly, James, that's what you're going to do. I've had a word with the Brits. You can skip the last three weeks of your spell here. You'd finished the formal stuff anyway. And you're not going back to Kenya until you're fit. I know you, you'll be back at work the next day.'

He hadn't exactly groaned in spirit, although he had always been reluctant to spend time in the States. He knew why. Cari would like them both to settle there. She had resident rights and a good job with a big company. She was bearish on Kenya and their last experience there had done nothing to make her bullish. Still, a holiday would be OK.

Pendham came in jauntily enough, dressed in blazer and slacks, his tie loosened and the top shirt button undone. Must be off duty, Odhiambo thought.

'Ah, Odhiambo, Chief Inspector Odhiambo, I presume. Me Stanley. You speakum de pidgin English?'

'For God's sake, Pendham, let's not start all that again. Oddly enough, I'm pleased to see you. I can't get anything out of anybody.'

'Right you are. But you're a bloody fool, nevertheless; sticking yourself into the middle of that spider's web. You're lucky that thug didn't do for you. I'm told you've got a pretty thick skull. It's what's inside that's lacking.'

'It was the only way I could bring things to a head. I knew it was the Tamlyn woman, but couldn't prove it.'

'How did you know? The last time we spoke you didn't mention her.'

'I told you there was someone other than Bastian. But, no, as usual all you were interested in was insulting me. So I decided to force you to take notice. I knew you'd tail me to the house. But you took your time coming in. Gave them plenty of chance to finish me off.'

Pendham smiled.

'We got a bug on to the outside, so down there in the bushes we were able to listen to your little drama. You should go on the stage. You'd be good in some murder mystery – the set-piece denouement scene. Anyway, we've picked up the local bomb planter, a young no-hoper, and now they're all grassing on each other. Well, all except the woman – she's a cool customer, but the others are pointing their dirty little fingers at her. So we don't need you, Odhiambo, if you want to head back to your jungle – or do I gather your wife wants you over in the States where she can keep an eye on you?'

'What about the Gregsons? Have you got anything out of them?'

'Yep. It's as the Tamlyn woman told you; Mrs Gregson wanted to make Mahendra look silly out of jealousy over his affair with Mrs Deane. But she admits Angela made a phone call after she told her about her little joke. When he turned up dead she, Mrs Gregson that is, was in a panic. She confessed to her husband and he went and searched Mahendra's room and destroyed her note. Mrs Tamlyn assured her the murder must have been a coincidence. I think after Mrs Deane's death they were both worried, but it doesn't look as if they suspected the old school friend. We could get them on destroying evidence, but I don't know if the powers that be will let us. Him being a diplomat and all.'

Pendham spat out 'diplomat' as if it was a dirty word. Odhiambo laughed.

'And what about the foreigner, Jan?'

'Yes, I think he was the main mover and shaker of the whole drug operation, with the woman as the brains. It's a big operation, it seems. I can't believe that when they started to blow up boats and so on they thought they would get away with it. But I guess someone like him is used to closing down a leaking operation and getting away. Nigel's death was a bonus. I think they'd have done for him anyway – probably got him on the boat with Menherian.'

'Well, we'll all be out of your hair soon, Pendham. And I should think after all this they might decide to send people like me somewhere else for our seminars for a while. So you'll be free from all those ex-colonials that you resent.'

Pendham looked at the man in the bed. Suddenly he sat down in the chair beside the bed, a symbolic gesture that made Odhiambo look at him in surprise.

'Good riddance too to most of them. But I'll tell you something which I shall deny if you ever throw it back at me. You've got a bit more to you than I gave you credit for, OK? So now you can sod off, right?' Pendham paused. 'And one last thing. I've got a message to pass on. From a certain lady. She told me to get the words right. She said to tell you this. She won't come to see you as your wife is here to look after you. She can put all that's happened behind her now and believes you can too. She wishes you and your wife well and hopes that you go on to greater things.' Pendham paused again. 'So there's the message, Odhiambo. I suppose she was talking only of the murders, wasn't she? Oh boy, you Africans.' He got up and moved to the door. Then he looked back one last time.

'I saw a film once with two blokes like us, so I'll use the last line. You take care now, you hear me?'

Odhiambo watched him go and lay and thought. Then he shook his head, raised his good hand and wiped the dampness away from below his eyes.